"Kyrie! This is Ragan Orr, aboard the *Deneb-3*. Kyrie, we had to contact you, rules or no rules, and we have no choice. We've been on all circuits for the last hour. The Watchers are dead, Kyrie. And we've got something going on the scanner; had it for the last six hours. It's Hish, your Kaleen's city. It's covered with an opaque bubble. At ground level, the scanner shows that those entering or leaving the city don't even know the bubble exists."

"Ragan, this is Kyrie. One thing I know—it's all coming down again, only this time worse. There are two things I want from you right now. I want the scoutship back and I want full belt power! If I don't get 'em, it may just be that you can kiss me, the Fregisians, and all of Camelot good-bye; not to mention what might also happen to the Fomalhaut binaries. . . ."

CAMELOT
IN
ORBIT

~~~~~~~~~~~~~~~~~~~~~~~~~~~~~~

Arthur H. Landis

DAW BOOKS, INC.

DONALD A. WOLLHEIM, PUBLISHER

1301 Avenue of the Americas
New York, N. Y.   10019

FIRST PRINTING, NOVEMBER 1978

1 2 3 4 5 6 7 8 9

PRINTED IN U.S.A.

The red-gold orb of mighty Fomalhaut I blazed for brief seconds through a wind-blown rift in the lowering snow clouds. The effect was prismatic, causing hoar frost on granite walls, crenellated turrets, and even the bulk of great Castle Glagmaron to sparkle with a myriad of colors. The bridge to the castle gates, now rimed and hung with icicles, glowed too with an iridescence similar to Terra's mythical "Bifrost Bridge"—that beauteous link 'twixt the world of men and mighty Asgaard.

All very poetic, if viewed from the comfort of a hovering spacecraft. But I wasn't in a hovering spacecraft. Indeed, I was seated on a wooden stool next to a wooden table, 'neath a most incongruous draping of weathered, purple canvas— my pavilion. . . .

Paradoxically, I was in full armor while dripping sweat in a surrounding temperature of five degrees Fahrenheit. I had just completed a series of jousting runs, thus the sweat. It was mid-winter on Fregis, Fomalhaut's second planet, thus the temperature. The place was the martial training field to the east of Glagmaron Castle in the country of Marack, most powerful of the five kingdoms of the northern continent of Marack.

The stool whereon I sat was next to that of my shield-companion Sir Rawl Fergis, nephew to Marack's Queen Tindil. Student squires were unlacing our plates. To the Fregisian eye we were alike as two peas in a pod; each of us weighing in at about one-ninety, and with a height of 6'1". But the likeness ended there. For whereas Rawl's fur was auburn and real, mine was jet-black and of a gene-cultured origin. Rawl's eyes were purple-blue; *all* Fregisians' eyes were purple-blue. Mine were brown, beneath purple-blue contacts. Lastly, I had twice the strength he had, since I came from a planet with twice the mass. An important factor, too, in a world of mayhem, was that an imposed neural preconditioning, infused

5

during the hours of sleep prior to planetfall, had made me a master of all Fregisian weaponry.

Even the beauteous stones of my swordbelt were not just "stones." They were a link to certain death-dealing laser beams, were I granted the power to use them, and to various other "things," including a communications potential with the starship Deneb-3, now, hopefully, orbiting Fregis. . . .

I reached for the pitcher of sviss which but short minutes before had been gog-milk, changed now by my companion's shouted "words." Rawl once confessed to me that he'd learned but three things of magick at Glagmaron City's Collegium: the thing of the sviss, *skilled* lute playing, and a spell for love—to be used three times only. He'd used all three on the Lady Caroween, daughter to the Lord Breen Hoggle Fitz; wasted them actually, since I'd been told later that Caroween would have used the three she had on him.

Snow lay in drifts upon the ground, sailed lazily through the air in puffs and swirls from fat pummeled clouds; all pushed in our direction by a cold wind. I sampled the sviss, rolled its tartness around my tongue and swallowed. Pleased, I emptied the cup.

Rawl refilled it, said casually, "With that frown 'twixt your eyes, Sir Collin, I'm bound to think you've a second thought as to our gerd hunt."

"To the hunt, no! To the company we'll be keeping, yes!" I nodded down the field toward one of a number of pavilions around which were a half-dozen warriors and dottle mounts. "Sir Soolis, yon young Lord of Bleese has had no love for me of late. Now he seeks me out—and with the gift of a riding gerd, *if* we can take it. Why would he do this?"

"Why else? You're the 'Collin.' Heeeeyyyy—" Rawl squinted at me with laughter in his eyes. "You've qualms of *Soolis?* Why, my lord, did he come at us with all the Bleesian Army, just you and I and Hoggle could take the lot of them. Nay, lord. He'll play no tricks; though I wish to the gods he'd try."

" 'Tis the thing of the eyes," I said softly.

He was instantly alert. "You think again of the Dark One, of the Kaleen?"

"I do."

"Then you believe it true, what you said at council—that he's come again to Marack?"

"I do," I repeated.

Rawl's grin grew wider, the original blithe spirit. His eyes shone. "Would it were true, my lord. This time we'll pursue the bastard across the River-sea. We'll take the whole of Om. We'll storm the gates of Hish itself. . . ."

I sighed. "He knows our strength now. I doubt we'll have that chance."

"Our magick, too, was greater."

" 'Twas not *our* magick," I said, unthinking.

"You mean, 'twas yours?"

"Nay." I shrugged impatiently. "But 'twas *not* ours."

He frowned. At the far pavilion the stocky Sir Soolis, bereft now of armor, was donning a fresh jupon and furs, . . .

In Galactic Foundation listings, Fregis was called *Camelot;* the indisputable facts being that other than a classical, medieval culture and the like, spells, enchantments, and dark wizardry, as practiced by Fregis' sorcerers, really worked. Moreover, the planet was an occultists', alchemists', metaphysicists' paradise. . . .

Foundation Center had been aware of this anomaly for quite some time. Indeed, over a period of two galactic centuries assigned *Watchers*—opposite-sexed pairs with a high compatibility potential—had forever apprised them of these facts.

To read a *Camelot* report had been a joy indeed, excepting the one received six months before predicting the onset of a dark and terrible sorcery to encompass the entire planet. Unless we moved quickly, the report had said, the forces for progress, the five kingdoms of the north, would be ruined, destroyed. The result? Chaos! A new dark age, and worse, for all the foreseeable future of the beauteous water-world of Fregis-Camelot.

Not liking the prognostication one damned bit, the Foundation had moved instantly to insert a bit of magick of its own, scientific magick! In essence, *me*, Kyrie Fern, an Adjuster-manipulator of the socio-evolutionary processes—the sly introducer at dark campfires of the sharpened stick and the gut-stringed bow. At the Court of Marack, I had passed myself off as Sir Harl Lenti. I had also been accepted—for my prodigious deeds—as their "Collin mythos," reborn. He who had returned to save the Northlands from darkest peril!

A graduate of the Foundation's Collegium, I'd become, at age thirty, somewhat of a genius in the art of "adjusting." The very man for the job, said the Prime Council, except that Camelot was one gigantic game of misdirection. On the one hand the "play" involved an extra-universal, alien intruder re-

7

ferred to as the *Kaleen,* or the "Dark One"; with his opponents, other than Marackians, etc., being the host-occupants of a half-dozen cuddly, button-eyed, wet-nosed, fat-fannied, normally useless tree dwellers called Pug Boos. The Foundation *and* the Prime Council hadn't the whiff of an idea of what the job really was. And I, after six months of a great and bloody war, wild sorcery, and a seething chaos of events involving a pot-pourri of the most lovable and zany friends that a humanoid could have—and the most evil of enemies— was just beginning to find out!

I glanced toward the Lord of Bleese. He was seated and smacking his lips over the steaming contents of a stirrup cup. "The man's smart," Rawl said bluntly. "He makes haste slowly, since our good Lord Hoggle-Fitz is still at joust." A roar from the lists where Hoggle was no doubt pummeling somebody, backed up this statement.

Toward the east then and sharp on the frozen air came the shrill notes of a trumpet, to be followed by a lusty feminine hallooing from many voices. I turned to stare in that direction; focused my contacts to four magnitudes. A covey of riders had topped the road up from Glagmaron City on the banks of the Cyr below. Their colors were those of my betrothed, Murie Nigaard Caronne, the Princess of Marack.

I nudged the squinting Rawl. The squires had finished with our plate-mail so that we now sat in padded jupon and chain long-shirts. I waved them away. " 'Tis the Princess," I told Rawl softly. "Your lady's with her."

He frowned, half arose, and sat again; said, puzzled, "But 'tis only four days. They were to be gone a week."

She'd spotted my colors—the field being not all that broad from the bluff's edge to the bridge. An instant wheeling of her mount in a shower of ice shards from off the cobbles, and she charged toward me as she'd seemingly charged the gates.

At first sight, I'd thought she but raced the threat of the storm clouds. But her ride toward me, headlong, precipitous, gutsy, was not only symptomatic of her character, but suggested, too, a possibility of peril.

Her dottle skidded to a whoooing halt within but six feet of us. We moved not a muscle. 'Twould have been un-Marackian to do so. A second dottle arrived just as precipitously, skidded, fat-fanny to the ground, at about fifteen feet to our right, deliberately. Its lithesome rider, with the cowl of her cloak flung back to expose her flaming red hair, was the Lady Caroween, dainty Valkyrie daughter to our Lord of

8

Great Ortmund, Breen Hoggle-Fitz. Rawl rose instantly to go to her.

The remaining six maidens of the entourage, one of whom held a trumpet and smiled most sweetly, halted respectfully some twenty paces to the princess' rear. Their dottles wheeed a greeting to our own.

The princess dealt a resounding whack to her mount's broad bottom so that it knelt before me with a pained look in its big blue eyes. Its six paws were instantly tucked beneath the warmth of its belly.

"My Lord Collin," she began, though her aura of urgency still allowed for a sparkling eye and a baiting grin, "When last we spoke, sir, you said you'd had your fill of lance and 'flats'—'till Ormon's Day, come spring. But here you are again. . . ."

She referred to my challenging colors, a sprig of violets against a field of gold, which flew from a great lance in the midst of a half hundred or more pavilions, each flaunting the blazonry of this lord or that. All around us on the line of a dozen lists, as many as a hundred belted knights, or *heggles,* inclusive of the Lady Caroween's father, were unseating each other in thunderous crashes of lance on shield, or were fighting a'foot with sword flats in melees of screaming, cursing chaos.

From the corner of one eye I say that the Lord of Breese, though mounted now, still held back to sit and stare in our direction. I ignored him.

"My Lady," I said, absolving myself with a careless shrug of any guilt, "there's simply nought else left to do." I'd moved forward to offer a hand, were she inclined to leave her lacquered, wooden saddle. She wasn't. I winked deliberately, allowing a twinkle to touch my right contact. Her returned stare was in every way as bold.

I sighed inwardly. Each new setting wherein I saw her renewed my belief that she was truly *the* fairy-tale princess, right out of the archaic "Crock of Gold." She had golden hair, golden *fur,* saucy blue-purple eyes, a quite elfish face with dainty, slightly pointed ears—though this last was no salient feature of Fregisians—and a forever demanding tilt to her chin. Petite, she was beautifully formed. Pound for pound, she was also the match of any warrior with sword or faldirk. . . .

She wore a white and gold cloak with voluminous sleeves, furred inside and out and reaching to her soft-booted calves. The cowl was thrown back. Being but loosely belted it was open now, allowing for the sight of padded, blue-velvet ski pants, with pullover to match. A white scarf was at her throat.

Beneath her altogether feminine boldness, however, I had sensed, indeed, knew instantly, that my princess was a very worried female.

I offered my half-filled cup, said softly, "You've returned early, my love. I've missed you."

She drained the cup, grinned saucily, scratched her nose and said, "Well! Have you, now? I should visit my cousin more often. I'd be there yet, sir—" and she fixed me hard with her eyes—*"had I not spoken in dream last night to my good Dame Malion!"*

I reached by reflex to my belt, pressing the stud for extended "null" so's to protect our group from whatever "mind" games the Dark One might just be up to. She'd referred to her "Court-appointed Companion," and she'd kept her voice deliberately low.

"Are you sure," I queried, "that 'twas not but a simple, normal dream?"

"'Twas neither simple nor normal, Collin. There's peril, sir, to my father."

"No nightmares?" I persisted—"No over-eating, of gog-meat pot-pies? I do recall, my lady—"

"'Twas *magick*, Sir Lenti—of the kind that *you* know well!"

"Tell me of it."

She said shortly, "There's no time." Her gaze had been drawn to my left, down the line of pavilions from whence there now came a clumping of dottle paws.

My eyes followed hers. The Lord of Bleese with two attendants was approaching. I instantly held up a hand to stay him. And because I was who I was he promptly halted. Murie continued: "I go to my dame now, Collin. We'll speak at sup . . . But know one thing: if 'twixt the hours of now and then the Lord Gen-Rondin arrives to Castle Glagmaron, then do you come quickly to my father's side. For Marack will surely be in deadly danger."

I shrugged, said softly, "The danger's never left us, Murie. So guard yourself, for I'll be gone 'til sup. I've a thing to look into."

She frowned. "By the gods, Collin, I speak of peril beyond danger. Why leave me now, sir?"

"'Tis but a ride of ten miles," I said shortly. "But it must be done."

She forced a smile. "Well, kiss me then, for I've missed you too."

Her dottle, kneeling, had brought her small, snow-maiden face to a level with my own. My steel shirt being a barrier to anything more daring, I kissed her, open-eyed, and with a casual though possessive hand placed gently on her thigh. Her eyes searched mine avidly, as if she sought some quick revealing truth.

I cautioned in one small ear: "From now on, love, do not look thusly into the eyes of our sorcerer, Fairwyn. Tell this to the king and your mother—and to your close friend Caroween."

She gasped, said tight against my throat, " 'Tis true then, what you said before at council—that the Dark One's returned; that some among our lords might be possessed, like unto that which my dame has told me, too?"

"I *think* 'tis true. I'll know for sure tonight."

She drew away, kissed me again, smiled grimly, then drew the circle of the god, Ormon, upon her breast. And then, because she could do it, she winked at me, signalled her escort and her red-haired shield-maiden, and whistled her dottle to its feet.

It stomped its six fat paws to rid them of unmelted ice, whoooed loudly and led off toward the castle. The bridge, now that red Fomalhaut had fled, was again a somber gray. Fresh snow-flurries touched all the plain around us. An idiot's time, I mused wryly, for to go a'gerd hunting.

It was just then that I noticed the presence of Hooli the Court Pug Boo. He'd been hidden by Murie's cloak. Now he clung to it for dear life, lest he be bounced from off her dottle's rump. Round, symmetrical, Hooli was hardly two feet in height. His legs and arms were short, sturdy; his ears fur-tufted, on a puff-ball head. I was again reminded of the first time I'd seen him, when I'd whimsically compared him to a cuddly toy I'd owned in the dreams or the play of my childhood. . . .

Hooli was a number of things. First, he was a leaf-eating tree-dweller, indigenous to the southern—Kaleen-controlled—continent of Om. He was also one of the Court Pug Boos sacred to the kingdoms and the gods of the northern continent. He was, specifically, however, *the* entity-occupant of the Pug Boo attached to the Marackian Court.

Exactly who or what this entity-occupant was, I hadn't the slightest idea. I knew only that without his aid all our efforts at the previous battle of Dunguring, in the northern land of

11

Kelb where we had smashed and driven the hordes of the Dark One, the Kaleen, into the River Sea, would have come to nought. For it had been his, *Hooli's* magick, about which Rawl had spoken.

All the more reason then for my resurgent fear of new dangers all around us—for Hooli and his cohorts, Pawbi, Dahkti, Jindil, and Chuuk, had disappeared, ceased to occupy their hosts immediately after that battle. For six long months I'd had no contact with him. And in that time, while I awaited the return of the Foundation Starship, *Deneb-3*, I'd become obsessed with the insidious idea that I, Kyrie Fern, *Adjuster*, was quite alone now; had been left, indeed, *saddled*, with the awful responsibility for every vestige of life on Camelot-Fregis. . . .

With the first coming of snow rumors had become rife of riders on ice-bound roads where they would not normally be; of strange guests in the castles of certain lords; of ships and dark visitors to seacoast towns and villages. I'd even enjoined a preliminary discussion some weeks before with the king and the lords of the privy council. To no avail. True evidence was lacking, they said, for a sequestering of this lord or that. Come spring, 'twould all be checked out. And too, Dunguring, to them, with its two hundred thousand dead, was both the greatest battle and the greatest victory of all time. How then, they reasoned, could *any* enemy recover so quickly? Need I add that it was impossible to convey the simple fact that while it was winter in Marack, it was the softest of summers in Om?

They'd listened, true, inclusive of the king himself. But they did so only because I was the Collin—their *hero-my-thos-savior;* that and the fact that no man alive, Kaleen possessed or otherwise, would challenge the Collin's sword. . . .

Two final things had brought the stew to boiling. But one week past my courier, the student warrior, Hargis, had returned from Klimpinge, a seacoast town, with the dread news that the two Foundation *Watchers* had been murdered—by a cloud, so it was told to him, of ebon-black with points of diamond light, that had burst the door of their bedroom in the inn which they used as a front, and entered to take their breath—and so, their lives. And then, on the very day in fact when Murie'd left to visit her cousin, I'd watched alarmed as our venerable and aged sorcerer, Fairwyn, had slumped in his chair at the king's table, his hands folded corpse-like upon his

12

withered breast while his pale eyes stared to nowhere. And so he remained throughout the meal—raptly listening to some strange and distant drum.

To compound the problem further, Hooli, for whatever his reasons, had tossed a cosmic wrench into my communications mechanism; this prior to his disappearance. The result? I no longer knew if I could even contact the Deneb-3. They *were* in orbit. I knew that. But I'd tried and failed. For this reason I'd deprived myself of "null" protection (a negation of all gravitational-magnetic lines of force), in the hope that they'd ignore the rules and contact me. In effect, whenever "null" was off *all* circuits were open. . . .

I sighed, turned to Rawl. But Hooli had suddenly glanced back to me so that I could see his runny nose and shoe-button eyes. An almost subliminal four-color print was instantly etched upon the retinal optics of my brain. It was of Hooli—dressed in a centuries-old, Terran, British admiral's cap and sword. He had a patch over one eye; one arm was missing, and the hand of the other grasped the rail of a certain well-known flagship. Need I add that the bombs bursting in air all around him were in the best tradition of a place called "Trafalgar"?

The scene's duration was accompanied by a voice inside my head—mine, of course; his way of communicating. It sounded as if it came from the deepest pits of Terra's mythical "hell."

"*Beware the jabberwock, Buby!*" The words were sepulchral—deliberately designed to startle—"*The jaws that bite; the claws that catch!*"

And that was it. A single second of Hooli's nonsense. Or was it Hooli? I shook my head, gasped and drew a deep breath. I then quick-focused my contacts to six mags so that I was nose to nose with the little bastard. I searched his face. No light shone from those flat little eyes. There was no saucy wink, no hasty thumb-to-nose. For Hooli, my only ally, brains-wise, was definitely *not* in residence.

Dark were the fulsome clouds as we rode out; dark, too, were my thoughts. Rawl strummed his magick lute—each note perfection. He sang amusing porno-ditties whilst the rest of us, my student-warriors, Charney, Tober, and Hargis, together with the boisterous Lord Hoggle-Fitz and the master swordsman, Griswall, joined in—as did Gen-Soolis, who rode to my left, and his two swordsmen, who brought up the rear.

Aside from the Kaleen's magick, I'd trust my mini-entou-

13

rage against all the fiends of Camelot's *ghast*, such was their prowess. Breen Hoggle-Fitz was a middle-aged giant of a man who loved nothing better than a fight before each meal and one before bedtime. He was honest, loyal, brave—beyond the meaning of the words. He was also, paradoxically, both brilliant and stupid. The dour Griswall, short, stocky, terrible in his strength, had the singular reputation of having killed three hundred men. A previous commander of the King's Guard, he now trained the young warriors assigned to my service. I welcomed his courage and his level head—an attribute too often lacking in Fregisians. My students were what they were, survivors of battles—brave, skillful, *smart*. As for Rawl, my happy lute player, were he pitted against me, and were I deprived of my "edge" of superior strength—I'd be a dead man. . . .

And Sir Soolis? Well, he was young, a good warrior, loyal to the king, and until quite recently a friendly sort who on one occasion had shared a cup with Rawl and me. But three days ago he'd challenged me to a run of the lance, which was not unusual, excepting that in no way was he in my class. For his honor's sake I'd thought to do him easy. But he'd ridden at me—*Kaleen possessed*—to kill me if he could. I'd caught him square on shield's center, sent him a full forty feet beyond his dottle's charging rump—and straight to bed for a good two days to ease the pain of his landing.

This morning he'd come again, all smiles; the madness lurking still, but in a way that only I could tell. . . . A gerd, he'd told me lightly, had been spotted by a retainer of his. 'Twas a young one. He'd make it a gift to me if we could capture it; this, for his folly and to show he bore no grudge. The "games-plan" was obviously to incite my interest so I would go where he would lead. The Dark One seemed never to know that I could *see* his presence in the eyes of his captive hosts, he was that stupid, or that *alien* to Camelot's reality.

A gerd-mount in battle, as opposed to a dottle, is every warrior's dream. Hoggle had owned one, and oft boasted of its courage. So here we were, gerd hunting; my comrades for the chase, myself to find through Gen Soolis where the Kaleen would lead me. I doubted much there'd be a gerd there. Most likely there'd be a dark and cowled wizard. . . .

We passed through the cobbled streets of the steelpoint, snow-bound castle city of Glagmaron, and out to the forest-girt fields to the north and west. We crossed the sinuous,

14

winding Cyr River three times ere we reached the great woods wherein the gerd was supposed to be. The threat of more snow became fact. Now, however, it was still intermittent, coming in gusts and random puffs of cotton flakes. The temperature fell ever lower so that our dottles, with their thick winter fur, fairly pranced their joy at the freshness of it all. . . .

But we found no gerd, nor even the presence of one. Had we done so the dottles would have smelled him—and moaned their terror. For a gerd is to a dottle as is a Terran wolf to a sheep dog—mortal enemies. A gentle dottle, who is at best but two-thirds the size of a gerd, will run his fat legs off to escape one. Moreover, when a gerd is actually found, the "hunt" is done by man—on foot!

Still we searched, shouted, blew our horns through bush, conifer, and ghostly stands of bare-limbed hardwoods, and plunged into deep drifts and against the whipping slash of branches and thorn-bracken.

"By the gods, Sir Collin," Gen-Soolls finally cried—and his chagrin seemed almost real—"I'll ask your pardon, sir. I should have brought the lad as guide. 'Tis that I'd thought I'd placed the site of the beast so solid in my mind."

I felt almost sorry for him. The act of possession, of control from so far a distance—Hish and Kaleen's dark Omnian capital, was a full eight thousand miles—waned and glowed, depending upon the degree of the Kaleen's attention. Poor Soolls was but a single pawn, in a horde of pawns; just as I was but a single enemy which he had now, perforce, to reckon with.

"A gerd's a gerd," I yelled in answer, above the clatter of a fall of great icicles which I had knocked from a branch. "If he's here at all, he'll be here tomorrow too. Let's to home!" But I wondered, *had* something gone wrong? Had he failed the liaison the Kaleen had prepared for him? For the briefest of seconds I questioned my own thinking. Mayhap it was all but a creeping paranoia, with the "reappearance" of Hooli as a part of the madness.

But the thought was negative. Hooli was real—if for no other reason than the eye-patch and the admiral's cap. . . .

We forced our way out of a copse of trees and on to the brow of a hillock where we surveyed the terrain to the west. Great Fomalhaut was now low on the horizon; for though it was still mid-afternoon, it was also winter. . . .

Our Lord Hoggle-Fitz, his great bulk wrapped to the ears in furs, his bulbous eyes watering in the frozen air, said sharply, "Our Collin's right. Let's to hearth and sup, sirs. The more so, me, for I've work to do. I've to compose a tri-part prayer," he pompously confessed, "to our sweet gods, Ormon, Wimbily, and precious Harris—for the Queen's feast day."

Hoggle, though a stout sword in melee or onset, and lovable too, was also a one-of-a-kind "grand original." He was that Camelotian-Fregisian rarity, the *religious fanatic*—and this in a land of a non-proliferation of deities.

Sir Fergis, glancing to me, raised tired eyebrows. He said softly, "I agree. Let's to home, Collin. Such piety *must* be served." His dottle Kaati, stomped and whoooed an affirmative.

But our young Lord Gen-Soolis who'd been staring silently to the depths of two ravines leading off from the hill's slopes, said loudly, "Hold! For by the gods I swear *I* can smell the bastard where these miserable mounts of ours do not! I'll tell you now. He's in one of those gulleys!"

The bald-faced lie evoked instant frowns from all my stalwarts. Dour Griswall grunted, spat. My students laughed. But I looked to Gen-Soolis' eyes; saw instantly what I'd expected to see. He was *full-possessed!* The eyes, no longer purple-blue, were hellish black. Black as the roiling clouds that seemed suddenly to press round us; to be joined by a roaring thunder—quite alien to snowstorms.

A faint, electrifying tingle touched on us too; a final proof of the Dark One's presence. I looked to the others, saw their startled glances, hands reaching to sword hafts. I quick pressed the "null" stone at my belt; extended protection to its full radius of a mile. There'd be no Kaleen seizures here! A thread he had to our sad Soolis, and perhaps to his swordsmen too; most certainly to whatever awaited us below—but not to us. I'd see to that!

All eyes had switched to Soolis. Had I so much as whistled, he'd have been carved into so many pieces. But my sole purpose in being here was to meet with whatever the Kaleen had conjured up—and best it—as proof to the Court of the Dark One's return.

So I dug my spurs into fat Henery's belly and reined him tight so that his forelegs pawed the air. While he wheeled in protest, I whirled him wildly, shouting to Rawl: "Follow me on, sir! This Kaleen's bastard has a penchant for yon south ravine! And do you," I yelled to Hoggle and Griswall, "take the north gulley. But be warned of this traitor's tricks, for 'twill be no *gerd* that you'll come upon!"

I led off instantly, giving them no time to talk. Shield to

the fore and with the long, venom-tipped lance to my right hand—gerds must be tranquilized for capture—I rode hard down the south fork. Rawl was to my immediate rear. The mad Gen-Soolis and his men stormed after us. Behind, on the slow wind, I heard the thunder of paws above Hoggle's shouted orders. . . .

For seconds we plunged down what seemed a shallow ledge. It widened quickly, but 'twas still a ledge. Below, at some fifteen feet, was the parallel sloping floor of the ravine itself. Brush grew from its sides. Its sandy bottom—it was a dry-wash, actually—was covered by a foot of snow.

We rounded a sudden bend. 'Twas at that point that Henery stopped; but he didn't just *stop!* All six great paws skidded, clung suddenly, desperately to the frozen earth for purchase, while the fur all round his body stood out in magnetized rigidity, a spine-chilling adjunct to his scream of total terror.

He had reason to scream. I confess it now that my own hair, from nape to crown actually gripped my skull with a tightness to bulge my eyes.

For there in all its ghastly horror, and at a distance of less than sixty feet—was the *jabberwock!*

Poor Henery, his great body trembling with an uncontrollable fear, sank to the knees of his last two pair of legs while he tried desperately to hide his head between his front paws. I thought he'd surely die of fright right then and there.

I'd flung myself instantly from the saddle; shield cast aside, I seized my greatsword in my left hand whilst keeping my lance in my right. Rawl repeated my every move, leaving his whoooing, moaning Kaati, to join me at the lip of the ledge.

The horror below was a full fifteen feet in width, twenty-five in length, and perhaps eight in height. It had four horned and segmented legs on either side and a monstrous curled stinger to its rear—which I judged for a length of thirty feet or more. Two great clawed appendages were to the front, as were a dual set of frightful mandibles 'neath a ring of eyes on what I presumed was its head. Ghastly chitinous hairs—they were antennae, really—stuck out from all its body. It was both arachnid and scorpion; truly the stuff of nightmares. . . .

Rawl coughed. I knew instinctively that he fought for speech 'gainst the tightness of his throat. He was crouched to my left, his weapons pointed. He managed hoarsely: "There lies our death, Sir Lenti. For by the gods, when that thing moves he'll cover a hundred yards in a single second."

17

"Indeed," I said, and my throat, too, was dry, a grating rasp. "But why then does it sit there? Surely it sees us?"

"Fear not Collin!" a voice screamed maniacally to my rear, "It sees you! 'Tis your *gerd*, my lord! *'Tis your new mount, oh greatest of swordsmen!"*

A quick glance to my rear revealed Gen-Soolis, dancing and writhing in ecstasy—or *agony*. He seemed now as some true fiend. His eyes, all bleeding, protruded from their sockets. His face worked, the features twisting the very flesh from off his skull. Blood from burst vessels streamed from his nose and ears. His very spittle was a spindrift froth about his face. He stood some fifteen feet from us. Behind him were his two attendants, mad too, but not so much as he. . . .

Rawl yelled, "Quick, Collin. It moves!"

I turned again to the monster. And as I did so that other, pitiful monster, my Lord of Breese, catapulted his body toward me; his arms outstretched to shove me to the creature's grasp. *"Ride your gerd!"* His bloodied throat screamed out the words. "Ride it, *savior!* Ride it, *Collin!"*

With a "controlled person," however, there is always that extra second 'twixt the thought of the possessor and the act of the host. . . . I had time to step aside and to put out a foot so that the Dark One's surrogate went tumbling through the frigid air to land within twenty feet of those dread mandibles.

We watched, fixed hard on the scene before us. The creature'd obviously seen him coming. But its reflexes were unnatural, slow. Its great claws moved as if in some deep and viscous fluid. Its segmented tail with the deadly sting came up and over its back in *slow motion*. Still it struck—to literally pin poor Soolis to the ground. He'd turned in the air in his tumbling so that he'd landed, feet toward the monster. With the sting through his back he still tried to raise himself on his two hands. His mouth was a gaping horror. The cords of his neck were as two cables. And thus he died—from the sting's venom, or the strike itself, and I know not which.

Screams from our rear then caused us both to look back—to Gen-Soolis' two charging swordsmen. We'd no desire to kill them, but we had no choice. With my left hand I brought my greatsword round to cut through the swordarm, rib-cage, and heart of the man nearest me. Rawl took the head of his attacker and kicked the body to the ravine's floor. . . .

Still the thing below had not *really* moved. Moreover, it seemed hard-pressed, barely able even to withdraw its sting.

Something was quite definitely wrong with the Dark One's "emissary." By the gods, I thought, could it be that? And then I began a silent laugh inside my head. The Great Sorcerer, as he was oft' referred to by Fregisians, had failed again. Detail was never his forte; indeed, 'twas beneath him. So in his arrogance he'd not thought his problem through.

I remembered the monster now, for I'd scanned it as I'd scanned all life forms and all terrain prior to planet-fall. It was a *meeg,* indigenous to the tropical swamplands of Kerch. And Rawl had been right! It could run, or leap, a hundred yards in a single second—in the swamplands of Kerch, that is. In Marack, *in the dead of winter,* and with the temperature at minus zero, it couldn't run, or leap, two inches. Indeed, since it was cold blooded, any movement at all, *now,* was a bloody damned miracle. I wondered just how long since the Kaleen had put it there. What an anomaly: the science for a matter-to-energy conversion—and back again—and then such lack of foresight. . . .

"Rawl," I said softly, happily—

But he interrupted, saying, "Collin," and his voice held a hollow sadness, "you've been right all along. The Dark One's here; in that thing. Now allow *me,* my lord, to a first attempt at tickling its guts with my lance. If I win, I've gained the honor—and you've not been risked. If I lose—well, you're the 'Collin,' sir; 'twill be your problem then. . . ."

He had not the knowledge I had—only the courage he'd been born with. I put a hand to his sword arm. "Nay, comrade. There's no need. We've already won. A few more minutes and the damn thing's dead, frozen stiff. The Kaleen's brains have in no way matched his magick. Score one for Marack!"

I then began to laugh, hysterically, in relief. Rawl looked to me in awe, then to the *meeeg,* until he too began to laugh. Soon we were embracing and pounding each other's backs. We even did a little dance on the icy ledge in our joy at the Kaleen's stupidity. For make no mistake, had that thing possessed its potential, the both of us would have been dead, our fluids sucked, our bodies rent. Of all life on Camelot-Fregis, only the great Vunn, and one other, so I'm told, can withstand the ferocity of the meeeg.

Finally, because we *were* warriors, we could resist temptation no longer. We slipped down from the ledge and approached the monster cautiously.

A single claw stirred and rose, upon which, with my greatsword in both hands, I hacked it off. The stinger came over its ghastly head again—but oh, so slowly. Rawl leapt, and slashed it off. In his exuberance he climbed up a horned leg and sought to plunge his sword through the carapace of its great back. It was much too hard. But he needn't have bothered. I'd moved to within a yard of the dread mandibles and the ring of ebon eyes—and watched them die, one by one, as the thing itself died.

He climbed down and we stood together staring 'til we heard a halooing from the head of the gulley. Rawl answered quickly with his horn. . . . Dead or alive, however, the horror of the creature would still be too much for the dottles of our companions, so we climbed again to the ledge to lead poor trembling Henery and the equally shaking Kaati to meet them on the trail.

Once round the bend we risked death again from Hoggle-Fitz who, with reins to saddlehorn, and with sword and lance to either hand, came on in such a storm as to almost ride us down. "By Ormon's love, Collin," he roared, catching himself at the last moment, and bringing his mount to whoooo and to raise its great forepaws, "what's a'foot? There's a stench to the air, sir, that has not at all to do with gerds."

I simply said, "Dismount and come with us." They did and we showed them the meeeg. They gasped, shuddered, and shook their heads accordingly, for no one in all the north had ever seen such a horror. While Tober hacked off a claw for the Privy Council to ponder, I told them of the Dark One's error—how he'd sent a thing through space and time (his magick), which on its own would die of cold in a single hour, and had done just that. I explained too of the possession of the Lord of Bleese and of his two swordsmen.

We returned to our dottles and led them again to the hill's top, where I thought to say a word or two on what might be happening even then at Castle Glagmaron.

Fomalhaut was truly low at that point, so that I doubted we'd make the castle before darkness. Still I held them to a dottle circle hoping to speak to them for a few minutes. First I switched off "null." I deemed it safe now, and more, I desperately needed the contact with the Deneb-3. Each second free of "null" could hasten that contact.

I'd hardly opened my mouth, however, when *pain*, the like of which I'd never known, struck from the webbed communications node imbedded at the base of my skull. The sheer agony of it drove me screaming from my saddle to the ground where I writhed in the snow to clutch my head with one hand and to fumble for the "null" stone with the other. But it was too late. A thousand scalpels touched an equal number of nerve-end ganglia. And then—'twas a bursting *nova!*

I literally leaped into the air, so they told me later, screamed again—and came flat down upon my back, unconscious.

They thought me dead, my yell was that convincing. Rawl said it was sufficiently loud to raise the pop-link birds from the castle turrets ten miles away. Stout Hoggle in a babble of wild confusion was instantly off his mount, Alphus, and to his knees bellowing prayers to the blessed trinity. . . .

As for myself, well, in some dark recess of my mind where I apparently still lived, I mentally crouched and awaited the Dark One's onslaught. For now, I thought, the bastard really had me!

But nothing happened!

And then it did—a familiar voice, somewhat concerned: "Kyrie? Hey, Kyrie? You all right?" It was Ragan Orr aboard the Deneb-3.

I projected: "You've burned my brains you stupid sons-of-bitches!"

"Hey! Sorry!" The voice was Kriloy's.

"If I survive," I told the both of them, "I won't forget this."

Kriloy said placatingly, "Kyrie . . . We *had* to. We've got a priority. We waited. You didn't contact. We *had* to contact you and to hell with the 'book.' We've been on *all* circuits for the last hour, Greenwich. I repeat—we had no choice, Buby!"

"Damnnn you!"

"It worked."

"You bastards! I was *open* on all circuits."

Kriloy ignored my statement. He said instead, "The *Watchers* are dead, Kyrie."

"I *know* that."

"We've got something going on the scanner; had it for the last six hours. It's Hish, your Kaleen's city. It's covered with an opaque bubble. At ground level, however, the scanner shows that those entering or leaving the city don't even know the bubble exists. . . . Very strange."

I got interested. "Scanner malfunction?"

"Sheeeee!"

"Look, smart-ass, dust motes play hell with adjoined prismatic lenses."

Ragan cut in. "Forget the scanners. It's the city and the Kaleen we're worried about."

21

"And do you think I'm not? There's more than that. . . ."

"When we left you," Ragan said, "everything was roses."

"Not likely."

"Oh? So why didn't you speak up before we warped out?"

"The Pug Boos had snapped the umbilical. I couldn't contact. I still can't."

"But we can?"

"So it seems. . . ." I briefed them quickly then, telling them finally that the Boos (host occupiers), had disappeared. I held back the fact of Hooli's three-second return. . . .

Kriloy asked concernedly, "Where did they go?"

"I haven't the slightest. But one thing I do know, gentlemen, it's all coming down again, only this time worse. There are two things I want from you right now. I want the scoutship back—" (they'd denied it to me when I'd refused their orders in the midst of the battle of Dunguring), "—and I want *full belt power!* If I don't get 'em, it just may be that you can kiss me, the Fregisians, and all of Camelot good-bye; not to mention what might also happen to the Fomalhaut binaries. . . ."

"It's that bad?"

"Indeed it is."

"And *you* were just going to stick around, marry up with your little, golden-furred princess and try to find some way to let her know what you really were. . . ."

"Something like that. But I knew even then—"

Ragan interposed bluntly—"And if you're given these things?"

"Then there's a chance—a small one."

"You psyched the Kaleen before. You *won* the big one."

"My ass! Hear the truth, Bubys—I only helped. The Pug Boos were the power. I was the agent, kiddies; the catalyst!"

They were silent, debating. Then Ragan said softly, "O.K. You got 'em."

"Have you moved the ship?"

"It's where you left it; same coordinates; whatever. Now! some questions. . . ."

"Shoot."

"What's the source of Camelot's magick?"

"I'm not sure yet (a lie). When I am you'll be the first to know."

"All *right!* Now just who and what is the Kaleen?"

"We've gone over that one, in part, before. Now kiddies, time's running out and our friend, the Dark One, may even

22

have found a way to wire into this prattle. I'll do an instant tape at the earliest and get it to you on next contact."

Kriloy came in, persisting: "What of the hosts who occupy the Pug Boos? Who and what are they?"

"Kriloy," I answered solemnly, "I haven't the slightest."

"Do they have sufficient power to control the Kaleen?"

"I'd say, yes. Whether they'll return in time to use it is another matter."

Ragan said flatly, "You know of course that if it becomes a question of *alien* control of the binaries and the two systems—if they or *it*, the Kaleen, attempts this with no effort to contact, to reach some kind of understanding: well that's it. We'll take out both systems and that'll be an end to it!"

"Not without Foundation authority," I said tightly.

Kriloy said softly, "Relax, Kyrie. We're not *nova* happy. You know that—" and then, "That bubble over Hish seems to be stabilizing, at like maybe two hundred yards beyond the city's walls."

"What do you make of it?"

"It's not a force-field. We can penetrate. It's inorganic, too. But substance-wise—well, the scanners come up with absolutely *nothing*. It's like it wasn't really there!"

I drew a deep breath, said tersely, "Look! I meant it before. We may be being monitored. Cut off now. There are things to do and we're wasting time."

Kriloy said, "We'll be 'in' and 'out' from now on, *first priority;* no orbiting; no fixed positions. Keep an open 'H' circuit, Greenwich. We'll come in at *any* time!"

"Check, but I'm mostly on 'null' for protection—so keep *your* circuits open, I've got a hunch I can reach you now."

"Fair enough, Buby. We'll 'out' now. Bless you."

"Bless you too, the both of you. And may your Carpittl soup turn to Blofonus *drek* in your mouth for what you did to my head."

I heard a sort of duo-chuckling then—and that was it.

I had been lying prone in the snow for maybe ten minutes. Now I went through the motions of regaining consciousness. In effect, I snorted raucously, coughed, and sat up among the welter of furs they'd piled upon me.

"My Lord," I moaned emphatically to Hoggle-Fitz, who'd been on his knees shouting his prayers since I'd first fallen, "Desist. I beg of you. The weight of your words, sir, will do me in a'fore the hurt." I grabbed his arm, pulled myself to my knees.

Looking around, I said accusingly, "Whilst we dally here the devil himself, mayhap, has come to Glagmaron. Let's to saddle, sirs. But first," I shouted to Rawl, "a cup of your brew. For I'm a thirsty man who's had his eyeballs touched by death."

Rawl, grinning widely in relief that I lived, tossed me a leathern bag of sviss from off his saddle horn. Hoggle-Fitz wiped his nose and snorted profusely. Griswall, Charney, and the others all muttered, "My Lord, my lord," and the like, to hide their joy that I was back. Indeed their twilight ring of happy, sword-scarred faces exuded vibes to equal a Pug Boo's "goodness." . . .

"What happened, My Lord?" Rawl finally asked while I drank deeply from the bag. They all waited expectantly.

I wiped my lips. " 'Twas an affliction," I improvised. "A family curse on our great-great uncle, Oalen Lenti, for having poisoned the well of a certain householder named Munns. 'Twas laid on all male children to the third generation—three times to a man. I'm of the third generation, and *that* was the last time." I rubbed my head to ease the not-so-pretended hurt.

They all sighed. And because they were of Fregis-Camelot they believed me. "A little wind on my face," I told them, "and I'll be as fit as ever."

We mounted and made our way to the road. And then, with darkness fast falling, I led them off into a blinding snow-storm. No mind. The dottles could *smell* the road. Our race was with time, not with the snow.

"If nought has happened yet," I yelled to them in the maelstrom of pounding dottle paws; "if we are allowed to pass to our quarters for to bathe and such, then after go to the common hall. I'll join you there. In the meantime, my warning: Look not into the eyes of any man for more than two blinks of a lid—else you'll be Kaleen-possessed, a loss for Marack."

We continued on while the storm grew until at last we mounted the hill to the jousting field.

"By the gods, Collin!" Rawl cried suddenly, as we thun-dered toward the great bridge and the opened gates of Glag-maron Castle, "There's a thing about you, sir, that delights my soul. You 'oft swear against violence. *But to you all violence comes!* I'd not trade your company for the kingdoms of the world!"

We all laughed against the wind and rode direct into the mighty courtyard. Nothing at all seemed awry. Ostlers came quick through the cold to take our steaming dottles to the stables. The guards saluted us respectfully. There was, however, a man among them, chatting. He was a warrior-swordsman—and he wore the colors of the Lord Gen-Rondin. . . .

We parted, Griswall and the students to their proper quarters; Hoggle-Fitz to the king's wing, for he himself would soon be king of Great Ortmund; Rawl and me to our eyrie apartments in the turret-tower of the great east wing.

Situated some three hundred feet above the winding Cyr River, my apartment, to say the least, was drafty. In winter all the drapes in the castle would scarce suffice to stem the cold of the winds that forever shrieked through the stone lacework of my windows. Usually upon entering, I'd simply curse and fling myself beneath the sleeping furs. Not so now. Minded of my recently granted powers, I searched for a victim, and found him—a large insect akin to a Sarithian veeg or Terran roach. It basked in the warmth of the implanted floor pipes. I touched the belt laser stud. A needle of blue light reached out to tickle the veeg. I upped the power! Nothing happened—inside my head, that is. Any attempt to use ungranted power brought instant blackout. Instead there was a flash—*and the veeg was no longer with us!* But still the charge had seemed weak. I made a quick check of the power pack. Sure enough, there'd been a leak. There remained, at best, just four good jolts. . . .

Whatever! I still had it! Belt Power! I'd developed a plan, too. A spur of the moment flash of brilliance along the line of Terra's "Occam's Razor," wherein the simple solution is the best.

I quickly sponged in lukewarm water brought to the rooms of the castle by crude pumping devices through hollow cane poles. The temperature inside my apartment was the same as outside—zero—excepting around the bed where pipes were laid in the wooden floor. At that point it was, perhaps, forty above.

Admiring myself in the full-length mirror of polished bronze, I patted a bit of Rawl's special scent into the proper areas of my ebon fur. The hair on my head was black, too, and shoulder-length. My gene-grown fur was short, a half-inch, but fine and thick. It covered the greater part of my belly. I resembled a rather large mink.

The color of fur on Fregis-Camelot varied. Fortunately no tribe, gen, clan, or family was recognized by any specific shade. Therefore there was no problem of discriminatory differentiation.

The Lord Breen Hoggle-Fitz, for example, was something

of a *pinto,* being both auburn and black. A touch of gray was just beginning to appear with Fitz. That all, if they lived long enough, would *be* gray, was the catalyst, I think, to an acceptance of equality, other than class, by everyone—still, 'twas a rare color indeed for a Fregisian.

Splendiferously dressed, and armed with belt, small-sword and fal-dirk—I also wore light chain-mail 'neath my shirt—I slipped down the myriad of stone steps of the west-wing tower. At ground level I chose the shortcut of the open courtyard as opposed to the castle's labyrinthine corridors. The snow had again lessened. I switched off "null" so's to allow for an accumulation of flakes upon my furs. Fregisians have sharp eyes. I then returned to "null" and walked the rest of the distance dry.

A small herd of dottles wheeed and whoooed before the main entrance. The colors of their blankets were those of Kol-Rebis of Gleglyn, a city some fifty miles distant. Rebis was a member of the Privy Council. He'd left for the "Staading" holidays. I wondered now that he had returned so soon. He'd ridden hard. His dottles literally steamed in the cold.

A handful of his swordsmen and a few of the king's guards milled about in the great anteroom. Kol-Rebis had apparently gone on for audience with the king.

So? Gen-Soolis. Gen-Rondin. Fairwyn; possibly the Baron Rekisto—and who else? Kol-Rebis? If so, what a pity. I'd known him as a slow and easy knight of some distinction in both learning and the martial arts. He, like the brave Gen-Rondin, had made his mark at Dunguring and elsewhere. . . .

The common-room was to the left of the great hall. I shouldered my way through the crowds to cries of: "The Collin! The Collin! Make way!" My face was now known by everyone. The room was its usual bedlam. Fires roared at either end. Fog rose from heated sviss-pots and the snow-laden furs of guards and warriors. The usual brawl was in progress. Spotting my stalwarts at cards, I threaded my way to their table.

Seeing me, Rawl yelled, "Ho, Collin! You've survived the curse, sir. You look the better for it. Join us." He dipped a cup while to my rear the two foolish battlers were being hurled bodily to the courtyard's cooling balm of ice and flagstones.

I sat, watching their rapt and peaceful faces, which seemed unaffected by any previous suggestion of peril. Such, however, was hardly the case. 'Twas simply their way of saving

26

me embarrassment, if I'd erred, or of coming instantly to my side if I had not.

I sampled my cup, waiting patiently 'til their eyes had no recourse but to lift from their game to regard my somber countenance. Rawl grinned, said, "Well, sir, that looks familiar—'tis of swords and fights of arrows."

I shrugged. "Have you spoke of the meceg to anyone?"

They looked at me in disgust, saying "Nay!" in unison.

I said bluntly, "Nothing's changed. Indeed, the peril grows. We're needed now!"

The hoary Griswall grimaced. The very predictable Lord of Durst glared fiercely around him to say, "By Ormon, Collin! Are we beset? I've heard no pipes."

"'Tis not yet a thing of armies," I told them softly. "'Tis a thing that *we* must *do*. Think me mad if you will, but I'll ask you now to join with me this night in an adventure the like of which no one in all of Marack will ever have again."

Their eyes shone. Their indrawn breath was a whistling chorus.

Rawl grinned and shook his head. "Did I not say it? That *to you all violence comes?* I've always thought you mad, Collin. But 'tis a madness to be loved. I'm your man, sir, in any case."

Fitz glared fiercely round him once again, saying, "You have my sword as always, Collin. But *are* you mad? I'd lief know so's to offer the proper prayer. I'm minded of a pious theologian of Great Ortmund who 'oft said that—"

"We've little time," I said to all of them, dismissing Fitz's maunderings. "This is the way it will be: When sup is finished we'll make our farewells and meet in full armor, prepared to ride. No blazonry. 'Twill be but the first step of a most perilous journey. I will, of course, have somehow warned the king."

Griswall asked softly, "Just like that, my lord?"

"Aye," I answered. "Just like that."

Rawl hesitated. "Dare we know our destination?"

I looked him square in the eye. "Most certainly, cousin to be. *We ride to Hish!*"

"You joke."

"Nay, I do not."

Griswall breathed a corpse-like chuckle. Fitz exclaimed loudly, "By the gods, you *are* mad! I've a potion, sir—"

I shook my head. "No potions; nor will we speak again of madness." And then to Griswall—"We'll be taking Charney,

27

Hargis and Tober. See that they're warned. And they have a right to refuse, remember that."

"If 'tis for Marack," he answered bluntly, "no one has that right."

Rawl said soberly, "Hish, Collin, is not just ridden to. 'Tis a city whereat no northman's ever been. 'Tis across a raging winter sea; through many wild and hostile countries. To *ride* to Hish, my lord, is to bid good-bye to all we've known."

I sensed his meaning; saw it in the three pairs of eyes; the likelihood they'd never see the North again. I'll ask once more," I said softly, "Will you follow me in this?"

"You are Marack's Collin," they told me. "You are the savior of the North. How could we not—if *you* have asked us?"

I smiled. "Even if you think me mad?"

"That, too, considered."

"Give my your hands then, and pledge me."

They did, unmindful of the crowd around us—six calloused, sword-scarred hands to grasp mine strongly. . . .

I smiled then to give them heart. "By this time *tomorrow*, sirs," I told them, "we'll be as close to Hish as Dunguring was to Kelb, on the eve of battle. I promise you—thirty miles, no more. From there we'll scout the countryside—ere we advance to tweak the Kaleen's scabby nose."

Their eyes shone again, as I had known they would. They gasped and believed me. For I *was* the Collin.

And I? Well, I thrilled with them. And why not Hish? While we'd slept and played these last six months, the Dark One had acted. And he knew of me now—whereas before he'd only guessed. More! he knew of me as a link to a starship with its, to him, unknown potential for his destruction. What better place to hide then, than in Om itself—except we wouldn't hide! A surge of adrenaline, born of the node's first buzzing, was still with me. A danger, really, since the subconscious, oft' times the victim of id-ego euphoria, plays perilous games. We spoke briefly then of plans to insure our safe departure. . . .

We were late to the royal reception room. The king, usually bluff and hearty, was tense, disturbed. At sight of me he moved to speak but was stopped by a hurried whispering from Fairwyn who stood behind him. A cold and drafty castle-wind fluttered the aged sorcerer's beard. He paid it no mind, which was interesting, for he was a confessed hypochondriac who wore quilted clothing e'en in the heat of summer.

King Olith Caronne and Queen Murie Tindil led off to the dining hall. We took our places: myself to the princess' right hand; Rawl to Caroween's; Fitz to the rear of the four of us. . . .

Gen-Rondin was there, no longer friendly, but rather cold and haughty. A stranger peered from behind his eyes. Fel-Holdt of Svoss, commander in chief of the king's armies, was also present, along with the two great "Kolks," Lords Al-Tils and Kals of Logven. Fel-Holdt was free of the taint, and I was glad of that. They placed themselves behind us, their station in the hierarchy. To the rear came the Pug Boos, Hooli and Jindil—Jindil being recognized by a circle round one eye. They were asleep, lying on cushions carried by lackeys.

"My Lady," I murmured to Murie as we picked up the royal cadence, "my regrets in this thing of Gen-Rondin. A certain indisposition—"

She gnawed her lip and eyed me angrily. "By the gods, sir," she whispered, "play me no games. I know of your monster, love, and of poor Gen-Soolis. . . ."

Damn Rawl! I thought. He must have run to Caroween after all; though in Fregisian protocol, to tell his betrothed was in no way a breach of trust. . . .

"I also know of your 'indisposition,' " Murie was saying. "A seizure, sir? And I was not told?"

"It was nothing, a lowly spell."

"Indeed? Look to my father. Is that, too a 'lowly spell'? If you'd been here—"

"The two are unconnected,"

"By the pits of *Ghast*, Collin. I'm to be your wife, remember?"

"Murie," I said, still *sotto voce*, "we will indeed be wed. But Om is indeed again in Marack. And I must lead in this. Do you understand?"

Tears brimmed her eyes, but she looked to me and nodded.

The pomp and splendor of Marackian royalty is equaled in no feudal society anywhere; nor is it surpassed. This night, as usual, it was beauteous, dazzling. It was also tinsel and running dye. We, of course, sat at the king's table; being doubly flanked by two lines of tables at right angles to our centered three. All rose to bow their heads to the king and to his light and airy queen. He simply seated himself and the nightly feasting began. Indeed, at that precise moment a veritable parade of trays and service poured forth from the kitchens. In the summer past, the viands had been great roasts and shanks of meat from all manner of strange beasts; tureens of gravies sufficient to drown a midget; puddings, pastries, birds in every shape and size—and an endless pouring of varied wines, sviss, and other alcoholic beverages. *Now* it was but a simple fare of gog-meat, winter vegetables, sviss, and thin wines. . . . Gaiety too had waned, for winter's grip was hard upon the Court: no partying; no hunting; no colorful tournaments—no bloody battles!

The "solstice," of course, would be celebrated shortly, along with the "Staading," the day of the "granting of life" by the hallowed trinity of Ormon, the father, Wimbily, the mother, and Harris, the "lost child," who, when found, would, like the Collin mythos, *me*, restores the Northern peoples to the greatness they once had owned. In this respect, I'd oft' thought that the Pug Boos, who knew of their real history, had allowed a bit of race memory to remain so as to soften the trauma of true greatness, when it would one day be returned to them.

Whatever, for the moment even the advent of this most religious of all days had yet to grab the citizenry. . . .

Our plain food done, we settled to drinks and entertainment. A trained snow-carnivore was first. It was a kuul, all white but with Fregisian blue eyes, great ripping fangs to scare a gerd, and taloned pads. It curled its huge, six-legged body into a ball and rolled this way and that to the command of its trainer. The kuul, possessing the high I.Q. of all Fregisian fauna, peered cautiously between the digits of one of its pads so as not to run into anything.

Watching, Murie slipped a hand into mine and pressed her head to my shoulder. She was usually not demonstrative. Other than our pre-nuptial "carryings on," I'd have thought her cold. Now, as I responded to this small advance, I saw two tears upon her cheeks, while her blue-purple eyes stared up at me, deliberately, and with a piquant sadness. By the gods, I thought, she's at it again; though she loved me she'd ever be queen to my role of consort—in waiting. . . . In effect, she'd "control me" one way or the other. I grinned, squeezed her small hand in turn and winked at her.

Among the many bits of wisdom that I, Kyrie Fern, will bequeath to posterity is the solidly researched fact that the female of the humanoid species, in transit from barbarism to what is preciously known as civilization, invariably attempts at one time or another in a relationship to make an utter ass, dubot, or flimpl, of the male of the species—even her beloved, or rather, *especially* her beloved; at the least she is at all times most willing to use her *person* to her advantage. I'd call it instinctive retribution for male-inflicted wrongs across the millennia of evolution. The pattern's in-grained—programmed! I, for one, suspect a Puckish God! I speak from experience. . . .

Betrothals on Fregis-Camelot—in this case, mine to the Princess Murie Nigaard Caronne, only child to the king and queen of Marack—take exactly one year; this from a posting of banns to consummation. Prior to an official announcement of a marriage-to-be; *anything* is permissible 'twixt the consenting parties. *After* the banns, the two parties are put on ice for the duration of the *full twelve months!*

That the court had conspired to neglect to inform me of this fact was the understatement of the Fregisian year. Not that they hadn't hinted, for indeed they had. But who, I ask, in the full euphoria of an "oft-requitted chase," would believe in hints? For six months therefore I'd been forced to adapt myself to the burning fact that delightful dalliance in sylvan gog-meadows, camp tents, and castle "nooks," were over—*kaput!* And, too, in my own eyes I had indeed become the "consort marionette" to my bit of saucy pulchritude as she seemingly went, uncaring, about her business of being *the* princess.

Moreover, and this perhaps was the greater blow, the sure knowledge that I, at age thirty—*I*, a Foundation *Adjuster* with sufficient carnal knowledge (Galactic), to last a lifetime; *I*, the hero-victor of Dunguring—that *I* could become so concerned by "non-access" to a certain delightful *tush,* had left me, to say the least—with a new Achilles heel.

I stared again. She *was* beautiful. My fate. My trap! She wore a velvet dress of purple and silver which, together with her marigold hair, sparkling tiara, and soft-molded outline of breast and belly, near drove me to my knees. She was cameo-perfect. If ever I tired of being the Collin, I had only to think of Murie—of that I was certain.

In control again, I thought to reassure her before telling her of our departure. In this last respect two tables below the salt held upwards of a hundred student-warriors all pledged to Grisswall and myself. Another table serviced a company of Fitz's men, swordsmen from Great Ortmund. Hoggle, of course, sat with us at the king's table. And finally one section of the castle guards was commanded by a sergeant loyal to

Fel-Holdt, whom Hoggle had warned 'gainst Fairwyn's eyes.

At the "high table" were the lords, Gen-Rondin, Kol-Rebis of Gleglyn, the brave and courteous Rekisto, aging now but always full of fight; the kolbs (barons), Al-Tils and Kals of Logven, Caril, kolb of Doriis, Gen-Baios of Drees, Fel-Holdt of Svoss, and a dozen others. Counting ourselves, a majority of the Privy Council were in attendance.

Of those present, I settled for Gen-Rondin, Fairwyn, Uurs of Klimpinge, Kol-Rebis—now that I'd seen him, watched his eyes—and Caril, the new commander of the castle guard, as definitely being the Kaleen's men. A pity; I'd known them all as brothers at Dunguring.

My job, in part, was to free them too.

"Murie," I began, "I've a serious thing to tell you. We'll be leaving tonight, I, Rawl, Griswall, and Fitz. There is a thing we must do. . . ."

She went all white; stared at me as if I'd told her the world would end at cock's-crow. "Where?" she asked.

"I cannot tell you."

"But Collin, my lord—how can you leave my father now?"

I said, "I'll explain after—"

A shouted ruckus interrupted from without, amid a caterwaul of loudly whoooing dottles. Two minstrels who'd taken the place of the kuul stopped their playing. Knights and warriors stood yelling to their feet. Hands reached for sword hafts. . . . Then three young knights burst through the doors in a mad dash to fling themselves before the king. The guards, pursuing, seized them, put blades to their throats, and waited.

The king stared silently, then gestured to the guards to withdraw. He nodded to Fairwyn who was court spokesman.

Our aged sorcerer, struggling to his feet, cried out, "Who be you, sirs? How dare you thusly to come before our liege?"

Murie's hand clutched mine still tighter. Rawl, teeth bared in an evil grin, said *sotto voce*, "Well, Collin, here's 'entertainment,' and that's a fact."

Bidden to rise by the king, the three doffed their coats to reveal the heraldic colors of Kelb, the seacoast kingdom wherein Dunguring had been fought. Hard cakes of ice clung to their garments. A steam of fog rose round their persons. The leader was young, strong. His wild eyes reflected the rigors of a difficult journey.

He shouted hoarsely: "Your most gracious majesties, and my lords and sirs—" he bowed his head briefly—"Forgive our rudeness. 'Tis that we've no time for the protocol of entry. We bring the plea of Laratis, our newly crowned of Kelb. He begs your aid and sends warning of dire peril. I'm bidden to tell you, sire, that our capital of Corchoon *is under siege!*"

Fairwyn angrily interrupted: "How speak you, sir, of peril and siege? The North's at peace. Dunguring's all behind us.""

The young knight ignored him, turned direct to the king, crying, "Dunguring's *not* behind us. *For 'tis the very dead from off that field who ring our capital!*"

There was a great silence then—followed by a gasp of total horror to sweep the hall like a soughing wind. An attack by two hundred thousand mouldering corpse-men was no pretty thing to contemplate. There were instant screams from the women and roars of anger and dread from the warriors. More! There began a weeping for the fact that if this were true, then among the dead would be the sons and brothers of those who sat this very moment at the king's tables— Fairwyn, normally prone to instant panic in any crisis, stood strangely calm.

Corpse-men! Dead-alives! The curse of the North! So much so that for countless years no one would dare the night except with a company of armed men. 'Twas a trick of the Dark One—to rule the night! He'd done it deliberately, sporadically, activating the dead to kill the living, or to seize a child or a woman, supposedly for some dark purpose in far-off Om. The fear instilled was quite effective.

I'd been the first in living memory to challenge that fear; to shame others to join me in the challenge. Indeed, 'twas I, the risen "Collin," who'd brought the warrior hordes of Gheese and Ferlach to the rescue of Marack on the field of Dunguring, forcing them to ride through *two* nights to do it. And we'd fought dead-alives at Gortfin and other places.

Now, however, the Kaleen had apparently conjured up an army, though we knew—I and the Pug Boos—that he had neither the skill nor the power to use such a horde effectively.

I watched Fairwyn closely, certain that this risen horror was no surprise to him. Normally, a threat to the House of Marack would elicit his immediate "words" and a spinning of the proper "web" so as to insure the king's protection. Now he did nothing.

The spoken "words" of a sorcerer-king-protector could produce a form of "null," but with certain differences. It was degradable for one thing, and lasted but a few hours. It was also accompanied by a slight fog. Fregisians, the Dark One must have reasoned, needed visual proof that their sorcery

33

was working. . . . For it was he who was the originator of all magick on Fregis-Camelot. Actually, though I still did not fully understand it, it was derived of a certain power over the planet's magnetic field, and he'd given it to the priests of the religion he'd created for the people in the south—the better to hold them in thralldom.

Osmosis-wise, however, the "magick" had crept north, jumped the River Sea and come into the possession of Northern priests. The *gestalt* effect of five thousand years of practice was such that the practitioners of the North had surpassed in many ways the priests of the South, having found, through trial and error, new combinations of sound—the secret to it all—that worked. In no way, however, could they equal the Kaleen. And too, to all who practiced it, North *or* South—it still was *magick!*

I watched the king closely. Indeed, I'd kept an eye on him since we'd first gone to the reception room. One thing was sure, though he was reacting to either the lies or threats of Fairwyn and the others, he was *not* Kaleen possessed. I wondered of that. Had the Dark One tried and failed? Had the king a power of which even I was unaware?

He rose to speak, in defiance of Fairwyn's glare. "Tell us," he commanded, and his voice was heavy, tired, "of those risen dead. We know of the Dark One's power. But never, to our knowledge, have those from a stricken field returned to attack the living."

Fairwyn stood suddenly rigid, his skinny hands all folded on his breast. King Caronne seated himself again and waited, chin in hand, for the "why" of it. . . .

To continued cries of dread and sounds of weeping, the young warrior told his tale: "They appeared a week ago," he said. "The people of a village were killed and eaten. Since then the countryside's been ravaged so that the folk have fled in terror to Corchoon. The fighting's been fierce. 'Tis a thing on our part of a hacking and a collecting of parts for burning. As for the dead-alives, when one of ours is seized he is torn asunder and his parts devoured, though our sorcerer, Kalfi, tells us that 'tis *not* the flesh of life that sustains the life in them."

"And all is done at night?" Fel-Holdt questioned loudly.

"At first, yes," the young knight answered. "But on the morn I left Corchoon, thousands had gathered in the bright sun to come before the city's walls. There were six of us when we started out. Three we lost while we chopped our

34

way through a mile of corpses; our poor dottles screaming the while in their terror."

"When did you leave Corchoon, sir?" the king asked courteously.

"Two days ago, Sire."

"Then you rode the night."

"The night, sirs," the young man said proudly, "will never again hold fear for Kelbians. For like your 'Collin,' we've fought the very fiends themselves." His tired eyes flashed; the first sign I'd seen of pride in deed.

There were thunderous cheers all around.

Fel-Holdt, Lord of Svoss, stern, patriarchal, Marshall of all Marack's armies, then rose to face the king. "Sire," he cried, his voice icy-calm, "From unnatural battle such as this true men will naturally turn and shudder. Yet 'tis thrust upon us and must be fought. Your army, in winter quarters at Castle Gortfin, is a third of the way 'twixt here and Corchoon. I say send to that army now! Direct it at once to the aid of our Kelbian brothers. And more!" he cried fiercely to shouts of "Aye" throughout the hall, "Until the problem's solved, guard all our graveyards day and night! See to it there's no more burying. The pyre, the burning vat, my liege, is the only way 'til this new challenge is over. . . ."

Then the Baron Rekisto received the king's nod and spoke, and the lords, Al-Tils and Kols of Logven, and Gen-Baios of Drees. All asked that aid be sent post-haste to Kelb. There was no disagreement.

Then Gen-Rondin rose to stand next to Fairwyn, who seemed again in a trance, also to endorse the need for action. But he took it one step further. Rondin was tall, heavy, his mien positive. A warrior-juror of Marack's courts, he had earned much respect. And he deserved it—except for now. "My king," he began, and his blazing eyes were of whatever it was that dwelt in Hishian darkness, "the task confronting our northern lands would be best served by sending our Collin to command the force at Gortfin. Where fighting's simple, Sire, we need but strength and valor. But where there's magick, there do we need the Collin. For above all other in the 'art,' our warlocks, sorcerers, witches—his magick is the best!"

Lord Uurs of Klimpinge, a smiling visage of darksome plot, rose instantly to acclaim the words of Rondin—and Kol-Rebis too, and Caril. The latter's face was so twisted in a grotesquerie of hate that I wondered that those around me seemed not to see what I saw. They stood to cheer and to

35

shout and clap for the "Collin." Need it be said that the whole hall followed suit?

I'd been right! A diversion was in motion right now. Though the Dark One had expected me to be dead, sucked dry by that damned meeg, he could still tie my hands—and along with me, Marack's army, in an unending, useless battle with dead men.

The shouting was sufficient to cause a guttering of the winter candles. Strange shadows flew and writhed on walls and ceilings. It was a beauteous and fearful sight, that wintry hall; that seated mass of warriors, knights, and ladies. It was an arras blown with snow-smells, the perfume of conifers; of wax, cooked animals, sweat—and from some, the pungent smell of awful fear. . . .

Neat! Oh so neat a trap! Except it was set for Fregisians, not Terran *Adjusters*. I'd change it all right now. I stepped to Fitz, bent to his hairy ear and spelled out precisely what I wanted. He looked to me in awe, groaned hoarsely, "Vuuns, my lord: our thirty thousand? Well, then we'll see to it—Fel-Holdt and me!"

Upon which I arose to the still thundering acclaim around me and held high my hands to the king. "Sire," I cried, "I've a question. If Kelb's attacked, what then of Ferlach, Gheese, and Great Ortmund? Have we had couriers from these lands? Do corpse-men walk upon *their* roads, besiege *their* cities? 'Tis a thing to know. Moreover, Sire, in this last respect, since our good Lord of Great Ortmund, Breen Hoggle-Fitz of Durst, leaves at dawn's light for that fair country to check it out. He'll stop at Gortfin first to lend a hand if need be. . . ."

"Nay!" roared Hoggle-Fitz on cue, whilst rising to his feet. "I'll not wait for dawn's light. I'll ride the night, too, sirs! And I do petition my friend and colleague, Fel-Holdt, to ride with me and to command the king's army in this affair. For I submit, my lords, that though I love our Collin, Marack's army should be led by Marack's Marshall. . . ."

"Would you demean our risen savior?" The spittle flew with the instant shriek from Rondin's mouth.

By the gods, we had him!

"Nay, nay, good Gen!" I called. "In no way doth our Lord of Ortmund demean me. I'd remind you, sir, that our Lord of Svoss is commander by right and not by accident. He's a proven strategist, the best we have. And besides, sirs, *I* ride to Ferlach and Gheese with Sir Rawl Fergis. Those goodly kings, Chitar and Draslich must still be warned." I then deliberately spread my arms as if to encompass all within that hall and cried, "And I do assure my friend, the Lord of Rondin, that if aught befalls our army at Corchoon, I'll join them there. . . . *He can count on it!*"

They cheered for that too and clapped again. Indeed, when Gen had asked that I command Marack's forces, my student-warriors had leapt to their feet to offer their swords. Now they volunteered to accompany me south. I could see Griswall restraining them. Catching his eye, I beckoned him to me.

A glance at Rondin showed him staring to Fairwyn. And that worthy, back from wherever he'd been, simply smiled. They both looked to the king who chose to ignore them, reaching instead for his flagon of sviss.

Since I wasn't meeeg-meat, they'd wanted me in Kelb. Still, they seemed not unhappy now that both Fel-Holdt and Fitz would be out of the way whilst I, with Rawl, would be off to the countries of the southwest. I'm sure they still thought they could plan some sort of entrapment—except, of course, we'd be in neither Ferlach nor Gheese. Nor would the Marackian army march to Kelb! I'd given Fitz his orders!

I felt quite smug about it.

The king arose to duly thank the heralds, his voice low, monotone. He then sent them to the warrior's room of the chirurgeons, masseurs, and gnostics, to be bathed, massaged, and tended. He promised an early audience on the morrow.

It was agreed then that Fel-Holdt would command. The discussion of tactics began, 'neath a pall of gloom. Normally a call to battle, border skirmish, punitive expedition, or the like was cause for wassail. But now the fighting would be with the corpse-men, and there was no joy. The canons of northern chivalry had no writ for such as this. There would be no glory, only horror. The expression of each warrior and knight was of disgust, repugnance, unease. Most simply wished to be somewhere else—and not from fear.

I told Rawl what Fitz would do. I told Griswall too, when he came to our table; also that he should prepare the mounts for our party and to somehow keep those hundred student-warriors at arms and ready—until we were safely on our way.

To my left, stout Hoggle, with a Fregisian's mercurial ability to dispense with worry once a solution had been offered to a problem, leaned across his daughter's pert slenderness to discourse with Rawl on the powers of *exorcism* as being done to a dead-alive in Ortmund. "But the man was a charlatan,"

Fitz roared to the bored Sir Fergis. "Though a taker of drugs, he was alive as you and me."

Rawl screwed up his eyes. "Did he actually lay claim to being a dead-alive?"

"Nay," Fitz said. " 'Twas that he was *accused*."

"Then he was no charlatan."

"But indeed he was, sir," Hoggle shouted.

"You say 'accused.' How then, sir? 'Twas no idea of his?"

"Why the guilt's clear. He *acted* thusly, when actually he wasn't. That's when the priest was called."

"Why?"

"Why? To drive the demon from him. And I must say that our good priest of Dernim Church arrived none too soon."

"What demon, sir?"

"The one that made him take the tistle-weed, the drug."

"Then surely," Rawl opined, grinning widely, "if he'd not himself laid claim to being a corpse-man; if in fact a demon had made him take the weed in the first place—then how, sir, can *he* be called a charlatan?"

Hoggle-Fitz breathed deeply at that and batted his large and bulbous eyes. He finally said sternly to Caroween, "Keep a close rein on this one, my dear. He has much to learn and I'd not see you burdened with the foolishments of an addle-pate."

"Your pardon, father-in-law to be," Rawl said with a straight face. " 'Tis as the world knows, I've only that of the 'sviss' to my credit. . . ."

Hoggle guffawed. "Would you could do it with water, sirrah! A well's oft' more handy than a mooly-gog's udder." He arose then to make his arrangements with Fel-Holdt for departure, pausing to whisper in my ear. "What we do, Collin," he said, "is rebellion. If you're wrong, 'twill mean our lives."

" 'Tis no rebellion," I replied shortly. "The king's a captive now. Believe me. We'll come to you, my lord. You can count on it."

He breathed deeply, pressed my shoulder and continued to his task. Upon which, Murie, no longer able to contain herself, pulled my face around to stare into my eyes. She hissed, "All right, my *love*, you'll tell me now what I must know—right *now!*"

Beneath the table my hand quick-grasped her silky thigh, moved up to her silky belly. "Hey," I said. "My every thought's for you. You know that."

"Hey, yourself. And I do *not* know that."

38

"Some things are not easily explained, here—and there's little time."

"Well *try*, you bastard!" Her blue eyes were flashing fire. For a second I thought he'd got her, the Dark One. But we were still on "null."

I put my mouth to a delicately pointed ear as if to kiss her. Instead I whispered, "List well, my love. Though I've volunteered to go with Rawl to Gheese and Ferlach, we'll not be going there."

—A surge had begun toward the entrance to the hall. More and more followed; each first bending the knee to the king. The thing of the corpse-men was oppressive, a thing they knew not how to deal with. Many were off to the temples in the city below to purchase spells and amulets from the priests, and to pray, perhaps, that a loved one was not among the risen dead. I watched from the corner of one eye as some of the finest knights in Marack made bold to take their leave. . . .

Murie'd lifted her chin. "Is my father, at least, to know your destination?"

"Perhaps."

"By the gods, Collin, you tell me nothing."

"I mean to see you shortly, when we've retired."

A smattering of applause swept the tables. We rose with the others to bow our heads to the queen's passing. Some of her ladies followed—a signal for Murie and Caroween. Rawl captured Caroween's hands against her departure.

Murie's eyes searched mine. "Do you mean in my rooms?"

"Or in mine."

She frowned, then licked her lips thoughtfully. "By Ormon, love, you're suddenly waxing bolder. Could it be," and she raised an appraising eyebrow—"that what's been needed is a small crisis to stir your bollocks?"

I could only look at her and gape—stupidly.

"Well, really," she said, with a certain accusing testiness; alluding obviously to the fact that we'd not bedded since the posting of banns, "Where *have* you *been*?" And since we'd both risen, she stood on tiptoe to brush my lips with hers and to laugh and to seize Caroween's hand and follow in the wake of the queen.

I stared after her, helpless, damning my conditioned adherence to protocol—my *idiot* abstinence. And she had the effrontery, the absolute gall to pause, look back, and make a moue.

A moue, to the uninitiated, is an expression, a weapon,

really, used only by the female of the species. Supposedly it absolves them of responsibility for *anything*. . . . Beyond the petulant grimace, as it is so described by the dictionary, a moue is actually the alpha and the omega of insouciance. It is, in the archaic, the facial expression of "Not tonight, Henry!" "Go to your room!" and, "Oh, it's *you!*"

By the gods! I thought, for a wave of lust seemed suddenly to permeate my entire being; by bloody damned Buddah-Jesus! If I was off to die in the Dark One's city, and there was every chance that I would, I'd sure as hell not leave *her* here. "Stop them, Rawl," I said flatly, "and hold them 'til I return."

He left instantly to do my bidding, whilst I hurried to the group around the king. "Sire," I said, when I'd shouldered my way through the press of bodies, "I'll take my leave, too, since your nephew and myself will be leaving at the same time as our Lords of Svoss and Ortmund."

He studied me thoughtfully, sadly; or so it seemed. The glowering Gen-Rondin and the reedy Fairwyn flanked him on either side. The number of castle guards behind the "high table" seemed larger than usual. A thought, transient but by no means alien, touched my mind: How easy it would be to kill all our enemies right now! And save the king! But it wasn't that easy, and I knew it. And even if I won, exactly *what* would I have gained? *Nyet!* The idea itself was distraction; for all was created toward one end—to allow for time; to allow for the Dark One to do whatever he had to do. And that "whatever" was what it was all about. And I, by the gods, would stop him. The field was *Hish*, not Glagmaron!

The king was saying softly, "I would that the waiting was over, Sir Lenti; that my daughter and yourself were safely wed."

I answered lightly, "Were that the case, Sire, I'd take her with me. There's no finer rider in all of Marack than the princess."

"Well then." He forced a hollow laugh. "Were I the gallant, I'd take her anyway. Where should a princess be, but at the side of her consort." His eyes lifted, stared hard into mine. . . . I'd received a *command*, and I knew it.

I grinned broadly to show myself in favor of the "joke," said quickly, "Well, if I had not such fear of my lady's 'maiden' wrath, Sire, I'd do just that."

The Lords Al-Tils and Gen-Gaios both clapped at this, midst a smattering of laughter. Hoggle had joined me too. I glanced toward Rondin and Fairwyn as myself and the Lord of Ortmund bent a final knee. The aged sorcerer was whispering "words," his eyes glaring blackly at Fitz and me. I laughed aloud—and glared right back. I no longer cared that he knew that I *knew*. A "mind control" he couldn't do. "Null" served us well—and I mean each person within the hall not yet controlled. They could send the guard against me. But I doubted much that the Dark One was ready to accept such a tactic, just yet. . . .

I said softly to Fitz, "Return quickly to Fel-Holdt. Do not leave his side again 'til you're safe at Gortfin Castle. Tell him what you will, but leave now. For the moment you have the important job—*to secure the army for Marack and the North!*"

He nodded, made the triple-circle upon his chest.

"A last thing," I murmured. "I've the king's order to take his daughter with me. With your permission, I'll take yours too."

"By the gods, Collin!" he exclaimed—his breath, right in my face, would melt a jousting lance—"do you remember where you go?"

"Wherever I go, old friend, your Caroween is safest, and she be with me."

At that he crushed my hand with his, shed instant tears, and spun upon his heel to return to Fel-Holdt.

Not wasting a second I returned to my trio, telling them the plan had changed: "An order from the king. You'll come with us, Murie, Caroween; right now! We leave before the hour's through—light armor, furs; nought else. We'll meet in the courtyard. If there's the slightest hint of danger, don't wait. Come direct to us. . . . That too is an order."

"And *my* father?" the hothead Caroween asked.

"What else? He sends his love."

Her eyes brimmed too with instant tears. They left hurriedly then to bid the queen good night. I saw with some satisfaction that Fitz and Fel-Holdt—the latter with a following of five swordsmen and Fitz with his tableful of Ortmundian stalwarts—were also leaving. Rawl deftly snatched a bottle whilst we collected our cloaks, and we too left the hall.

In his apartment, on the same level as mine, we acted as each other's squire in donning gear. I'd sent a lackey to alert Griswall. Each fumbling second was like a minute for I doubted much that the Dark One would allow us to leave without some attempt; especially since I had the odd premonition that he, through his surrogates, now knew that the princess would leave with me. We had to get to the scoutship immediately. Without it, in the vernacular of the archaic, we'd really be "in the soup."

Within thirty minutes we were armed, cloaked, packed and ready; still we took an extra minute or so to toast each other with the last of the sviss. I was not at all surprised, therefore, when we finally entered the courtyard to find Fitz, Fel-Holdt and all their entourage already mounted. Moreover, their departure awaited but the opening of the gates. Fitz, shouting, blaspheming—no contradiction, for even his blasphemy was a form of prayer—was hurrying the guards to do just that.

I walked direct to the Lord of Svoss, gave him my hand and said bluntly: "Trust my Lord of Ortmund, sir. He's the king's man ere he'll ever himself be king. Be assured too, that the fate of Marack will certainly depend upon your arms. Stay to Gortfin! You'll hear from us directly!"

The stern and sharp-faced marshall made the triple-circle and cross upon his mailed chest. He answered briefly, but from the depths of his being: "May the gods be with us all tonight, Sir Lenti." He looked toward the gates.

They were opening amid echoing shouts of guards from those other gates of the outer walls. I glanced quickly to the myriad torches lighting the broad steps to the oaken doors of the entrance. Murie and Caroween were as yet nowhere in sight. We mounted up. With the two girls we'd number eight. Griswall and our three swordsmen had brought a herd of twenty-four dottles to supplement our personal mounts.

Small chance their knowing that we would ride but twenty miles.

Seeing us, Hoggle-Fitz rode hastily back. His huge dottle, Alphus, reared upon four of its six legs while its fore-pair pawed the frozen air.

"Do you leave with us, Collin," he shouted, causing his Alphus to stomp in a half circle. "If not, I bid you good journey now." Both he and Fel-Holdt were equally impressive in cloaked mail and towering helms. Greatswords and shields were slung to their backs. Fitz had managed a running herd of better than two hundred dottles.

Excepting the night and the two four-hour dottle grazing periods, all Northern warriors rode straight through to wherever they were going; thus the practice of an accompanying herd, or pack. The stamina of mount and man was a thing to see. I had twice the strength of any Fregisian, Terra having double the mass of Fregis-Camelot. But I'd not their staying power. At the end of any lengthy trip I was a mess; whereas they were fresh, ready for anything. Indeed, my riding weakness had long been known in joke as the Collin's "curse." Much sport was made of it.

I sat astride a fully recovered Henery. He'd also been my mount when I'd fought the Kaleen's champion, the great Gol Bades, on the field of Dunguring. I'd won. But poor Henery had lost an ear, for which he'd never forgiven me. Now Henery reared to Alphus. And he too waved his foremost set of doggy-paws—a dottle greeting.

"Nay, sir," I yelled to Hoggle's question, "we've to wait, as you can see."

He sought to say more. But that hardened warrior, Fel-Holdt, seeing the gates full open, refused to dally when haste was of the utmost. He'd taken our words of warning quite seriously. "All on!" he shouted. "NOW!" And he led the entourage off, with the wheeing, whoooing dottle herd in happy, dog-like pursuit.

Hoggle-Fitz, whirling Alphus in a great scattering of ice from off the flagstones, had time only to cry to Rawl: "Look to my daughter, Sir! You've a father's love what ere your faults." Then he raised both mailed fists in high salute, shouting: *"For Marack!"*

We answered, crying, "God's speed, my lord! For Ormon and the *king!*"

And they were gone. . . .

We waited silently to one side of the torch-lit entrance, in the lee of the castle wall. Above, in a primal sky patched with snow clouds that had never left us, silvered Ripple, smallest of Fregis' two moons, made a hurried transit from one cloud bank to another; to be followed shortly by Capil, the larger. The guards at both entrance and opened gate stomped their feet and waved their arms to aid their frozen misery. Except for an occasional snort from our steaming dottles, the quiet was awesome. . . .

Then they came running—not from the grandiose entrance, as expected, but from a minor exit of that monstrous pile of slate and granite. Hargis had dismounted to check the cinch belt of Murie's saddle. I motioned him to hurry.

They were two short and bulky figures, mailed, cloaked, and with the hafts of small-swords showing above their shoulders. Except for a certain arrogance and a feminine wriggle in every lengthy stride, they could have been what they seemed, two warriors of the king—albeit, shortened by a head. Another oddity that would set them apart from the king's standard warrior was the small furry creature dressed in a warm suit, a blue-knitted cap with a huge red pompon, and with something akin to "booties" and "mittens" which clung to the travel bag on Murie's shoulder.

I sighed, "Oh, Jesu-Magnus!" knowing she'd made those clothes herself.

They ran straight to us, vaulting into the empty saddles of the mounts being held for them. Murie yelled, "Let's to it, Collin! They'll be on us in an instant!"

But Hargis still worked at the cinch. So while we whirled this way and that, keeping our eyes to the entrance and gate, she explained breathlessly—"We went to bid my father adieu and were met in the hall by Fairwyn and Gen Rondin. They sought to detain us, but we broke from them. And because we are fleet of foot we lost them in the corridors—and here we are!"

"Seeing you dressed, armed—and with *that*"—I pointed to Hooli—"I'm sure now that they know you leave with us."

Hargis to saddle again, I led them in a parallel trot along the castle wall so as to not upset the guards and to bid them a proper salute before riding for the gates. Murie's voice came over my shoulder—"Aye, Collin. But there was no other way."

It was just then that I felt a tingling—and a need to *move*, and quick.

The desire scarce preceded a sudden, bellowing shout, crying, *"Treason! Treason to the King!"* coming from the entrance.

We drove instantly toward the gates. But, being humanoid, we hesitated for the nth part of a second to glance back to the source of the shouting. A fully armed Gen-Rondin stood in the torchlight of the entrance. The doors had been flung full open and a horde of guards were streaming out upon the broad steps toward us.

Rondin continued, screaming: *"Seize* them! They've taken the Princess! *Seize them!"* And his voice was all amplified, you can bet—but not enough so that we failed to hear the whistling, tearing sound that came from above. Indeed, even as I recognized it for what it was, Rondin's cries were drowned by a great crash of granite upon the flagstones—on the very spot where we'd just been!

Score *two* for Marack. The granite blocks had crushed the lives from a dozen or so of our would-be captors. They'd moved too fast. Blood splashed the flagstones. The remainder fell back in terror; looked up to see what I saw.

At a hundred feet above the courtyard a turreted abutment

was now minus its crenellated stonework. Fairwyn stood on the remaining flat-space, all shining in a warlock's aura of red and purple light. His skinny arms raised in a mad obeisance to the primal skies, he shrieked his "words." He looked three times his actual size. Blue lightning played around him.

At the first screams of Rondin, Griswall had whistled shrilly, keeping it up. In answer, there now came from the direction of the stables, and in a thunder of dottle paws, our hundred student warriors. They came on in a maelstrom of swinging swords, driving between us and the castle guards—a complete surprise!

We in turn rode hard for the gates, to seize them and the portcullis, lest it descend to bar our flight. Thirty guards held the gatehouse. Most were confused, stunned. Still some stood forth to stop us. After all, they *were* Marackian warriors! Their sergeant, a burly giant of a man, bent low, seeking to hamstring poor Henery. . . . I rose full in my stirrups and with one whistling stroke swept both screaming head and sword arm from his body. Rawl killed two men in as many seconds, as did Griswall. Our three young swordsmen each slew his opposite. The remainder fell back in terror to mingle with those who'd made no move against us.

All this took place in a spate of seconds. Such is the way of *true* combat. Fighting raged around the great steps. Our students, though mounted, were still outnumbered. Their dottles found purchase difficult upon the icy flagstones.

I cupped my hands, shouting, "Break off! We've seized the gate!" And they did, falling back across the bodies of the slain. At once there came from above a seering blaze of great lightning to crisp a dozen of them. Some screamed in agony. Our dottles cried their fear. The warriors of Gen-Rondin and the Lord Caril cheered and moved to charge the courtyard.

Roaring, "*Hold, Fairwyn!* 'Tis the *Collin* who opposes you now," I whirled Henery back from the gate, stood again to my stirrups, my armor all glowing *bright*. I'd switched on the ion activisor, affecting sulphur compounds in the steel. The guards of Caril cried in awe. I shouted, "Withdraw now, lest I turn your very lightnings back upon you!"

But like Gen-Soolis before him, the Kaleen had him, fully. His eyes were wild. Spittle flew from his mouth. "Base traitor," he shrieked, "the evidence is there! You've seized the princess!"

Upon which Murie yelled from behind my shoulder, "You lie, you foul-fiend, bastard!" But her small voice was lost in the reverberations of Fairwyn's words.

45

"The truth, sir sorcerer," I roared again, "is that 'tis *you* who've seized the *king!*"

At that very moment another bolt of blue-white death, sufficient to render both myself and poor Henery into our respective weights in suet, did it strike us, came crashing down.

It was *deflected*, for I'd stepped up "null" to full. More! At that precise instant I triggered the stud for laser action. A thin blue beam struck straight and true, needling our erstwhile "timid" sorcerer to the heart. He screamed once, grabbed his skinny chest and toppled from the platform. His aged body, bone-dry, feather-light, seemed but one more snowflake as it fell—albeit, larger. I'd actually loved that old man. 'Twas one more debt the Dark One owed me. . . .

"Follow on!" I cried then, midst an enveloping stench of fire and brimstone. We wheeled to thunder through the gates and on down the narrow lane 'twixt the great double walls of Glagmaron castle. Our students, cheering, rode hard in our wake.

The second, outer gate lay two hundred yards to the left. There too was a portcullis and drawbridge; though there was no moat, just a chasm—a deep ravine.

War pipes shrilled now in the freezing air. All the castles' myriad inhabitants were astir. Kettledrums beat wild staccatos of alarm. More amplified cries of "treason" preceded us. The garrison of the main gate, some two hundred strong, were ready for our onslaught, albeit confused and wondering.

Our swords unsheathed, I'd have ridden straight into them. But Murie spurred suddenly ahead, rode direct to their shield front where she threw back her cowl to reveal the royal curls of Marack, whilst flashing her dottle's painted paws right in their faces. She yelled, "Down swords! To your knees, you sons-of-bitches! 'Tis your Princess who commands you. If you want more—well, here's our Collin too, your risen savior!"

The young guard's-captain, clearly impressed, went instantly to one knee and offered his sword. Still he said, "The voices say 'treason,' my princess. First 'twas your father's sorcerer, Fairwyn; now 'tis the Lord Caril, my commander. What would you have of me?"

Murie's eyes blazed. "Why I'd have you clear the bridge, sir. *Now!*"

I'd ridden up. I said bluntly, "There's no time, Captain. Stand aside. Your Fairwyn's dead. The Lord Gen-Rondin and Caril now hold our king for Hish."

"Then, sir, let's fight them."

"We will. But first the princess must reach the safety of the army. —Now, for the last time, stand aside!"

"And do you not," Murie yelled, her royal anger rising, "I'll burn your bloody souls to hell when I return!"

"Lead off," I told her. "Quickly!" And I whacked her dottle's rump. . . .

She did so, riding at them, sword bared; fat Hooli with his pompon still clinging to her furs. They parted like Terra's fabled "Red Sea." I think the sight of Hooli did it. The remainder of my hundred students followed after.

"If you truly love the king," I shouted to the captain, "then raise the bridge when we've crossed over."

"I'll do it, Collin!" His voice rang proudly in the rising, snow-laden wind as we, Rawl, Griswall, and our three swordsmen, who'd stayed with me, rode 'neath the portcullis and out upon the bridge. Only a handful attempted to stop us. But their hearts weren't in it. Rawl cut their leader down. Our swordsmen slew the others where they stood.

We'd barely made it across when the great bulk of the bridge shuddered and began to rise. Simultaneously with this there came a thunder of dottle paws from within the inner walls. Seconds later we heard the clash of swords and the shouts of men in battle. But we did not look back. We'd have seen nothing anyway, for the snow came down heavy then, making the night an instant, stygian blackness. . . .

On the south road the dottles took over. They could follow a road or a footpath unerringly. As stated, they could *smell* a road. And too, unlike the Terran horse, a dottle *knew* what a road was.

We parted at the crossroads, our students ordered on to join with Fitz and Fel-Holdt at Gortfin Castle. Two pairs of them I sent to the kings of Ferlach and Gheese. They were to be told that our own King Caronne had been seized by controlled creatures of the Dark One; that Kelb was besieged by corpse-men; that Marack's armies remained free to accept mine and the princess' orders, and that they, too, should hold themselves in readiness for any call; their sorcerers maintaining a protective fog at all times until I could get to them— which would be *soon!*

Then we drove south, pounding over the frozen, iron-hard earth of the "great road," to the unshod, cushioned thuds of our dottle's fat and leathery paws.

Murie rode as a veritable Valkyrie, sword bared and ready, her golden hair all frosted with the driven snow. Her eyes

47

sparkled with a strange euphoria. She obviously dearly loved her role as shield-maiden.

I yelled against the biting wind: "That was indeed a show back there, my princess, though I'm minded to say that I think you dwelt too hard on 'burning.' "

Upon which she sheathed her sword, burst into tears, grabbed that pea-brained, dressed-up Hooli from off her dottle's rump to cuddle him and cry: "Hey, Hooli! Tell this miserable lord of mine—who's slain his hundred many times—that I'd not hurt a single one of all I threaten. 'Tis what's expected."

"Sweet Buddah-Muhammad!" I leaned across to hold her—and we were galloping at twenty miles per hour—and to force a rubbing of noses while the snow blew and the wind whistled, all in the dark forest around us.

She finally blinked and grinned, and ran a pink tongue 'round my lips whilst pressing a small hand to the warmth of my belly. I said to her nearest pointed ear, "You were wondrous brave. You saved the bridge for us, you know."

Upon which she returned Hooli to her dottle's rump where he again clung to her waist for dear life as we thundered through the night.

The spot where I'd left the scoutship was more familiar in my mind's eye now, than was Kriloy's smirking face. We reached it in exactly one hour. I then took them off the road and up the bluff to where but six short months before I'd first touched foot on Fregis-Camelot. I might add that the snow had again stopped; the clouds had parted, and Capil had joined us on his second journey to help light the darkness. Dismounted, we gathered at a base of standing trees, leafless, skeletal—eldritch; all in a broad hollow, or fold of the hill.

Rawl eyed the area warily. One hand strayed cautiously to his sword's haft; the other was tight round Caroween's waist. Charney, Tober, and Hargis, too, stared round them, wondering, while Griswall toed an ice-hard hummock, his craggy features frowning, curious.

I looked them over, paused for some seconds, and then said, "Now I'll ask a foolish question: What do dottles do in weather like this, when there's no stable for warmth—and worse, no food?"

Stout Tober, prone to ear scratching when puzzled, did exactly that and said, "Why, my lord, I'm sure you know the answer. In winter a dottle's fur is thick. His food is turf and tree moss. Tame dottles oft' sicken when enclosed too much

48

at snow time. They are sent off to the forests, on their own—to guarantee their lives."

"Well then. Unsaddle our mounts and turn the whole herd out. They'll be on their own for now."

They simply looked at me as if I had gone mad.

Murie asked the obvious question: "And what of us, Collin, if they are sent away?"

"Trust me. There's nought to fear." I put an arm about her shoulder.

Our three student warriors began the unsaddling. It was a strange experience. Like all men of Fregis-Camelot, I'd come to know and to *love* dottles for what they were. A Terran saying has to do with a "dog" being "man's best friend." Well, excepting that dottles were herbivorous, they *were* dogs. I.Q.-wise, they were "dolphins." Actually, a fat-bellied, sweet-smelling, blue-eyed, six-pawed, lovable, two-ton dottle—who would give you a wet and blubbery kiss at the slightest excuse—was unlike anything in galactic lore. . . .

This was made even clearer when Henery and the others rejoined the herd. Tober, a dottle-warden's son, simply pointed to the heavy growth around us and said softly—"Go home! Go home! Go *home!*"

They tossed their woolly manes and waved their rumps, not certain he meant it. Then when we did nothing, they skittishly tripped here and there, wheeeing and whoooing. Finally, after Tober admonished them again, they lined up, bowed their heads as if to say "good-bye," and left us single file. Henery being the last, he sounded a final, echoing, "aloha" whooo, and disappeared over the bluff.

Rawl tossed his leathern bottle of converted sviss to me and said bluntly, "What now, Collin?"

They all waited, flat-eyed; even Murie. "Well," I said, "there's nought for it, is there—but to go where the climate's warmer."

I took Murie's hand, bade the others follow. We stumbled through the deep snow to the back of the hill. The storm had died again. An odd "earth light" illuminated the frozen hummocks, great conifers, and endless stands of deciduous quasi-oaks—all phantom-like in their barrenness. The question suddenly plagued me; the one I'd dared not think about: What if they hadn't given me the ship after all?

I'd soon find out!

I waved them to the protection of an overhanging rock, pressed the proper stud for field activation and pronounced the *numbers* loudly and clearly (an embryo galactic parallel

49

of Camelot's magick): "Three-seven! Two-nine! Four-one!" And I waited. . . . And slowly, slowly, the little scoutship phased in, snub-nosed and competent. I called again, and its door opened. . . . In utter silence I herded them into it, Hooli riding on Murie's shoulder. I then switched the entire ship to "null," switched *off* the belt—and breathed a sustained sigh of relief.

I explained nothing. I simply gave orders to strip and to relax, setting the example myself. We unburdened ourselves of furs and armor, keeping only our jupons, linen breeks and boots. A scoutship's built for four; I settled to the master-swivel, put Murie, Rawl and Caroween in the remaining three. Griswall and our swordsmen I consigned to "steerage," in the combined relax-eat-and-sleep quarters. The bunk beds unfolded for them.

They showed no awe at the coming of the scoutship. Indeed, they entered it with a certain Marackian *savoir-faire*. After all was I not the Collin? The greatest "warlock" of them all? Such magick could be expected. But then, as I lifted to a hundred thousand feet; continued on to an orbit of fifty miles, the enormity of what was happening began to reach them. They stared, wide-eyed, through the little craft's translucent nose.

Space, from orbit, is but an infinity of blackest black. It has long been known in deep-space psychiatry that if there were only *that* to see, a sentient with knowledge of what he saw could not survive the experience. . . . But to see also within that great and awful abyss, ten thousand times ten million spheres of light, in clusters, whirls, pinwheels—to *see* those planets, suns, those sparkling islands in diamond colors, all hard and brilliant—to *see* all that—was to witness infinity; to *know*, for the first time, that there was a final answer to the final question. . . .

Rawl, staring, said quietly, "A memory comes back, Collin."

"I guessed it would."

"And will you take it from me this time, too?"

"No. Nor did I ever."

"Then who—or what?"

I ignored his question. "What *do* you remember?"

"All that." He gestured toward the stars. "I've seen it all before—and from a 'thing' like this."

"And so have I," Murie said softly. And the others chorused, "And me, and me. . . ."

"What else?" I asked, curious. "What more do you remember?"

But that was it. Just a hint of race memory, which the Pug Boos had kept alive.

They were silent then, just looking, staring, hardly breathing, at all that beauty.

Then finally Murie asked with a small subdued voice, as if now I was a stranger to them all, "Well, my lord? I would imagine that you know the 'why' of all this too?"

"There's little time," I said. "But—would you like to know?"

They nodded mutely.

And so I told them; risking nothing, since I could indeed remove their memory again. And I broke out a few bottles of Terran wine to ease the pain, or the joy of it. . . .

"To know the 'why' of it all," I explained solemnly, "is to know yourselves and the Dark One, too; for your fate has been linked with his for a full five thousand years."

And then I told them what the Pug Boos had told me; making it as simple as I could so they'd at least understand a part of it: The Dark One was a single member of an alien life form. He'd been the first of his kind to pass through a space warp from his parallel universe to the Fomalhaut, binary system. The warp, or "gateway"—alien created—had been set up on Alpha, first planet of Fomalhaut II, now visibly blazing at some two billions of miles. As the first of a potential horde, the Dark One's purpose was to search for proper hosts among Alpha's life forms. . . .

But—strange quirk of fate, the Dark One had passed through the "gateway" and into the midst of a nuclear holocaust, unleashed by Alpha's warring humanoids.

Enter the Pug Boos, who consider themselves *Universal Adjusters* as opposed to our simple *galactic* status. Whatever. The Boos had been keeping a close eye on Alpha. At the very last moment they moved to transfer its humanoid remnants to Fregis, the second planet of Fomalhaut I. They sought three things, actually: to save the remnant humanoids whilst destroying their memories so they would be forced to evolve again; to destroy the first intruding, alien ship; and finally, to guarantee there would be no life of any kind for future aliens to occupy—*they sterilized Alpha!*

Unbeknownst to the Pug Boos, however, the alien, which was the Dark One, had escaped its ship prior to destruction and had successfully occupied a single Alphian *life form*. The Boos had provided twelve great ships wherein the Alphians had crossed the void 'twixt the two systems. The Dark One seized one. It landed in the far south—and Hish was founded. The great Reptilian Vuuns seized one—and thus their caretakers. One crashed, with a subsequent release of radioactive materials—and thus the mutant Yorns. Six of the remaining nine landed in the north, on the continent of Marack—thus the men of Marack, Ferlack, Kelb, Gheese, and Great Ortmund. The remaining three came to ground on the isles and southern shores of the River Sea—thus Kerch and Seligal.

All ships were then destroyed by the Boos, as were all memories of Alpha. All this I told them, except I made no mention of the Pug Boo's influence. The Alphian ships were *theirs*, I said, for such was their greatness then. . . .

I'd shifted the little scout-ship nose-down, toward Fregis as it turned on its twenty-six hour, axial spin. I reached to take Murie's hand. "Look now to your world," I said, "for there's nought like it anywhere. There are your ice caps." I tried to explain this simply, too—"your snow lands, as you call them. And there, 'neath the northern cap and winding about your northern hemisphere is your great land of Marack, and the countries of Marack, Ferlach, Kelb, and the others." I pointed them out, and they marvelled. "And there," I said, "beyond the mighty River Sea, is the southern world of Om. See all the isles between? Those are the Seligs wherein," I forced a laugh, "I gained my spurs 'gainst Selig pirates."

At my side I heard a faint but royal "Hmmmmmpppphhhh!"

"The Om you see," I continued, "is not so dark after all, is it? Indeed, much of it is a verdant land of jungle and great trees. And over there to the east are high mountains. And further to the east and south are the mountains of Ilt, where live the Vuuns. And directly south," I said—and we were slowly drifting south—"all, too, is green. 'Tis like Marack, except there be great moorlands, too, and sea towns alike to Klimpinge. And finally, there's land like unto yours on the edge of the snow lands, in Marack's province of Fleege." I tipped Murie's chin so that I could look into her eyes—"Remember?" *I* come from Fleege."

She whispered, "*You* come from the pits of *Ghast*, my love." and sank her nails into my wrist.

Oddly, Griswall was the only one to retain presence of mind as to our job. He asked calmly, "My Lord Collin, whereat is Hish, this foul one's lair, who has troubled us so much these full five thousand years? I would see it, sir, a'fore we land to take it."

The sheer arrogance of his statement forced them from their reveries of the fairy world upon which they gazed. Rawl burst out laughing. Behind him I heard Charney's and Tober's hacking chuckles. . . .

But Rawl said seriously, "Collin—or whatever you are—"

"Hold!" I said sharply. "I will ask you all to create no differences in your minds 'twixt me and you—for there is none. I am what you are, no more, no less. My home is here, on Marack. But there is my home too—" and I waved a hand to the spheres, "as it is also *yours!* The answers to all questions, sirs, and my lady, will best be found in the doing of what we have to do. Now in terms of *that*, you're pledged with me to go to Hish. To the men of Om, we'll be as pirate princes, Rawl and me—come to seek more trade with Om. We'll have good gold to prick their interest. We'll display the heraldry of two lords of those Isles. . . . And we'll spend our time 'twixt now and sleep in an exchange of Selig and its ways."

Griswall asked bluntly, "What do we seek in Hish, my lord?"

"The source of the Dark One's power. Our task is to destroy it."

Rawl grinned, his humor returned. "And how will we do that, my heart's friend?"

I grinned right back so's to add to the levity. I said, "In this adventure, sir, I'm not quite sure."

Murie said, "My lord? *You* do not know?"

"Nay, my love. But it must be done in the next few days. If not," and I looked to all of them, "then mayhap our beauteous world will die. Do you understand me?"

I need not have said that. For they were warriors of Camelot-Fregis. More! They were also Alphlauis, my potential equal in every way. And too, *that* at least they would understand. For though having a potential for being my equal, I doubted much that even a fragment of what I had told them meant more than a beauteous fairy tale to a child at bedtime. . . .

The continents of Marack and Om wound round the planet in such a way that the greater part of the north was experiencing day whilst Om experienced night.

I descended to treetop level on the west coast, even as twilight and darkness reached toward the city of Hish, some five hundred miles to the east. Our power source, Fregis-wise, was the use of anti-power; of a "falling," for lack of a better word, along the lines of the planet's magnetism. We were in "null" plus "five," which involved a distortion factor, producing something akin to *invisibility*. We turned inland from the seacoast town of Geretz with its hundreds of dromonds, feluccas and trading and fishing vessels, to follow the narrow road to the Kaleen's capital.

We arrived within thirty miles of the city simultaneously with the sinking of great Fomalhaut I's blood-red orb into the western sea behind us. All in that direction was now reds and purples, mixed with the striated colors of a southern *borealis*. The city of Hish lay dark—doubly so now for its new, protective bubble.

We hovered, saw roads to the cardinal compass points; saw vague villages in forest clearings, moorlike savannahs; saw here and there a ghostly castle. In most ways it was not at all unlike the North.

"We'll need mounts," I said, "so we'd best settle next a castle."

Rawl said, "Prisoners, too, for to ask the way of things. A question, Collin. We know of the Dark One's power. Does yours match it?"

I laughed, pleased at his blunt lack of guile. "Would that it did," I told them.

"But that of the lightning bolt, and Fairwyn's death; 'twas something new."

"Aye. But 'twas a limited thing. The fact is that when you are near me, or in this 'ship,' you are safe from a 'mind' seizure, or 'transference.' But in no way can I protect anyone 'gainst a purely physical attack. And I, too, with you, must suffer the threat of sword, spear, arrow, or stone from arbalest and sling."

Rawl grinned happily. "Well! We've a purpose after all. I'd have taken it poorly, Collin, had you brought us along to 'mind your gear.'"

We grounded in a darkling vale hidden from the road on all sides by great trees and heavy underbrush. We dined on starship rations. They loved it; especially the Terran wines we used to wash it down. Griswall was particularly cheered. "By Ormon, Collin," he announced, "I'd thought your province of Fleege to be a barren, one-crop land. But this"—and he held up a flagon of hearty Riesling—"reveals that you've much to tempt the palate."

54

But Murie looked only sad. And I guessed that she'd sensed a thing she had never known before—that power does not necessarily lie in the hands of kings alone. And too, with me she felt a true estrangement, about which she knew not what to do. . . .

Giving Hooli to Griswall, I sent him and our student-warriors to sleep outside the ship. "If aught disturbs you," I told him, "you have only to press upon this darkened circle." I showed him where it was, one of four at the quadrant points of the door's almost invisible line, an emergency entry.

The bunk beds were in line, one above the other; thus providing for privacy. . . . Within minutes Murie's hand reached from above to search for mine. She found it and lowered herself to join me. She was warm and sweetly naked. Thirst has no time for prattle, and we'd a full six months' abstinence behind us . . . An eon later she snuggled against my naked chest to murmur, "Now tell me true, my love—what now will become of *us?*"

" 'Tis as always—I be Harl Lenti, Marack's 'Collin,' consort to the Princess Murie Nigaard Caronne, whom I will wed when this small business is over. . . ."

"Nay," she said sharply. "Speak not in joke. I'm still a princess, sir, and not a child."

I leaned up on one elbow, my eyes but inches from her own. "List me good, my princess," I said. "And keep it well within your head and heart. Though I be not from Fregis, still are we one and the same, you and I. For I have told you that you, too, are not originally from *here*. Didst ever pause to wonder that except for Pug Boos, all other animals of this world have six legs?"

She frowned, screwed up her eyes. "No, my lord."

"Well, Murie, you also have but two. And so do I—and there you have it."

(How's that for brilliance in *Adjuster* parlance?)

"Have what, my lord?"

"Why, the thing of the legs. It means that you, like me, do come from somewhere else."

"And a mooly-gog, sir," she said with a cat-like, toothy grin, "has *seven* titties and gives milk. Where do they come from?"

She was indeed a warlike Alphian. "Murie," I told her, holding her tight to keep from being bitten, "forget it! Allow me, my love, these few sweet moments to tell you—to *show* you how much I've missed you."

55

"Oh, ho? Well, there too, sir, are you shaky. *My* door's been open all these nights."

"Dwell not on past error," I pleaded. "I didn't *know!*"

"Collin—" and she wound her slender legs around me, "You waste our time. The riddle of the Pug Boo legs and gog-tits is best left to theologians. We, sir, might easily die tomorrow. I therefore command you to cease your chatter and to keep your arms about me, and love me—for this night!"

Dawn disclosed red Fomalhaut as hugely hanging in the east. Rain clouds, all shaped like ghostly ghouls ringed the horizon. We showered, the girls and Rawl marveling at soaps, colognes, and the like. Griswall and the others, having bathed in a rivulet that split the narrow vale, were fully armed and ready when we hailed them. 'Twas just then we found that Hooli had left us.

Murie at first was too stunned to cry. Indeed, considering the veneration given Pug Boos by all Northerners, a soberness lay hard upon them all. There could be no greater portent of disaster than for a king to lose his Pug Boo. Hooli's new clothes were scattered all about, causing Murie to finally burst into a paroxysm of crying—that he'd been eaten by some beast.

"Nay, nay, my lady." 'Twas Griswall who hastened to calm her. " 'Tis not like that. In fact," and he glanced to me before he snorted, hawked and spat, "there are more Boos in yonder copse," and he pointed to a grove of great deciduous trees, "than ever there were in Marack.".

I watched them narrowly. They had to know it sometime—that Pug Boos did not come from Ormon's "heaven." . . .

Following Griswall's finger, they stared amazed. On almost every limb of every tree there sat a Pug Boo. Hooli had simply shed his clothes—to rejoin the herd.

Great Ap, the Vuun, had told me in the long ago that the Boos were simple leaf-eaters who lived in the South. "And if the trees do not leaf properly," he'd said solemnly, "the Boos but wait and stare, and finally fall to the ground, quite dead."

"Thet are *that* stupid?" I'd asked.

"They are."

And he was so right. For when we walked among them, they showed no fear of us at all. They simply stared—and ate, and ate, and ate!

"Murie," I finally laughed. "They're all alike. Consider

56

then that *all* are Hooli! Pick a Boo—*any* Boo. We'll get him for you."

"By the gods, Collin!" Her face was instantly white with anger, "I will *not* 'pick a Boo'! If Hooli were there, he'd know me. Something has got him—and it's your fault!"

At that moment an intruding thunder of dottle paws sounded upon a distant road so that I quick looked toward the east, focusing my contacts. At six miles I espied a company of mutant Yorns, all streaming north from Hish. "There'll be no time now for Hooli," I said grimly. "We'll seek him out when we return. Let's to the road . . ."

I had no plan, really, except to get mounts and quick. I phased out the scoutship, ignoring Murie's still dark and angry looks and led them all on a quick climb to the road. If riders came by we'd either purchase their mounts, or take them. I doubted the latter would be necessary, however, since *gold* has a most salutary effect upon humanoids—everywhere.

For the first time as we waited, I viewed the world of Om around me. I had thought it would be, hemispherically, exactly as Marack was, in summer. It was—but not quite. There was an extra "something" that made it different. Birds flew and twittered. Butterflies fluttered. Small animals peered at us from the safety of mouldering logs, thorned brush and trees. In the distance two fighting kottees—Fregislan grizzlies—roared. It was all so pastoral. Except that the clouds seemed much darker, more ominous; the water where Griswall and the others had bathed, less clear, more bitter in taste. And too, as I focused upon the great trees and the myriad flowers—I saw a "difference." It seemed manifest in an odd lack of "control": thick, heavy leaves; boughs and tendrils that writhed and grasped; riotous colors; cloying, heavy perfumes. The lightness, the sweetness of simple beauty was *not* there. The very atmosphere was morbid, oppressive. I was reminded of the words of the Keelian philosopher, Arditch, to the effect that, "Tyranny, on any world, will influence in manifest ways the physical essence of that world." But somehow I think I'd known that no violets would grow in Omnian vales . . .

Still, it was not too disquieting.

There was a sudden hallooing then, toward the east, and an accompanying thud of dottle paws. From around the bend in the near distance a young knight came riding at full gallop. He wore only a light chain-shirt, was armed with sword and shield, and controlled his dottle with his knees. His displayed blazonry was the same as that which waved from the twin-turrets of a castle a mile or so to the west.

His poor dottle was winded, lathered too, from blubbery nose to tail. It resembled a large laundry bag on wash day. Indeed, considering, I would not have stopped him. But young Charney, anxious to be the first to do a deed in Om, *any* deed, sprang to the road and literally flung himself at the dottle's harness. That beast, true to its training, came to a skidding halt, panting as would a gog in heat, and waving its fat rump.

The young knight attempted to flatten Charney with his shield's edge, but my man was too quick for him. Hargis and Tober then dragged him from the saddle. He was strong—and desperate. It was all the two of them could do to wrestle him to the ground.

He'd hardly had time to shout, "By Hoom Tet, had I another sword arm, I'd take the lot of you," when around the same bend came two more knights, six men-at-arms, and four great Yorns—all obviously in pursuit.

Tober, glancing up from his perch on the Omnian's chest, had the presence of mind to whistle a shrill halting order, causing the oncoming mounts to slow their pace somewhat.

It was our turn—and we had no choice—for drawn swords on Fregis-Camelot will kill you first; ask questions later. And theirs were out and ready.

They came on three abreast. We'd leapt to mid-road. Ducking the fat nose of the mount to the right, I came up to drive my sword full through the rider's chest; upon which I jumped to plant my feet square on his dottle's rump. Balanced solidly, I brought my greatsword around and back to take the heads of the first two of the second three. I then skewered the last man of that trio by throwing myself full at him. My weapon freed, I seated myself in the saddle and whirled to face the others of the column.

Rawl, on my left, had gone under the head of his adversary's dottle to plunge his shortsword to the hilt in the man's armpit. He too then hurled the body down, mounted, and came to join me. The canny Griswall had simply grabbed the center dottle's tender nose, bent the squalling animal to its knees, whilst his blade went full over the neck—as the Terran matador to the bull—to take the rider through the throat.

Six men we'd killed, in as many seconds—nay! eight! For Rawl, all blood-mad and heated—he was also under the eyes of his lady, or so he told me later—drove full on the halting column to take the head of one and the arm of another, who

58

instantly fell screaming from the saddle to run into the woods. He'd obviously not last long. The hulking Yorns, half again in size and strength to *true* men, though slow in reflex and lacking much in brains, were the only ones left alive. Their leader, a contradiction, wisely led them in a mad dash across a field to a thick forest close to the road to the north where they ranged their mounts with their backs to the tree boles. We followed to confront them. 'Twas obvious they'd sell their lives dearly.

Our stalwarts rode up, the young knight with them; no longer complaining. Indeed, he was literally shouting his joy at his deliverance. "By Hoom Tet's fat-thighed lover," he yelled to me; he'd sensed I was the leader, "such sword-play, sir, I've never seen before. From whence came you all? Hey! But you've a strange blazonry indeed. Who *are* you?"

His accent was difficult. Considering the distance from Om to Marack, in space and *years*, we were lucky to understand him at all. Ignoring his questions, I asked, "What of these?" pointing to the Yorns.

"Why, kill them, sirrah! They're the Lord Haken's bought-en swordsmen from the 'pack' of Twill. They're better than most."

"We want their dottles, not their lives."

"*Not* kill them?" He looked to me in wonder.

"'Tis only the mounts we want," Griswall echoed me grimly.

"Well! 'Tis mounts you shall have. For know you, sirs, that I am Lors Sernas and yon is my father's castle. I was girl stealing and got caught at it. I would have taken Lord Haken's daughter, Buusti. Now he'll take *my* head, if he can get it." Lors Sernas seemed to have instantly forgotten the Yorns.

But I had not. I stared hard at their leader. He stared back, dull-eyed. I tried a mind-thing, saying without words: "I have no wish to kill you. Give us your dottles and you may go free."

He answered in kind, proving that the lower animals are oft more receptive to simple telepathy. His thoughts came haltingly, "How do I know you do not lie?"

"Because I say so."

"But how do we *know?*"

I looked around us, studied the road. Murie and Caroween came up, also on captured dottles. "The forest is thick," I told the Yorn. "Pursuit would be difficult. We will return to the road. Do you send us one dottle at a time; each Yorn fleeing into the trees when his mount has gone. We will not pursue, I swear it."

While I talked, my hand was up for silence and to stay Rawl and the others from attacking. The Yorn's voice came again. "Go to the road—far down. And we will send the dottles."

"Do not try to flee."

"We will send them."

Upon which I wheeled my mount and said aloud, "Leave these and come with me."

Caroween said in her direct way, "A Yorn, my Lord Collin, is a fiend of *Ghast*. So sayeth my father who, as is well known, is a pious man."

"Indeed he is," I muttered, but continued toward the road.

The young Omnian, whose fur was as black as mine, was large-eyed, slack-lipped, and possessed of an oddly nervous laugh. He'd been ogling Caroween with an appraising eye. He said to her, "I'm thinking your father's a follower of our roguish Hoom Tet. For how else, my dear, could so pious a man beget so beauteous a daughter?" He chuckled at Caroween's instant frown. "Nay, nay!" he exclaimed, "be not so wroth. 'Tis known that worshippers of Hoom Tet couple only with the fairest—and thus their offspring."

"My father," the redhead retorted icily, "worships the Trinity of Ormon, Wimbiliy, and the precious Harris. I doubt me, sir, that he'd care a day-old bun for your silly Hum Toot."

We'd reached the road. The gay and laughing Lors Sernas dismissed with a true cavalier's shrug the sincerity of Caroween's words. "They're unknown here," he said lightly of the Ormon trio. Which meant to me that Om had many deities. "But come, sirs," and he changed the subject. "Break fast with me in my father's castle. I'll guarantee that for saving the life of his only son, you'll have the pick of his dottle herd. On second thought," he mused reflectively, "you may not! I've called to mind that he's good friend to Lord Haken, whose daughter I've abused somewhat. And too, back there are Haken's men, all slain by *you!* Nay. I'm inclined to believe that the matter might not sit well with my 'pod' at all. He follows not the teachings of Hoom Tet, but rather those of the bloody Kroom—who lacks somewhat in humor."

We'd gone some distance down the road and halted. The first dottle was on the way; the first Yorn had disappeared into the trees.

"Perhaps," the young knight concluded, screwing up his

60

eyes in what was obviously painful thought, " 'twould be best to steal the dottles."

"From whom?" Rawl asked.

"From my father, of course."

Rawl, quite conscious of the glitter in the loose-lipped Omnian's eyes as he continued to ogle Caroween, said sharply, "Your prattle, sir, doth match the caterwaul of yon tic-tic birds—who no doubt derive their inspiration too from that same Homm Tot you praise so much. But whether or not we go to your castle, I'd advise you to keep your eyes from off my lady."

"Oh, ho, ho!" the jolly fellow said. "Why this hearty's a Hoom Tet man himself and doesn't know it. Who else would risk his life and limb for a simple, well-turned buttock?" He winked owlishly at the rest of us and pursed his red lips.

"Sir!" Rawl admonished stonily. "One more such remark and I'll split your grin down to your ballocks—and that's a fact."

A second and a third dottle joined us, tongues lolling, blue eyes beaming. The fourth was on his way. The Yorn leader held up a mailed fist in farewell and disappeared into the trees. This, while our Omnian gallant pranced his mount, combed his hair and mustaches with his fingers, and winked directly to Caroween. She too, at this point, could hardly contain her laughter. He said saucily to Rawl: " 'Tis moot, sir, as to who'll split whose grin. But *I* fight not for honor, only love—if 'tis promised me before my sword's unsheathed." Again he looked direct to Caroween.

He'd gone too far. Rawl roared, "By Ormon!" and stood full in his stirrups to snick his greatsword from its scabbard. But Murie quick-drove her dottle hard 'twixt him and the Omnian saying sharply, "Hold! Cousin! We've more important things than to take a head with every idiot challenge. This foolish knight but jests with you. Is this not true, sir?" She turned to Sernas.

But Sernas was already gasping, for Caroween had the point of her small-sword to the man's carotid artery. Her laughter was indeed short lived.

Murie said admiringly, "By the gods! Here's loyalty—*and* love!" She turned to me. "I'd mark it well, my lord."

Rawl grinned and shrugged. Catching my eye, he surreptitiously winked. For above all else my shieldman too had a sense of humor.

I said sternly to our ribald gallant, "We appreciate your

concern, young sir. But we've eight mounts now. Hish is but thirty miles. We should be in quarters by nightfall."

I had wheeled as I spoke to lead them casually off in that direction. When we came to the bodies of Haken's men, I ordered that they be dragged from the road. It took but a minute and we were off again. Murie rode at my side. Rawl, Caroween, and Griswall followed, with the others to the rear. Then suddenly the Omnian, who'd simply been sitting and watching in mid-road, came trotting fast to join us.

He doffed his velvet cap. "Your pardon, lords and sirs," he said. "I tend to joke when jokes are out of place—and I've many a scar to show for it. But I've just remembered that the lords from four hundred miles around will be to my father's either this night or tomorrow's, and I disremember which. The Lord Haken will be there, which means that I should not 'til this thing of his daughter—" He stopped, screwed up his eyes and looked quite worried. "May I ride with you?"

I shrugged, looked to Rawl and Murie.

Murie nodded. Caroween said nothing at all. Rawl said, "Well, why not?—An he keep a tight rein on his parts." Like all Fregisians, Sir Rawl Fergis held not the slightest grudge in victory or defeat. It was a part of their training, Pug Boo infused, I think, else they'd have long since killed each other off.

The young man grinned, said lightly, "Though your heraldry's unknown to me, I thank you." He touched Rawl's arm in friendship. "I'd still suggest, however, that your taste is much to our Hoom Tet's liking."

I interposed bluntly, "Don't press your luck, Omnian." And then, "Why do these lords all gather at your fathers?"

"Why else? To complain about our gracious Dark One's taxes. Who be you to not know that this is the time when all gather to rant and rave at our lord and master—and then to do nought about it for another year."

I answered haughtily, "We're from the Selig Isles, sir. We be merchant-princes; warriors! We would create more trade with Om—'mongst other things."

He "oooohed and aaahed" in amazement, causing my student-warriors to wink and roll their eyes, and to each begin a tale of Seligian adventures, the one more violent than the next, wherein, of course *they* figured prominently.

As we rode dark lightning lashed the horizon and great thunder followed like the rolling drums of distant armies. Since we were again even with the place of the scoutboat, I glanced to the grove of trees beyond the vale where the Boos

had been feeding. 'Twas a premonition perhaps, or better—
I'd *seen*, I swear, a flash of color there. I focused my contacts, a simple, muscular twitch of the eyclids. . . .

"Oh, copulating Buddah-Jesus-Og!" I could hardly keep
from shouting out. For there *he* sat on a lower branch,
watching—and grinning.

It was Hooli! *The real Hooli!* How did I know? Well, he'd
retrieved the blue-velvet tam with the red pompon that Murie
had made for him. He was *wearing* it, the little basketball-
headed bastard! It was his way of letting me know that he
was back. He couldn't just say, "Hi, there!" inside my head.

I upped the focus to ten mags so that his round fat face,
his shoebutton eyes and runny nose were just two feet from
my own. He knew exactly when I did it. He winked at me.
He *winked*, stuck out a pink tongue and waved a leaf—after
first taking a bite out of it.

I said not a word; just kept trotting along so that soon he
was far behind us. He would join us later—in his own sweet
time.

A wave of relief; indeed, a wave of Pug Boo "goodness"
washed all my body. I sighed, hugely, causing Murie to look
up to me, startled. A burden had slipped from my shoulders.
My blood pressure was down twenty points. All this though I
knew quite well that Hooli's help was the long-run, general
kind. He could cure you of cancer. More, He could "reach"
inside you and cure *all* your diseases. *But!* If your beating
heart was about to be ripped from its chest-cage by one of
the Kaleen's cowled wizards—well, that was your problem.

Rawl was saying: "Oh many's the sea battles we've had
with the Ferlachians, sir; the men of Kelb, too. Strong warriors, all of them. The Marackians are the best, however.
Pray hard to your Hoom Tot, Sir Sernas, that you never meet
a Marackian with time on his hands for a run of the lance.
'Twould be too bad for you, I fear."

I closed my eyes, allowing my new-found euphoria to
settle. Murie's hand reached out to take my own, softly, quietly. She said nothing, sensing my mood and my need. "They
had to know," I told myself, Kriloy, Ragan, and Riisfil, the
Starship's commander. I had to tell them that Hooli was
back; that we were in Om right now—approaching the Dark
One's lair. I'd do an "instant tape." There was no other way.
The question was: had the Deneb remained in orbit?

I composed it mentally as we rode; recorded it simultaneously. I told them everything, then pressed the stud for

contact; depriving us of "null" protection at the same time. One second—two—Blessed Muhammad! They were there and I had 'em!

"In! In!" I shouted mentally, and "saw" the flash of the code numbers to receive. I "named" the code for tape transfer—*and did it!* Then I was out and "null" was back. And that was that. The whole thing took ten seconds. . . .

I opened my eyes, lifted Murie's hand to my lips, returned it and said peremptorily to our Omnian, "Tell us of Hish, sir, and of your master, the Dark One."

He sucked in his breath, hesitated, and then said slyly: "Is he not your master too?" He crossed himself with a facsimile of the Terran "tau" cross, the one used in two-times-two.

I did the same upon my breast, causing Murie and Caroween to gasp and to bounce their curls at this obsequious apostasy. "Oh, indeed he is," I said. "But we're so far away. You must realize that though we give obeisance the relationship's much looser. As for controls, well they're nonexistent, except for a priest or two. . . ."

"By the gods, my lords." The Omnian's spittle fairly flew in his enthusiasm. "If what you say is true, I beg you to allow me to return with you."

I said nothing, waiting.

" 'Tis," he confessed, "that I'm one of those come home these two months from distant Kelb, where the great Gol Bades lost his life to Marack's sorcerer-champion, the 'Collin.' I saw this with my own eyes, being one of the few to escape later to Kerch and from there by coaster to our port of Geretz. . . ."

We listened, amazed, while he told us *his* side of the battle of Dunguring. The more so was it strange for the fact that we, the perpetrators of his misfortune were riding toward Hish, with him, *to finish the job.*

A most interesting aspect of his service, he explained, was that he'd commanded a company of Kelbian men-at-arms, from whom he'd learned about the North. The Kelbians, he said, had been against their prince who'd sold himself to the Dark One, a thing *he* could hardly argue with. And more! He'd learned from them how the northern countries functioned—with kings, grand councils, city and town councils, with burgomasters and such, and a form of "freedom" totally alien to the South. He'd been deeply intrigued by the way of it.

He confessed, too, that since he'd been back, he and others with similar experiences had discussed these freedoms among themselves and with others. And there were those who were beginning to listen—thus his fear. For, as he put it, he'd no desire at all to lead, or even to participate in a fruitless revolt 'gainst a god, *the greatest sorcerer of them all.* And to have, as he said dryly: "My guts drawn out, my belly filled with stones, and then to be put in the sun to die."

"So you found," I suggested, "that the North is more powerful than the South?"

"Not at all. For even on their own ground, sir, our Kaleen controls some leaders—and hence whole hordes of warriors. What have they to equal that? No Northman could survive a single day in Om."

"They were outnumbered at Dunguring," Griswall said bluntly. "Any yet they won."

"True."

"And what of their magick?" Rawl asked.

"Most potent. But the Dark One's, as you *must* know, is greater still. Methinks, sirrahs, that their real weapon is their strange freedom to do almost what they wish."

I sighed. " 'Tis something like that in the Selig Isles. Basically we're pirates. And though bound loosely to the Kaleen we, generally, are masters of our houses. Much more, perhaps, than in the North. How does that differ from here, your homeland?"

"Why, sir, here in each town there is *the* sorcerer of the Kaleen, who some say," he hinted broadly, "are but extensions of the Dark One himself. Here are no city councils— only garrisons and priests. No man has a say in anything— 'cepting the lords of castles and lands like my father. But his council too consists of warriors and priests. And all must bow to the Dark One."

"Hast no collegiums to study magick?" Rawl baited.

Lors Sernas laughed. "I knew not what a collegium was 'til those of Kelb informed me."

"We've none in Selig either," Rawl said hastily.

"Tell me," I asked. "Who will we see to discuss the reasons for our visit?"

"Why *the* sorcerer, of course."

"The Kaleen's extension?"

"Aye."

"So we were told in Geretz. But why not the Kaleen himself?"

His eyes instantly widened. His loose mouth twitched. The blood drained from his foolish, sybarite face. He choked.

65

"You *must* be mad! No one in all of time has *seen* the Kaleen and lived!"

I smiled. "How would you know this?"

"So it is written. The Dark One is our *god!*"

"Greater than Hoom Tet?" Griswall queried.

Lors Sernas' responding grin was sickly, weak. "Hoom Tet," he whispered, "but lives in the Kaleen's shadow."

"The Kaleen's not all that great in the North," Rawl said.

"He will be some day."

"Do you really believe that?"

"Yes. I do not like to, but I do."

I asked, "Does *he* inhabit the house of the temple where I'm to see the sorcerer tomorrow?"

"Some say yes, but who's to know?"

"Perhaps *the* sorcerer," I grinned.

The young knight said frankly, "I like not the direction of this conversation."

I laughed and so did Rawl. Our stalwarts echoed us. "Young Sir?" I plagued him again, "Tell us of your god, Hoom Tet, and how he differs from the Kaleen."

His expression saddened. "You jest with me. I'm sure now that I should have stayed to home."

I apologized quickly. " 'Tis that we live too far from Om," I explained. "We're not familiar with 'controls.' Indeed, we'll take a tip from you—and watch our mouths."

As we neared the city, traffic grew heavier. Carts laden with vegetables and all manner of provender crowded the narrow way; challenged us for our mid-road position. Each time I graciously signalled our group to give way. Our Selig banner and simple blazonry caused many a head to turn. Trees fronting two villages through which we passed displayed the hanged bodies of a dozen men and women. . . .

"Why?" I asked of Sernas.

He shrugged, uncaring. "Taxes. Unlicensed witchcraft."

We continued on. Companies of brutal men-at-arms and Yorns were everywhere now—in every village; on every side road. The folk all hastily made way for them. To those who didn't move fast enough, they were simply beaten by spear butt and sword flat. No mercy was shown. And strangely, none seemed expected.

I thought again of the parable of "tyranny" and its effect upon the color of flowers. The effect upon people, humanoids, was equally obvious.

66

The "cloud" as described by Kriloy was there all right. It ballooned over the city as a great, translucent mushroom. From below it seemed as a ground fog. I watched our Omnian closely, looking for some kind of reaction. There was none.

I asked calmly, "Is that not some kind of a mist ahead? 'Tis strange for a summer's afternoon."

He smiled, squinted his eyes. I knew by the expression that he saw nothing. Yet he replied: "The Kaleen oft' does such things. Who is to know his reasons?"

Even this would not have bothered me, except that my Marackians, too, *saw nothing*.

Whatever it was we rode right through it with no ill effects. At the bronzed west gates, we were challenged by the guards as to our origins and purpose. But oddly, they demanded no papers as proof of origin. The very insularity of the Dark One's capital of some fifty-thousand souls had made of it an almost "open" city. No one, apparently, in all the five millennia of his rule had ever dared present himself as being other than what he was. We were given squares of metal, numbered, and with the date of entry.

The metal felt strangely warm. As a precaution I switched off "null" to check it. The heat continued, inexplicably. I returned us to "null" again.

Markets teemed in the city's outer regions; the areas closest to the four gates. Foodstuffs abounded, and artifacts, precious stones, and clothing. There was even a dottle corral, with a half-hundred or so of the beasts for sale. They looked quite sad—and I had never seen a *saddened* dottle.

The clouds, fast gathering over Hish, now damped our clothes with large sporadic raindrops. Toward the west the clouded sky was red, denoting Fomalhaut's sinking toward the sea. I figured we had two hours still of daylight. "Find us," I said to our Omnian tag-along, "suitable quarters appropriate to our needs and station. We'll pay in gold."

"Of Selig?" He beamed mercurially, his fears all banished. "I've never seen a Selig gold piece."

"And you won't now," Rawl told him. "We're pirates, sir. We've no use for the myriad captured pieces from this land or that. We melt 'em down. The 'pieces' of Selig, my Omnian friend, are but different weights of purest gold . . ."

"By Hoom Tet!" Sernas exclaimed, "You do know how to live."

Hish as a city was an admixture of a Terran "Arabian Nights," the mythical "Aztlan," and of the great stone hulk of forbidden "Gabtsville" on Procyon-4, with its ten thousand secret towers. It was in no way an ugly city. But it was a foreboding place. The very atmosphere held within it an almost palpable touch of fear. . . . It was a round city. Its streets, concentric circles from the center, with others from hub to rim, as spokes upon a wheel. We rode through pedestrian crowds and all manner of carts and palanquins down the broad avenue from the west gate to the great central plaza. In its precise center was the Dark One's temple. It was—a *pyramid!* Its size was equal to that of the Terran Cheops. All 'round the glistening, polished, black-marble overlay of its four triangled sides, and at a distance of perhaps five hundred feet were the temples of other Gods, each placed in servile balance to the center—as night flowers to the moon.

We sat our dottles like gaping farmers, in awe of what we saw. Worshipers thronged to every temple. A small line of supplicants dared even the Yorn guards before the single entrance to the pyramid. I asked of Sernas, "Which one of these doth serve your Hoom Tet?"

He hung his head and pointed. And, lo! 'twas the smallest of the lot.

I said, "Take us to it. We would see what you have to offer." This, over Murie's and Caroween's darksome mutterings.

It was as seedy inside as it was unkempt and dirty outside. The carven, sculpted god himself—mounted in the courtyard—was an obscenely fat, naked, lewdly grinning gargoyle of a Bacchus-Dionysian type. He had bulging red eyes, a fantastic belly, and a great phallus which seemed—by Muhammad-Og, yes!—directed right through the doors toward the very entrance of the Dark One's pyramid. Though the Kaleen himself was bereft of humor, such, apparently, was not true of the wags who'd "invented" Hoom Tet. . . .

The courtyard before the inner temple was a welter of tangled weeds, cracked flagstones, and bits of debris thrown all about. Lors Sernas chose not to take us inside the temple. He fell to his knees instead before the facsimile of his "Lord." My disgusted entourage simply stood and stared, whilst I, with a robber-baron's haughty gesture, gave a few pieces of purest gold to young priest-attendants in threadbare, wine-stained robes. Their eyes glittered. Their paeans of praise were loud, for both Hoom Tet and myself. There'd be an orgy that night, for sure, and mayhap for many more to come.

We collected our praying Omnian and returned to the plaza. I said in an aside to Rawl, "Remember this moment, swordsman. Where one cannot light a candle, 'tis still possible to plant a seed."

I doubt he understood me.

Lors Sernas then guided us through masses of citizenry and the ever-watchful hundreds of warriors and fierce Yorns, to quarters in the eastern section. These were in the wing of a palace devoted to visiting lords, who occasionally came to revel in the delights of the city which, I found from our Omnian, could on occasion rival Terra's "Sodom"; indeed, could be all that Hoom Tet himself could wish for. . . .

We were given separate rooms, baths, and a center salon for dining. Darkness being fast upon us, I sent Sir Sernas to see that a feast was properly prepared—and gave him solid gold to do the job. In the streets, as viewed from our balcony, the crowds—they had been to some sort of murderous event wherein men had fought to the death—were just beginning to thin.

I briefed our company, told them I would enter the pyramid on the morrow. If I failed to emerge within four hours, they were to return to the scoutship, cutting their way if need be. Oral numbers (galactic pronunciation), were given to Murie and Rawl along with instructions as to how to contact the Starship. One man of their choice would stay and watch. If I failed to return within twenty-four hours, they were to make that contact.

All this was accepted without comment.

We bathed and napped, and awoke to feast on Omnian delicacies. Later we drank and told more tales of battles on land and sea; these to Lors Sernas and three young friends he'd found to share his "luck"—all Hoom Tet men, of course. Each man of mine outdid himself in lies of butchery and derring-do. Our Omnians were pop-eyed.

Still, through it all a discerning eye would note that we remained quite sober, and at no time were our sword hafts but inches from our palms.

With Griswall setting a guard for the night, we retired, Murie and me, and made love and slept. At first, she'd taken time to suggest in a tone of censure that I'd seemed "quite taken" with that dirty Hoom Tet god of Sir Sernas'. "Indeed!" she admonished in heated whispers, "your until now well-hidden propensity for lechery, my lord, comes as a puzzling surprise."

"Even," I asked softly, while propped on an elbow, and with errant fingers caressing her wetted belly and the softness of her inner thighs—"even if all my lechery is saved for you alone?"

At that precise moment I touched her gently but with a controlled deliberation so that she cried out and seized me too. There was then a series of thrashings accompanied by a Hoom Tet chorus of sighs and moans, wherein I held her close, tight, helpless—saying: "Let us hear no more of Hoom Tet's supposed influence. For those who truly love," I said, with fingers crossed, "the mind's set to it; the body's kept in shape for it. Look to yourself! Look to me! A pox on Hoom Tet—for *we've* no need of *him* at all!"

She clung to me all tight and grasping, moaning softly, "Forgive me, Collin. Were all men the likes of you, no Hoom Tet *would* be needed."

I murmured sweetly—"The same with you, my lady."

He slipped as usual into a dream that had no meaning. When he visited, he did it his way; with a display of painfully archaic scenes, dress, idiom, and an infantile attempt at humor which he insisted was *mine*, and best understood by *me!* He came a'strolling with top hat, cane, and incongruous red galoshes. He paused beneath a Victorian gas light to lean upon the cane, shake a stubby digit at me and announce, with *my* voice: "Well! We've screwed up again. We've sent a boy to do a man's job. . . ."

I stared at him, wide-eyed, my lids still closed. I said, "You're late, *Jack*. And just who the bloody hell are you to criticize? Should I remind you of Dunguring's two hundred thousand dead—all down the drain? Do you understand me, you little chrysanthemum-headed son-of-a-bitch?"

He pointed his cane at me, said, *"BOOM!"* and wriggled his cupcake ears.

I said, "I'd love to see what you really look like."

"You wouldn't survive it, banana-nose."

"You let the Dark One take over poor Fairwyn, and then Gen-Rondin and the Royal House of Marack—why?"

"You're blaming *me?"*

"I am."

"Well blame yourself, Buby. You could have stopped it too, you know."

"How?"

"How? *How?* You have 'null' power. You could have kept close to him and guarded him as long as necessary."

"*He's* not possessed. And anyhow, how long would that be?"

"Forever."

"That's no answer."

"Quite right. It's as meaningless as your accusation. You're an *Adjuster*. Tell me, what exactly have you 'adjusted' these past six months?"

"Nothing! Not a damn thing! I've just boozed it up, hunted gerds, played at 'flat's, jousted, and sat around wondering what in the hell ever happened to *you!*"

He peered at me from between his legs. "Were I your superior, I'd nail your ass. . . ."

"Well, where were you?"

"Where else?—keeping an eye on the store."

"Why did you first interfere with Foundation contact— then give it back without my knowledge?"

He said seriously: "To the first question, no answer. To the second: so that your instant tapes could get through. I figured it was about time your Starship knew the score."

"Why now?"

"Cause in the vernacular of your past, Buby, *'It's all coming down'!* And they have a job as well as you."

"You're aware, of course, that *they* can blow Camelot-Fregis right out of the Fomalhaut system?"

"The Dark One, too, will shortly have that capability. That's why you're here."

"Hit me again?"

"That's why you're here—in the lair of the beast; to prevent him from doing it."

"Why the hell would he do it?"

"Oh, he wouldn't, intentionally. But one way or the other, you're here to stop him."

"At least we agree on something."

"Not quite. You see, if I'd saved the king and the privy council—or if you had; was still involved in precisely that, where would we be?"

"In Marack—In 'Fortress Glagmaron.' "

"Exactly, Buby. A dead end. So we moved king's knight to opponents' 'castle-check.' You're now in Hish, trog-brain, and you're nowhere else to go . . ."

"Are you suggesting that you programmed my head? I'm getting pretty damn mad at you, Hooli."

"Nyet. No programming. It was your own idea—except *we*

71

set the stage for your quite logical deduction. Whatever. As Great Ap the Vuun would say, 'Cheer up. You still have your mating animal.' " The top hat did a series of flips along the length of his stubby arm. He caught it neatly and broke into a heel-clicking shuffle. "From here on in," he burst into song, "the going gets rougher. . . ."

I sighed. "Does the Kaleen know I'm here?"

"Nope. He's spread too thin. You're safe until you begin to cause trouble."

"What can I expect?"

"Well, he can send Yorns against you, zap you with lightning, throw rocks, make it rain on you and the like. But mind-control is his greatest weapon—and against it you've got 'null.' . . . It's his potential we've got to worry about. He's finally organized Fregis' mag-field so that he can manipulate for a 'warp.' He's out to make a new 'gateway,' which he'll hold open while *retaining the field!* This gives him access to his erstwhile buddies—and *unlimited power!* Your friends and mine, my 'beamish boy' are marked for hosts to all the baddies."

"That's bloody dangerous—a warp within a mag-field."

"That's only part of it. Remember your deBroglie-Dirac and such?"

"School-book stuff: Total reversals in electro-mag complexes result in matter which cannot exist in its original universe. Ergo: the act of reversal creates an instantaneous 'hole punch' to another, parallel, accepting-universe—our key to instantaneous inter-galactic travel."

"And?"

"And what? How does this affect our problem?"

"It doesn't, really, except as before, just like on Alpha, *he'll* punch a 'warp,' not a 'hole.' And to hold such a warp *open* within a planet's mag-field demands tremendous energies. . . . He'll need a *sun,* Buby."

"And?"

"Well, Collin-Kyrie, if even a pinpoint warp is made in the proximity of a sun-star, a very *rugged* translation device is needed. Without it the star-magma, or flux, due to the potential or pressure gradient, will flow in at a rate to instantly destroy the device creating the warp. Do you read me, Poopchik?"

"Loud enough."

"If the device is on the surface of a planet, *the planet too is destroyed.*"

"And that's what he's doing?"

72

"Yup."

"Well, how did Alpha survive?"

"They *had* a rugged translation device."

"Well, the Dark One should have that knowledge."

"Nope. He never knew the secret. And he's no Edison. The one he's built will *fail!*"

"And his friends? What about them?"

"We doubt they even know he exists. To them he was swept away in the holocaust five thousand years ago."

"Sheeee!" Then I stared hard at him with my tight-shut eyes. The little bastard! Despite the life-and-death seriousness of the problem *he* was sitting on his reversed topper and paring his toenails with a penknife—no doubt to get his booties on easier. . . .

I asked bluntly: "Do you know the answer to all this?"

"No way. What are *you* going to do?"

"Simple. I'm going to get Great Ap, the Vuun—if he and his cohorts will do it—to fly in Marack's army. When I decide what to do with them, the *deus ex-machina* will strike again!"

At that he ran his penknife into his big toe and actually yowled, mentally, inside *my* head. He literally exploded. "Bleeding, bloody bojangles—and *you're* a galactic *Adjuster?*"

"I knew you'd like it."

"In the words of your Clemenceau: *'Merde!'*"

"And the Dark One's got opposition on his own turf, too."

"Really?" The little round head thrust forward so that the wet button nose touched mine—"And just why do you think you put down next to *that* particular castle?"

I asked lamely, "You know about the meeting tonight?"

"*Tomorrow,* meatball. Don't muff it."

I sighed, frowned. "Maybe I can spring a Magna Carta on 'em."

"Do it. Neutralize 'em; divide and rule—unless you want the whole Omnian potential to come down on your Mackian army; that is, if Great Ap goes along with your crazy scheme."

"Where will you be?" I asked angrily.

"With my learned compatriots, eating leaves. If I joined *you*, tiger, we'd all last fifteen minutes. . . ."

"I doubt that," I said huffily. "By the way, what about this bubble, this damned fog over the city? How do you account for it? What is it?"

"What fog?" Hooli asked sweetly. He began to pirouette

73

off into the recesses of my mind. "There's no *fog*, Buby. It's all in your head. Bye!" He waved a tiny hand that sparkled in my mind's blackness, and disappeared.

He'd done it again—managed to tell me absolutely nothing except to suggest that I should visit the Sernas castle tomorrow night. But he *was* right. For other than my blowing the Dark One through his own potential gateway, an unlikely prospect at best, I would need allies. Therefore, though I'd go to the pyramid tomorrow, I'd take no risks; for tomorrow night I had to be at the castle. The idea of the Dark One being confronted by an irate mob of robber barons waving a facsimile of the Magna Carta tickled my fancy. But I had no illusions. The Lords of Om would need a lot more than a rambling sheet of vellum to set their blood to boiling. They'd first of all need a "happening" to given them courage—something to show them that there actually was a limit to the Dark One's power; that he could be fought.

And suddenly I had the answer to that, too. A feeling of almost euphoric elation raced through each vein and artery. I, *Kyrie Fern* was back in the game again. Hooli's reappearance notwithstanding, the situation remained what it was and had been. And central to the whole charade was the fact that without *me* the Fomalhaut system hadn't the chance of a puff-ball in a hail-storm.

I would begin it now! Indeed, each second wasted could imperil us the more did I *not* do it now!

Rain lashed the gardens outside our windows and the streets of the darksome city beyond. I got up, walked naked to the balcony, looking instinctively toward the north and east where lay the Iltian range, the home of the greatest of all Fregisian creatures, the Vuuns!

At the time of Dunguring, I had established some rapport with them. Later, in terms of a mutual need against the threat of the Dark One, we had agreed on a single thought for emergency contact. I had given them a mind picture of the Andromeda nebulae (M 31), whereon the Vuuns could gaze for days on end and never sate their thirst for beauty, mystery, and knowledge.

As with the Boos, there would be no danger. For the telepathy of sentients, especially humanoids, compares in no way to the power use of a magnetic field. Indeed, to this day telepathy alone can bridge the gap 'twixt a sea's surface and an errant ship below, or direct itself to the *far* side of a moon or planet. And so it was taught as a part of Foundation curric-

74

ula, and I, perforce, had developed a certain median skill in the art of it.

As for the Vuuns, well, they were as great in intellect as they were in size. Their life span was a thousand years or more, so that by meditation, converse, and pure reason, they had long since acquainted themselves with the mysteries of the universe. Regarding their physical size, suffice it to say, had they been carnivorous all life would long since have disappeared on Camelot-Fregis.

I seated myself cross-legged on a cushion 'neath the balcony's awning. In both the near and far distance a pervasive clink of steel and harness and the thud of marching feet was audible. What had Lors Sernas told me?—that the garrison in Hish alone was twenty thousand? and that twice again that number could easily be drawn from a twenty-mile radius of countryside?

Uneasy indeed was the crown of Hish's ruler.

Slowly, slowly, I created an image within my head—Andromeda the beautiful, with its striated gasses and its myriad suns in a gem-like kaleidoscope of color. I held it, sharp, projecting, hypnotized somewhat with my own illusion.

And then, after what seemed an eon of time, a like impression formed to match my own; to superimpose itself upon my own. . ,.

"I *see* you, Collin!" The words of Great Ap, first among Vuuns, if such could be, came strongly. There followed a rushing inside my head as of some great maelstrom of raging waters, and then I seemed oncapsuled, suspended womb-like before the many mouths of the cave world of Ilt, deepset within the great volcanic mountains. All was snow and ice, with tiny trees, barely visible at the bottom of great chasms and precipices . . .

Down to the shelf of the central entrance I went, on past the mighty guardian Vuuns upon their translucent, glowing pillows. They rested, great leathern wings—when expanded they measured two hundred feet or more—all folded along the lengths of ghastly, mottled bodies; necks hunched back upon slate-gray, bone-slick shoulders; and head lying forward upon a breast that resembled nothing less than a monstrous kettledrum. Their hugely gleaming eyes were slitted, hellish red with greenish pupils.

I went then, seemingly in a dream, down the endless corridors to the great hall wherein, upon raised platforms and water cushions, were three great Vuuns; and one was Ap; or mayhap *all* were Ap!

75

"I *see* you, Great Ap," I mentally said to the center Vuun. "And so you do. What do you wish, Man-thing?"

"To speak of death—*our* death, and of what must be done to prevent it." I then told him exactly what had happened, withholding nothing, and what I intended doing. . . .

The three of them listened, silent, withdrawn. Their eyes had become fully lidded, the leathern, membranous lids coming up from the bottom. They seemed to sleep. But I knew different. I waited, looking again to right and left and down the many passageways all aglow with a Dantean, orange-red-purple light of far volcanic fires. The very mountain was catacombed; each passage Vuun-sized, like subways of antiquity. Around the periphery of the platforms was a small stream cut too from the very rock. Its water was heated, green, and phosphorescent. The temperature was considerable, though not uncomfortable.

"Collin!" The voice, though mental, was stentorian. I turned my mind's eye instantly to the now opened stare of the monstrous, reptilian *Lazarae* . . . .

"I hear."

"We would *see* for ourselves the Dark One's work—and so we went there. We do not fathom it. We were bold to ask him what he does, but he would not say. More. He has denied us further *sight*. And in his domain his power is such that we truly can no longer *see;* nor will he converse further. . . ."

"I have told you true, Ap, what he will do."

"We believe you; 'tis that we searched for error, no more. And too, before access was denied us, we found his thoughts to be—uncertain, fearful. In that alone there is great danger."

"His 'gateway,' Ap, will destroy us all—one way or the other." I drew a deep, mental breath, to halt the wavering of the 'scene'; to hold the 'picture' of it, and to hold Great Ap and all his creatures to the full power of my thoughts. "As stated," I continued bluntly, "within the hour I would ask that no less than five hundred of the Vuuns, and with body nets upon which *men* can climb and ride, begin the flight to Castle Gortfin in Marack. Thirty-thousand of the pick of our Northern warriors await you there. You will then transport them to the environs of Hish. You will know where to set them down, Great Ap, *by the fighting that will then be raging along the western road from the Kaleen's Dark Capital.* . . ."

"You speak riddles, Collin. What force is there in Om as of this instant which would challenge the Dark One?"

"There will *be* one, I promise you."

The great eyes stared, grew even larger, seeming to enter my own. For the first time I felt, nay, I was immersed in *their* communion. . . .

And then I was free, and Great Ap was saying. "You speak the truth, for nought is hidden when minds are once enjoined. As to whether it is the best thing to do is something else. An area of your thinking is denied us, you know—though 'tis not of your doing, but of some other force. We like it not, Man-thing, though we sense that like yourself it is not a thing of evil. So be it. It will be done. We will start within the hour!"

"How many hours to do the job?"

"To go to Marack, and then to Hish—no less than forty."

"I can expect you then at mid-afternoon on the day following tomorrow."

"Yes."

"Great Ap," I said solemnly, "if you do not come, it well may be that I will fail and all will die. . . ."

"We will come. Are they warned, those men of yours? For if but a single flight of arrows is launched against us—"

"They are warned. They will be ready."

"Then so be it, Collin!"

And just like that I was again sitting naked upon a cushion on the rain-swept balcony of our castle-wing in Hish. I arose to reenter our quarters and find a towel. My doughty Breen Hoggle-Fitz had indeed been warned. More. He was to have passed the word to Fel-Holdt and mayhap a dozen more. Upon Ap's arrival, Hoggle would have either convinced them of the need for this most monstrous thing in all their history—or he'd be a dead man. The mere thought of the task he'd accepted—to get thirty thousand Marackian warriors to mount the webbed bodies of five hundred great Vuuns, their erstwhile mortal enemies, and then to fly eight thousand miles in what would seem as a howling gale—was sufficient to depress even me.

But not for long. A Rubicon had been crossed, true. But there were still alternatives. . . .

Beneath the sheets again, I looked to Murie. She seemed delectably small beneath the soft-weave linen. Had she not been blowing bubbles and snoring delicately, I'd have thought she'd disappeared completely. I woke her up.

I roused them all before dawn since even a minute wasted could spell the difference between defeat or victory. The thin edge of great Fomalhaut was just above the eastern horizon when we finished our breakfast and hied ourselves to the temple pyramid. Even then at that early hour the streets were alive to a beehive of activity. In the area of the pyramid, supplicants thronged to revere the myriad of gods. Most were for the peripheral temples, including Hoom-Tet's; few were for the Kaleen. Hishians, I mused, were indeed early risers.

Actually, the time I had previously suggested—after which, if I had not returned they were to take other measures—was way off. Moreover, if I *had* been seized by the Dark One and they *had* waited four hours, it would most certainly have meant their seizure too. Such however was not the case.

The garrulous young Sernas led us to one of the many cafes and drinking spas spaced round the periphery of the great circle. They would await me there. As they seated themselves, I sensed their trepidation, sharply; their concern. More! Their *fear* followed me, enhancing my own as I walked rapidly across the five hundred feet of polished flagstones.

I wore hauberk and surcoat, but no weapons. Guardians at the great doors, young priest-warriors in black robes with drawn swords and cowls thrown back, answered my questions. They told me what I already knew, that the problem of trade was administrative. They advised me where to go. I replied courteously that I would still see a priest of authority so as to give my personal thanks to the Dark One, and vice-versa, and thus to have some proof of his good will to take back with me to the Selig Isles.

My wish was granted.

Once inside, I marched down a lengthy passageway to arrive finally at a great inner hall, the pyramid's very heart. Except for the Dark One's priest-wizard officiating at an obsidian altar at the hall's center, the place seemed empty. Corridors leading from it and around it, however, teemed with activity. Young priests, also of the warrior category, were everywhere. Other than myself there were less than a dozen supplicants. Each "interview" lasted but a few minutes. Indeed, my waiting time was twenty minutes, no more—during which I accomplished all I had come to do. . . .

Contact lenses, imbedded brain-nodes and a bit of electronic bat-sonar: it was all there inside my head. In the very lair of the beast, to quote an antiquated cliche, I quickly determined the exact layout of the inner rooms of the pyramid. The faintest of "molar" clicks plus additional sound factors, all assisted by an electronic control penetration, created an instant graph, or "stat" upon the reverse of my contacts. The stat was three-dimensional, defining distances, and outlining the sites of barracks, warehouses, numerous other rooms below us, a myriad of passageways, a larger room at a distance of two hundred feet above us, and one final, small room directly below the pyramid's peak. Tracing the pattern of that room's ceiling, I found an aperture, *the* opening to the skies. I knew then that I had the exact location of whatever mechanism it was that the Kaleen had created to do the job. I even had time to double check it before it became my turn to stand before the Dark One's facsimile.

Luck was still with me. For just as the guards at the city's gates had not had to deal with enemies for a full five thousand years, thus losing the fine edge of suspicion, so was this also true of the Kaleen's own representative—the extension of his very self.

The *thing's* torpor was more than apparent; indeed, the ritual was a study in dullness. Still did I know that all supplicants to the Dark One would have one prime thing in common—*fear!* When it was my turn, therefore, I acted accordingly. Actually, I hardly needed to. For as I too approached the dark and ominous creature holding forth at the obsidian altar, I confess to a sudden trembling, a small but noticeable weakening of the will.

The figure was tall; the black robe and cowl were all encompassing. Moreover, where even the sight of a shadowed face within the cowl might be expected—all was darkness. The voice, when it came, was sepulchral—as dead as that of the Hishian lord, Gol Bades, before I'd ripped asunder the various parts of his armor upon the great field of Dunguring—to find nothing inside.

The priest-wizard asked, "What is your desire? What would you of our living God's omnipotence?" *And the voice came from inside my head.*

My eyes flew open instantly, *deliberately,* denoting proper, startled fear. Then they dropped, looked away, while I allowed my hands to tremble slightly. "I am the Prince Til-Cares," I mumbled orally. "I am from the Selig Isles—here on the question of trade. . . ."

"Our god's house, Seligian," the hollow voice proclaimed, "is not the market place. What would you here?" The robe and cowl stood straight. The echoing voice inside my head evoked a phantasmagoria of death and tombs and dark, eternal night.

I fell dutifully to one knee, saying, " 'Tis that when I am through with administrative things, I'll then return to Selig. Therefore I'm come to pledge me once again to our god and to his office and person—for *I* am *his* man. And in this respect," and I bowed even lower, "I would beseech our god's beneficence, so's to take it back to Selig with me."

The outright cupidity of my petition made no mark at all on the wizard-priest. Indeed, I'm sure, 'twas the norm. And too, at that precise moment I'd chosen to place a small bar of purest gold upon the obsidian altar, admiring the while the sheen of the beauteous yellow against the black.

The darksome figure disdained to notice the offering. He raised a withered, blue-white hand to admonish me, saying, "Return then to your Selig Isles with this proof of your 'oneness' with the Dark One. You need but to press upon it and call—and *he* will answer. Use it not lightly, Seligian," the dread voice intoned, "or 'twill mean your death. . . ."

The raised hand put forth a corpse finger, and lo! upon the altar beside my piece of weighty gold was a circle of green metal with a centered orb of black. It gleamed and when I seized it, tingled to the touch as had the entry permits to the gates.

Then the hand dropped. The voice was silent. The cowled figure became as still as the horror it really was.

I bowed deeply in reflex, arose and backed away until I'd reached a respectable distance. I then simply turned and made my retreat to the passage that led to the single exit.

The whole thing, from the time I'd left the group until my return, had taken but forty minutes, no more. My eyes sought out Lors Sernas who sat to one side conversing with round-faced Charney. "Young sir," I told him bluntly, "the question of extended trade and its mutual benefits has been resolved with the Dark One. We will go now to your father's castle, for I would discuss it still further with all those gathered there."

He batted his protruding liquid eyes, asked weakly, "You've *seen* him? The Kaleen? He's told you this?"

"Do you doubt me, sir?" My voice was suddenly harsh and cold. I produced the pulsing green medallion, showed it to them all. The looks of horror upon Murie's and Caroween's faces and the hurried sacred circle of Ormon traced instantly upon seven breasts, was evidence of its power.

Young Sernas' face had gone dead white. He mumbled almost incoherently, saying, "My Lord, 'tis the mark of highest

80

favor." And then, as if he had suddenly thought of something awful, "I pray you, sir, think nought of what I said last night and the day before, about our Hoom Tet—who, as all know, is actually but slime in the wake of the greatest of them all."

"Hey, now." I winked and slapped his back, switched roles mercurially to assuage his fear, "Your Hoom Tet's not that bad—nor," I grinned, "is the Dark One all that good." This, while I turned the "null" stone again to *full* against any use of the talisman's power against me.

"Come!" I said to them all. "Let's to it. It's thirty miles to Sernas' castle. We must be there before noon. . . ."

Rawl, catching my eye, said softly, "I think me, *Collin*, that despite all else the game, as such, begins right now."

I replied just as softly, "Indeed it does—*right now!*"

Once beyond the gates—and there wasn't a one of us who didn't breathe a lusty sigh that we'd accomplished it all so easily—a cloudburst rain began. Despite it we kept to the road, fur cloaks all hunched against the driving wetness.

After a short while we passed through the village wherein we had last seen the dozen or so hanged citizens. On the previous day the bodies were fresh. Today they were decomposed. An indication, I thought, of what *Adjusters* had long concluded—that where tyranny reigns all things are tainted, and thus corruption's speeded.

Our dottles kept to their measured pace. We sheltered but once, a dottle browsing period in a barnlike building next to the road; shared it with a dozen or so soft-eyed gogs, all smelling of milk and with three calves to nuzzle the seven teats of each winsome mother. There is nothing on Fregis to equal the downright sweetness of a small fat gog-calf. Their loving nature is matched only by the excess of their stupidity. This last reminder tempered somewhat my sudden revulsion against the gog-meat jerky upon which we were all chewing. . . . Murie, concerned with my pensive silence, said softly, "My lord, you're not sharing."

"Nay, love," I replied, "I cannot. For the truth is, I play it all by ear."

But they had a right to know. So I sent Sernas to the road to check for Yorns and such while I told them what had transpired and, generally, that I hoped by the use of every trick in the bag to win the lords of Om, at least this batch of them in Sernas' castle, to our side.

"And which side may that be—now?" the doughty Griswall asked dryly. And I knew then that he—nay all of them—desperately needed some sort of reassurance beyond my mouthings of "play it by ear" and such. For, after all, I had been in the lair of the Dark One himself. Who was to know what had actually happened there?

Still I *was* their leader. Discipline and firmness was therefore the only way. "There is but one side, Griswall," I told him bluntly: "The side of freedom; *our* side; the side of Marack and the North. And do *you* not fault me, sir. For I remain who I am—the *Collin!*"

I made to continue, but before I'd even finished, Murie's fingers came lightly to my lips to stay my need to explain. She whispered softly, though all could hear her, "Hey, now, my lord, you've told us. There's no need for more."

"But there is," I said. "For nought but your good cousin and myself know that Hoggle-Fitz, our Lord of Dernim, will also be with us in this, the final bickering—" I grinned— "along with Fel-Holdt and the thirty thousand now waiting at Gortfin castle."

They gasped.

Rawl laughed aloud, saying, " 'Cepting that we don't know when they'll get here."

"We do now," I said.

"We do?"

"Aye. By mid-afternoon tomorrow the skies will be filled with Great Vuuns, bringing Marack's army; their objective, to join the force of fighting men which, hopefully, we'll be leading against the Dark One's city."

Murie, her eyebrows one solid arch, exclaimed, "And *you* play *this* by ear?" Her tone was incredulous.

"I've no choice. The time grows ever shorter 'twixt now and when the Dark One makes his effort."

Griswall, pondering, said soberly, "I ask forgiveness, Collin. My faith in you *did* lapse. It will not do so again."

I laughed. "Be not so hasty. It may well be that tomorrow's sun will see Great Vuuns and Marack's finest arrive to an empty highway—except for a gallows line whereon we'll all be dangling."

Sernas returned then to tell us that there were no Yorns in sight, nor any others. Discipline in Om had not the significance it had in Marack. In effect, why ride the rain when there was no need to? Tober whistled our dottles up and we set out again. As we rode, I laid the groundwork for a small part of my plan by explaining to Sernas my desire to share the controls of a mutual trade with the lords at his father's castle. The potential, as I described it, even with its limited freedom, caused his eyes to literally shine.

At the spot where we'd fought and slain the knights of Haken, I bade them pause and excused myself from the road for a privy purpose. With a well conditioned decorum they did what I'd expected they would do—stared dutifully in the opposite direction.

I went directly to the scoutship, phased it in, entered it, and turned its "null" full on. Its power was sufficient to disrupt the mag-field for a full fifteen miles in all directions, thus giving the castle a limited protection from the Dark One.

This, of course, would not apply to wizards and such, those who already had some sort of liaison with the pyramid. . . .

On the road again we leaned into a steady downpour. Indeed, the rain was such that when I'd remounted, I'd failed to see what Murie strove desperately to show me. When I finally glanced curiously to her dottle's nudging shoulder, I saw her *Cheshire* grin. Her purple, elvish eyes were gleaming. A toss of her rain-drenched curls suggested that I look back. I did. And there sat Hooli upon her dottle's rump. He'd put the booties back on, and the bright red tam was on his head— worn jauntily. With one hand he clutched Murie's sodden cloak; the other held a nibbled leaf. His expression was vacuous. But then, almost unnoticeably, his little round head turned ever so slightly. One beady black eye widened—and the bastard winked at me.

I drew a deep breath. "So he's back." I smiled to her joyous, piquant face.

She frowned, reminded no doubt of my previous callous suggestion. She said sternly, *"Pick a Boo,* indeed, you shameful bastard. I told you he'd return."

"Frankly, my dear," I answered softly, "I must confess, I'm furiously jealous. . . ."

She laughed delightedly, seized my arm and pressed her face against my shoulder. A half mile or so further on, we came to a bend in the road. We rounded it to see, in all its garish splendor, the castle of Lors Sernas' father.

It lay across a middling stream, now filled with a cloudburst spate of water. At first glance I saw that though large, it was still but half the size of great Castle Glagmaron. It was also without a moat or bridge. This caused me to wonder if in Om lords actually fought with lords. Considering the Dark One's tight control, I doubted it. Which meant that those ramparts, battlements, and arrow-slits were really against the people, the peasantry, should they seek in some manner to right a wrong, or to avenge themselves against some heinous act of tyranny, and bedamned to the Dark One's appointed swords!

Broad fields surrounded the entire pile of beauteous stone. Beyond the fields were more trees, some of them fruit-bearing. From the small river to the castle's entrance, all was an untilled greensward encompassing many tens of acres. Jousting runs were there, as well as marked battle squares for melees and the like. Now, in the falling rain, the greater part of all those acres were hidden by a myriad of pitched tents, like so many hundred mushrooms sprung from a sodden field. Their colors reminded me of country fairs and tournaments, such as I'd come to know at Glagmaron in summer. I judged the total of men-at-arms attached to the four hundred lords and barons I knew to be there, at no less than 5,000. The displayed blazonry, banners, pentacles, and standards were such that had the sun been shining I doubt our eyes would have survived it.

The bridge, I noted, was but loosely guarded at either end. Still, at a good three hundred yards from it, I instinctively slowed our pace.

And then—and then, I heard a small voice say, "Hold, Collin! Look up and back." And I did, and saw the faintest of yellow in the eastern sky. The rain had ceased, and suddenly, I grinned, knowing full well that Great Fomalhaut, on orders, would soon break through.

I put up a hand, yelling, "Hold!" I then said, "Let's dress ourselves a bit, do what we can to look presentable." They needed no urging. Fregisian-Alphians have an almost "Greek" thing about their persons and attire. Indeed, I'm sure that mirrors were re-invented before the wheel. So we doffed our smelly cloaks, combed our hair briskly, cleaned our boots, touched up our gear, and looked to the adjustment of our silken surcoats with the Seligian blazonry of Til-Cares and Til-Keeves—three golden dolphins against a black wave curl, and a blue ship's sail with red sword and gauntlet, respectively....

All in all, we gave such a spit and polish to our appearance that Rawl saw fit to acclaim us as most certainly fit to represent the Selig Isles to Lors Sernas' doughty father. In the midst of all the preening, I even took time to say jovially, deliberately, to our Omnian (and I'd talked to him at greater length upon the road concerning our project), "Well, sir, will

84

your father now look kindly upon you, if I name you *envoy* to myself and my companion, Prince Til-Keeves, in this thing of our mutual trade?"

The act of naming him envoy, of course, was a ploy with predictable results—so joins the warp and woof of spidered machinations.

He gasped. His eyes flew wide. He gulped, exclaiming aloud, "By Hoom Tet's scented belly, Prince, he would, indeed. But by all the gods, sir, do you really have permission? For you must know that 'tis a thing unheard of here."

Thinking I'd test him, I frowned, saying sharply, "Well, since you ask, the answer's 'no.' Nor do I care a fig one way or the other. But have no fear, envoy-to-be. All will go well. You'll find that profits and gain alone is the end product of what we do. . . . And young lord," I whispered owlishly, "fear not the Dark One. We of the North do not. Ours is the power, sir, and 'tis *we* who'll prevail. How else, indeed, do you think that I managed this?" I tossed the talisman gaily into the air. . . .

His face paled. But in our company, rife as it had been from the first hour with a certain apostasy, a certain disdain for the fears he'd lived with all his life, he too had changed; enough so's to allow his natural cupidity, plus his hate of the Dark One, to come to the fore. He cast all doubts to the heavens to mutter fiercely, "If what you say is true, my lord, even a tenth of it, then I'm your man. If not? Then Hoom-Tet's darkest curse upon you."

I laughed. "And what might that be?"

He grinned. "I doubt, sir, that you'd like it."

I'd spoken to him with such a cheery voice and with such a projected confidence that he actually had little recourse but to smile and agree. And, too, as stated, the promise of gold, power, and the freedom to use it is both a lever and fulcrum to move all humanoids.

We had, in the meantime, arrived at the bridge. Recognizing young Sernas, the guards bowed low, made way for us. Four stood at the far end. They were equipped with trumpets and drums; alarums and such against onsets. As we moved out onto the heavy planks, the sun, as I knew it would, burst through to our backs, sent great rays of golden, Pug Boo light, to focus on our persons. I beckoned the trumpeters, tossed them a handful of small gold, and bade them *blow!*

And they *blew*, put their lungs to it so that we needed no Pug Boo amplifier. Indeed, their blasts were such that those in the castle, too, were alerted. I then activized the ion sulphur effect in the iron of our armor so that we, too, glowed, ever so lightly, though clearly visible. And so we crossed the bridge to canter gaily over the great field with its mass of tents and warriors.

Bright sunlight seems always to have a magical appeal to humanoids; this, whatever and wherever the planet. With a reasonable temperature (between seventy and one hundred degrees Fahrenheit) they emerge like the fabled lemmings to enjoy its warmth and promise. No wonder the proliferation of sun gods. It was *the* single object most likely to receive worship in the first stages of barbarism.

And so it was in the fields and halls of great Castle Sernas. All were astir with the sun's appearance. Moreover, before ever we'd ridden through the mass of men-at-arms who'd surrounded us on every side to exclaim at our strange heraldry and colors, the gates, too, had been flung open and a crowd of lords, barons and knights came forth upon the steps to see and greet us.

We rode three abreast, myself, Murie, and Sernas leading, for after all, it *was* his father's castle. Then Rawl, Caroween, and Griswall; after them our three stalwarts. These last grinned widely and waved arrogant hands—as per my instructions—to their counterparts in Hishian armor.

Then a dozen or so great lords rode forth to take their place with the other nobility before the gates.

Young Sernas, his spirits ebullient, his loose-lipped, sybarite face all beaming with his newly acclaimed preeminence, cried loudly above the hubbub, "Well now, my Lord Til-Cares, that black-browed center figure is my father. Those lords so thick around him are the most powerful in these parts. That they've come out at all is a thing I've never seen before."

I nodded, though I doubted that all things would be sweetness and light. We halted at some ten paces from Lord Akin Sernas, for that was his full name. Ignoring the rest of us, he rose high in his stirrups and called to his son, yelling, "So you've come home, you damned gerd's whelp! And you dare to do this with the stench of your attack upon our Lord of Haken's daughter still foul upon your body. Better you died, sir, on that Northern field from which you so miraculously escaped. And who are these strangers?" He stared straight at me and his glare was menacing. "You'll find no safety in *their* company, I promise you." The spittle fair flew from his mouth.

Our young Omnian, startled, looked apprehensive. I sat my mount, my face expressionless. He then shouted in turn to his

86

father, and in an accusing voice: "These are men from the far-off Selig Isles, sir, here at *my* suggestion to discuss conditions of trade direct with you and your peers."

"At your suggestion? By the gods," the great Lord of Sernas thundered. He meant to say more but was interrupted by a black-browed lord of evil visage who, also yelling, had wheeled his mount to within a few paces of young Sernas.

"And by what right," he shouted, "do these 'men of Selig' murder my men upon the highway, fornicator? And look you close, my lord," he said to Sernas senior, those are *my* dottles they bestride, *my* saddles, *my* blankets! And you, you snot-nosed calf," he cried again to Lors, "have despoiled my daughter. Which means, sir, that I'll have your liver!"

"By the gods!" Young Sernas exploded in turn. "If that's your game, I'll have yours first!" Out came his sword, and his shield from off his shoulder. But Griswall drove instantly and skillfully between them, forcing young Sernas back upon our ranks where he sat his mount and looked quite helpless.

The tableau in which we now found ourselves was in no way to my liking (Hooli had set us up for better). Still, I had no choice but to make the best of it.

"My Lord of Sernas!" I called out boldly, sternly, nudging my dottle a pace beyond our line. " 'Tis true that we ride mounts taken from the men of your friend Lord Haken—for which we deeply beg his pardon. Moreover, we would make amends for his loss in any way he so desires. I will assure you now, sirs, that it is not the way of Seligians to murder strangers upon the highways. Our mounts were stolen while we slept. Had we the opportunity we would have purchased others with good Seligian gold. But, as we stepped out upon the road to petition whom we could, the Lord of Haken's men stormed down upon us, swords bared to take our lives. We but defended ourselves, sirs, no more. That his men died and we did not is but the vagary of chance. But," I continued flatly, "Between us as of gentle blood the problem should be minimal. In no way must it interfere with what we have come for—which should be of basic interest to us all."

"And that is?"

"The question of trade—*direct*, between you and us."

All chatter had ceased. The silence lingered while Sernas studied me. He was a big man, heavily muscled. His hair and beard were dark. His eyes and lips were as his son's, slack, red, and sensual. The richness of his garments proclaimed his wealth. His eyes then shifted from me to the others of my party, lingered on Caroween and Murie. He finally asked,

"Who are you really, sir, to come here with this reprobate? For know this, though he calls himself my son, *his* friendship will grant you no entry to my house. I ask again: Announce yourself as is the custom. . . ."

I sighed, rose high in my stirrups, the apparent protocol, to say strongly, "I, my lords, am the Prince, Til-Cares, of the Selig Isles. This is my Princess, the Lady Meeres." I touched Murie's arm. "With me is the Prince, Til-Keeves, and his Lady Carameer." I gestured. "The others are our squires and our master swordsman, Og-Grisald. And now that you know us, my lord, allow me to say that in our island-world of sea, wind, and ships, we have a thing called courtesy. Guests are given respect until proven false. None are left to sit their mounts outside our walls or to ply their ships before our harbor moles. As stated for the last time: We will most certainly make amends for the wrong done to the Lord Haken. But there still remains the other, the business about which we have come."

The Lord Haken cried, "What of my daughter, sir?"

" 'Tis no affair of mine. We but met this young lord on the road."

Haken continued—as Lord Sernas' advocate. "What business," he asked, "can you possibly have which is not now granted us by the beneficence of our living god?"

I shrugged. "You refer to your Dark One? Well, know this. I have his agreement to this meeting which, as stated, will be 'twixt yourselves and me alone."

At that they frowned and muttered, while Sernas pulled his beard and bit his lip. The muttering grew. For I'm sure they'd never heard such a proposition in living memory.

A man stepped forward, the one I'd been waiting for. His garb was the crimson robe, and he was the castle's priest-wizard. His black eyes glittered. "What proof," he demanded, "do you have for this suggestion of yours—which I deem *blasphemy?*"

I smiled, brought forth the green and glowing disc. Without a doubt each lord possessed one like it. But that I, an obvious outsider, should have one, too, was to my credit. The disc, catching the sun as it did, glowed strongly, and with a Pug Boo's added glitter. It must have seemed twice as big in their eyes. "The authority," I defined it flatly, "of your God!" Then I turned direct to Sernas. "My lord," I asked. "What *say* you? Is there courtesy to your house or is there not? If not, say so—and we'll be on our way."

The Lord of Sernas grinned, then laughed outright.

"Through all of that?" He waved a hand toward the five thousand warriors and knights. His laughter was joined by the roaring guffaws of others until, in ever widening circles, it reached the horizon of his tents.

I looked slowly around, screwed up my eyes as if counting heads. I said solemnly, "Well now, 'tis my thinking that our master-swordsman could do the job. He's killed three hundred men, you know. And that by accident. But if he did need help, well, what with the rest of us, I doubt me there'd be a problem."

At this bit of bravado the laughter mounted along with some applause which grew, too, as my words were passed to those who waited. For above all else, before ever they were warriors of Hish in Om, they had first been Alphians—true warriors who could appreciate a *man!*

Lord Akin Sernas rode forward then to take my hand; the others likewise. He shouted so that all could hear. "I welcome you, Prince of Selig. And let us hope, sir, that this business whereof you speak will compensate for the insolence of your words." Seeing his son beaming at this sudden twist of things, he scowled, said bluntly, "As for you, whelp, you'll defend yourself, you hear, against my Lord of Haken's charges."

"Why Pod," young Lors said blithely, "mayhap I'll marry the bitch and end the problem altogether. After all," he finished unconcernedly, while licking his red lips, "the girl's a fat-thighed, Hoom-Tet dream, and that's a fact." He seemed not the least bit disconcerted by either Haken's instant howl of rage or his father's overt grunt of disgust, but rode with us into the castle courtyard as would a returned conquering hero. . . . He was a young man, I mused, most difficult to like.

I wasted no time for there was none to waste. Two ploys had been put into motion. The lie that I had authority from the Dark One to do what I wished to do. The act of disassociation wherein I spoke of *their* god and not of *mine*. I had no doubt that all in the castle would soon be reminded of what I'd said by the priest-wizard himself, which was what I wanted. It could only strengthen my position. For whatever happened in the next few hours, one thing was certain: the priest-wizard would commit a cardinal error. Thinking the Dark One *all knowing*, he would await instructions rather than contact the Dark One directly. The longer he waited, the more the others (and I'd long decided that Omnians obeyed

89

their god through fear only), would rub their hands in glee, gain confidence in the fact that whatever I was up to, I was getting away with it. And victory would be theirs, too, and with no risk at all to themselves.

Though the risk for me was great, I was staking my all that the Dark One—busy with his gateway—cared not a mouldering fig for the annual nonsense at Castle Sernas. Moreover, unless he had direct knowledge of something awry, there would simply be no reason for him to move. The idea of trouble in *Om* would never cross his mind. For just as the city's gatekeepers and his priest-wizards of the pyramid had had no reason to think in terms of a meaningful enemy on his own turf, so was he, too, conditioned.

Precedent, I mused with a certain inner glow, was a most natural adjunct to *natural* history. Without it? Well how does one learn without history?

I sent Griswall and my student warriors to ride through the spread of tents and swarms of swordsmen to do one simple thing—to laugh, to slap myriad backs in friendship, and to share as many drinks, short of drunkenness, as they could. Their purpose? To insure that in the eyes of all who saw then they would seem the happiest, the most confident, and the freest of men; this, thought they quite obviously were not Kaleen possessed and, indeed, showed no evidence of a need of him at all. . . .

We were given rooms in Lord Akin Sernas' own quarters. This, since four hundred lords, barons, and the like, with their ladies, had descended upon him for Kaartag, the yearly meeting, so that he had already apportioned the remainder of the castle. Suffice it to say the estate and all its surrounding fields were crowded. Suffice it to say, too, that rooms in Sernas' quarters were the best. For no lord in all of Om, had he a choice, would give rooms next his privy apartments to priest-wizards or Kaleen supporters. So, in that sense, too, we had an extra measure of freedom.

I'd commissioned my gay young Lors Sernas to gather what drinking companions he could find and to create a *claque*, as it were, to shout in support of the questions of free trade between the Selig Isles and the Lords of Om, which I would bring to the night's meeting. With Sernas gone to his duties, I then held the others for a last word—that they must prepare themselves this night to face with me the fury the Dark One would unleash against us. For with any luck, before cock's crow our "Birnham wood" would have begun its perilous march to Hish's Dunsinane."

Alone at last on our sumptuous bed with its furs and scented sheets, my faery princess frowned darkly. "By the Gods, Collin," she said in teasing petulence, "you never cease to surprise me. Despite all you've told me, you can still lie there, sleep even, when for all we know, sir, the Dark One may have our souls before the hour's out."

" 'Tis like I said," I mumbled. "We play it all by ear."

"Huuummmmpppphhhh!"

She looked delicious in her diaphanous red shift.

"There's nought to do," I continued against my pillow, " 'till sup, 'til parley time." I flung myself about so's to end with my head upon her thighs. She ran her fingers through my hair. I mused aloud: "One thing, my dear. Rawl and I must get you and Caroween to the safety of the ship."

"That," she said, "you will most certainly *not* do." Her hand had tightened, pulling my hair so that my eyes teared.

"Murie. 'Tis best."

"I am your princess, sir! When my father's dead, I'll be your queen!"

" 'Tis why I'd hold you safe, for Marack."

She laughed shortly, kissed me, and lingered to say softly in my ear, "Play me no idiot games, Collin. For I know you now. 'Tis true that a lying lover's the best to be had in all the world—that is if his love is constant. But no man, Sir Lenti, including you, may use the power of his maloness for the express control of my person. Do you think for a second that our Caroween would shirk her duty because Rawl feared for her? 'Twould be demeaning. Do you think it would ever enter his mind to ask such foolishments? 'Twould be an insult! You say, love, you're from another world. . . ."

"I never did," I murmured.

"You say you're from another world," she persisted. "Well, look round you, Collin, and learn our ways before you judge and give your orders."

I sought to reply but she placed a finger to my lips. "There's but a single person," she continued—she'd moved to straddle me, all cutely naked, with her roanberry lips just inches from my own—"who gives orders to a *prince*. That person is the king—or the *queen* of Marack."

I saluted from the flat on my back. "I'm at your service, my love. You've but to ask—a meeg to slay; a castle taken; the Dark One fried and sizzling in his suet—"

She frowned, slapped my face hard—and pulled me to her.

The rain continued, a hypnotic patter conducive to reverie and dreams. Twilight came, then darkness. Murie left to join with Caroween in preparation for the festive dinner.

Rawl slipped in to tell me that our stalwarts were ready. And our young Omnian joined us for a few brief minutes, after which he left to be with his clique of newly organized supporters. These, we were told, were excellent swordsmen. They were also admirers of both his sexual peccadilloes and his iconoclastic spirit. The host, Rawl informed me, was also alive to the fact that something was in the wind. They eagerly looked forward to sup time. "How," he asked curiously, while juggling his fal-dirk to keep his fingers supple, "do you propose to handle what's bound to happen?"

I wasn't sure and I told him so. "Maybe I'll just promise 'em all they could wish, dazzle 'em, tell 'em anything. At some point our Dark One will have to move in, challenge us. When he does, we've got to pick up the gauntlet, boldly, so as to prove to our Omnians that we are as powerful as he is; that we can protect them with our power. In effect, old friend, we must *destroy* the Dark One's supporters in Castle Sernas in a way that no man who witnesses it will ever forget." I smiled at him flatly. "Are you up to it?"

His eyes glittered. He pounded a fist into a gloved hand, exclaimed ecstatically, "By the gods, Collin, to you *indeed* all trouble comes . . . I do hereby swear to you that though these next few hours or days do be my last upon this earth, still will I spend them with such joy in combat and bold splendor of battle, that my name *and* yours will be remembered through all the ages of the world. I swear this, Collin!"

His eyes were the eyes of Galahad, his spirit, Launcelot's. I said not a word but took his hand and pressed it. For seldom is it given to an historian of any age to witness a Roland declaring himself on the eve of *"Roncesvalles."*

We then tossed a skin of sviss back and forth and talked of this and that until the time came to dress and present ourselves to our ladies, and to Lord Sernas for the march to the dining hall.

From our baggage we'd rescued the best we had bought from the ship: light padded *jupons* with fur collars, linen breeks, chain mail of the finest steel; soft knee boots. Over it all were the silken surcoats with the blazonry of our two supposed princedoms—all sewn by our ladies. Dirks and greatswords were our weapons. Rawl wore a cap of green to match his colors. It was alive with the iridescent feathers of tic-tic birds. I wore, and for the first time, a golden chain. Pretentious? Yes. But when one is an *Adjuster*, one takes full advantage of the rewards of adjusting. . . .

The great hall was astir, fevered almost, awaiting something, it knew not what. Before, in the countless years of gatherings, protests, and railings against the pyramid and its master, the third day was simply one of gloom and depression; this, in the renewed realization that not a thing could or would be done, *ever*, against their *albatross*, their paradox of enemy, and God! Indeed, it was for precisely this reason that so many southern gods existed. If the Dark One had been less authoritarian, more sharing, he could have held them to him. As it was they obeyed him through fear and nothing else. He knew it. They knew it. So why not other gods who had no power, but who at least could create the pretense of opposition, an illusion to substitute for fact.

But on this *third* day there was no dullness. More. The very air was alive to an electric, tactile tension akin to the skies without where great crashing bolts of lightning played. The rain still fell in torrents, a muttered thrumming quite pleasant to the ear.

We'd asked that our squires be allowed to sit with us. This was granted. As honored guests we were then seated at the "high table" in proximity to Sernas himself. . . . To our left was our young Omnian and his warrior companions. As we entered, he rose instantly to toast us; the warriors followed suit, looking like so many dangerous birds of paradise. I bowed my head, gave them the "V" sign of benediction.

Most eyes, however, were by no means upon me. Murie was the prize, and Caroween! I doubt that such beauty had ever been seen in that southern world. Moreover, our two witches had made the most of what they had. Valkyries they remained. But *such* Valkyries! The fine and delicate links of their steel shirts were silver-washed so as to gleam and glitter with points of diamond light; this, in the glow of great tapers from the walls, and candles on the tables. Their hair, brushed to a lustrous, seawave froth, fell softly in a contrast of red and gold to their black-furred, *jupon* collars. And their embroidered surcoats were no surcoats at all, but diaphanous silken threads of all mingling in color to rival the iridescence of Rawl's bright tic-tic feathers. Thigh-high boots of softest leather covered their velvet breeks. And if my gold chain was in any way pretentious, well *they* wore diamond tiaras. "And why not?" Murie demanded afterward. "That's what they're for, sir! And *I* am a princess. So, too, is Caroween, or soon will be when her father takes his crown in Greatest Ort-mund."

The soft moving air was perfumed with spices, musk, and the scent of flowers. The food was good; the wines and liquors, excellent. The entertainment, however, had been set aside. The reason being that we were the entertainment, I and my seven swords!

Around the walls stood guards with bared swords. A full half of them, Yorns. They were Sernas' heraldry, a blue fist with spiked ball-and-chain against a field of crimson. In the North, when lords gathered, such a display would be offensive. Excepting in the hall of a king no swordsmen were allowed. In Om, however, the Dark One ruled. A balance existed—his balance. No castles were ever stormed; no battles won or lost. Life, for *all* Omnians, was one gigantic frustration. Guards, armor, weapons, all served a single purpose—to keep the populace in line, or to quell small bickerings. In effect, Om's lords simply played at being lords. For theirs was but a power allowed, a power permitted—to be taken away at will.

It was an unnatural state of affairs. no wonder the cruelty to their underlyings. No wonder, too, the proliferation of "witches," and those who would practice illegal *magick*!

Throughout the dinner my eyes searched the hall for those of the Kaleen's creatures whom I knew would be there. The priest-wizard, of course, sat with Lord Akin Sernas. Two acolytes sat half-way down the length of tables on either side, while among the lords themselves were two dozen or so who had the *look* of the possessed. There were some, of course, who truly worshipped the Dark One, believed him to be what all of history said he was, a true god among men.

The feasting over, toasts flew around like kisses at a picnic. Wine spilled, liquored fumes rose to the drafty ceiling. Lord Sernas, noting this, and wary lest things get out of hand, arose—to pound the table's top with his flagon and to call in a mighty voice for silence.

"Hear me all," he shouted. "The time has come to cease your swilling lest you reveal your natural talent for wallowing in gog-sties. Go duck your meaty heads in water if you must. But in justice, if not in courtesy to our guests, I ask that you sober up sufficiently to hear his words. I myself will listen closely, for I'm told that he brings a possibility for such freedom of action as our baronies have never had in all of time. Now hail with me these Selig princes." He raised his refilled, gold-worked flagon high. "Hail to the princes, Til-Cares and Til-Keeves, sea pirates by their own admission. Their cleansing, salt-wind breath might do this land a service."

They came to their feet shouting, "Hail Cares! Hail Keeves!" And we, too, arose to accept their greeting. Their voices and their pounding of the tables became thunderous. Even some of the Dark One's own had joined the cheering.

Again Lord Sernas cried for silence, and yet again, and still again. He finally smote the table, smashed some plates, dented his flagon, and ruined a platter-load of sweetmeats. The clatter then died, but slowly.

It was only when I held up both hands, fists clenched, that silence fell. Having their attention, I turned from left to right so that all could see me. When once I faced the host again, I cried out: "We would hail you, too, my lord, and all your friends. For I swear that seeing them thusly, I can honestly say that no gaggle of lusty swordsmen in all our islands could equal these gallants here tonight." I spoke to their hearts and egos, and they loved it. "Indeed, I roared, "I'd deem the lot of you true shipboard companions, worthy of any adventure where gold is seized, great deeds are done—and *freedom's* strongly fought for."

Again they yelled their pleasure. And we shouted with them and drained our cups and asked for more.

Once more I held my hands high. This time when the shouting died, I let it lay. When I spoke again, my voice was even, direct, serious, so as to command them and to make them feel a part already of whatever venture I might purpose.

"Sirs," I said solemnly, "Lords. Baron. Knights of Om! I am the Prince Til-Cares of the Selig Isles, which you must know doth sit astride the ship lanes from north to south. We are rich in both plunder and in tariffs which lay on all who pass through our domain. Your ships of Om are few and do but ply their trade along your west coast only. It is my understanding, sirs, that your real trade, what there is of it, is sent of necessity across your great continent over perilous land roads; this, being a journey of three thousand miles of arid desert and darksome jungle to the minor ports of Seligal and Kerch. Few are the caravans that set out; fewer still those that return. The risks are great—and not a thing protects them!

"Friends! I would end all that. I would ask you lords of Om that we, together, begin to establish warehouses, trade pacts; devise procedures for entry and exit to our countries, and begin to work for direct trade 'twixt *all* the North and *all* the South. More! I would ask you to join with the North in the creation of a joint and direct control of the seaports of the world!

"All this will we do ourselves, with interference from no one. For that which benefits Omnians will also profit us. I would add one small thing. Our world is huge, its boundaries limitless. There is room for every sword to claim, in justice, a rightful place for all its people. . . . I await your questions, sirs."

They came thick and fast. I answered them all without equivocation. Most wanted only to hear of gold, exploration, adventure and the like. But I had deliberately linked the whole with the strange word "freedom" and the rights of men—so there were some who dwelt upon those factors too.

Central, however, to all the questions was the daring newness of the plan itself. Everywhere there was rustling and argument; some even came to blows. Finally, after I'd answered a particularly complicated query—that the fleets of the North existed now, but such was not the case for Om— the company broke into more applause and shouts. I'd simply suggested that shipbuilders and master seamen might be *loaned* to Om until such time as they had sufficient ships and knowhow of their own. Lord Sernas was hard put to it to quiet them all again. But he did—with a threat to call the swordsmen from the walls to belay the most unruly.

Soft breezes wafted through the hall from somewhere, while we talked. The flames of the tapers danced, cast weird shadows to meld with the tableaus of tapestries depicting a thousand years of the dullest kind of history. A breathing spell. I had time to wonder just *when* the Dark One would awake to the fact that a teller of tales and a spinner of webs had invaded this small portion of his world; a portion wherein, as of the moment, even he was partially locked out. Then a baron stood up to ask the single question that I knew was foremost in minds of all. He was the Lord Gol-Spils, who, I'd been told, held a mighty keep on the road to Geretz.

"We must know more, sir," he demanded ponderously, "of this question of 'interference.' I find your suggestion that our god has actually stepped aside in this most difficult to believe. Indeed, if he has, 'twill be for the first time in living memory. Explain it more, sir."

It was most certainly the "heart of the matter." While he spoke, I'd kept my eyes hard on the priest-wizard. He made no move; sat watching, listening sharply. I answered straight away; "Well, sir, 'tis that I've been given this talisman here, and that is enough for me. It's simple when you think on it. All things work best where free rein's given to those who do the work. A centralization of controls oft proves a barrier to the job itself. The North has long known this.—Therein is derived their superiority in many things. . . ."

The hall itself seemed to gasp at that while the priest-wizard, shifting his greatsword from his shoulder in postured outrage, jumped to his feet. Though my heart pounded, *Adjuster* training allowed me a maintenance of composure equal to none. I even smiled at that gross behemoth, noting the while that his acolytes had also arisen as had a few dozen others, hands on sword hafts, ready to act upon whatever he would say or ask of them.

His voice, when he spoke, was harsh, penetrating. "Show us this authority, Northman. Give us your proof," he demanded. As stated, he was a huge man. His cowl was thrown back to disclose blue-purple eyes that literally blazed. His bush of hair and beard was as black as my own.

I grinned, presented the disc again, letting it shine for all to see.

He laughed contemptuously (I had known he would do that), and showed me *two* of his own; one like mine and another, a black one, which hung from his bull neck by a leathern thong. "It may be," he announced loudly, "that northern barbarians know little of our Dark One's grace. I'll change all that right now! Your bauble, *sir*, is for lords who pay heed to the Kaleen's laws; no more! Why then should you think it gives you some right to independence from controls?"

The trick was to show no fear, which was what I did. More! I displayed the opposite—supreme self-confidence, and incredulity. . . . "Why?" I repeated his question to the staring sea of faces. "Well, sir priest, *I* have always acted independently—as do all Northmen. I do so now, this very minute. The Dark One with all his power must surely know this. *I* think he does . . . To me, therefore, the gift of the 'bauble', of which you speak disparagingly, but underwrites this fact—as it should for all here gathered!"

His voice was an instant screaming rage of sound. "You lie! You blaspheming bastard!"

My eyebrows flew up in mock alarm as I shrugged helplessly, held my hands wide—and before those lords disassociated myself from such arrant hysteria. The ensuing silence, their indrawn breath—their *waiting*, all indicated that I had them, in part. So I simply laughed aloud and said, still laughing, and with all the arrogance I could master, "Why, on my sword, ill-mannered priest, I do *not* lie! If you, sir, are unfree, 'tis because you choose to be. And methinks, by the gods, that there's a certain craven glint to that look of yours that does me no honor at all to speak to you. Still I would say this one last thing, something that a northern child learns with his first breath: *'Only he who is not afraid to die is truly free!'* "

The gauntlet was now down and all there knew it; and not just for the priest-wizard, but for themselves, too.

A man, a stranger in their midst who had offered them a life they'd give their souls for, was actually challenging their Dark One's priest right there, before their very eyes. Some drew instantly back in abject terror. Others, white-faced, moved neither against me nor for me. But there were those I could see, whose eyes were aglow, whose blood was drunk with the heady scene. No doubt their hearts were pounding twice as hard as mine. I sensed, even then that they were ready, should I somehow achieve the miracle of "winning," to take the first small step, to join me in my daring—my obvious apostasy.

The wizard, figuratively, picked up the glove. He stepped boldly out around the "high table," moved to the great rectangular space between the rows. In the eerie candlelight he was as a monstrous, blood-red beetle. He drew his sword; upon which three great lords the size of Yorns stepped out to join him.

On cue, my Griswall then offered the first challenge, the final insult. He snickered and bared his sword from off his shoulder, nodded to me and said loudly, in a voice to match the wizard's, "Well now, my prince, and you too, my good Lord of Sernas, I beg that you give these gray hairs the honor of splitting yon piddling palm-reader's brisket from poisonous tongue to fatted ass. I'd dearly love—"

His words were than lost in a moaning wave of fear at what he'd said. Still, and believe me it did my heart good, there were a few of those who arose to applaud his courage, and my own daring. For I had stepped around the tables to confront the priest-wizard in the "arena." Griswall followed. But at my signal our remaining swords stayed where they were. . . .

The six hundred barons, knights, and ladies then became as

a silent tableau, a woven arras; so riveted to their seats were they at what was happening.

I called tauntingly—"And now, Priest, what would you? Do you really believe your lord will dare to stand against us, deny us this simple act of trade in peace and freedom? You've drawn your sword, sir. So have your followers. Should you not at least consult your god before you're slain?"

He'd been trying to do exactly that. Indeed, his face was already blue from a muttering of his *words*. And nothing had happened. The "null" of the scoutship was stronger than I had supposed. The complexity of the magnetic field had in no way been affected.

The Lords of Om, especially the tall Lord Sernas, were observing this *failure* with glittering eyes.

"Would you say, sir," I baited him further, "that your Dark One had deserted you? Or is it, perhaps, that in the presence of my own god—*he has no power?*"

"*Damn your blasphemy!*" His voice trembled with rage and hate.

At our own table, I sensed that the tension within my small group was already unbearable. I could see them, poised, hands on weapons; ready to move and instantly when I gave the signal. "Smile!" I'd told them. "Convince these Omnians of our confidence in ourselves. Be friendly, but haughty; arrogant, if you will. Above all, show no fear, lest we lose the battle before ever a sword is drawn."

I'd not told them all I'd planned. I'd saved the final ploy for their moment of darkest peril. . . .

"*Yes!*" I thundered at the priest-wizard. "My own, the *greatest* of gods. His name is ORMON! He's of the North. The very same who scourged the Dark One's hordes from off the bloodied plain of far Dunguring. Did you think for a single second, Priest," I asked contemptuously, "that I could stand here and call you foul fiend and oppressor of these noble lords if our ORMON was *not* more powerful? Call your Dark One *now*! Call him! I tell you, sir, you'll get no answer."

And try he did, while thirty knights and lords, plus his two acolytes stepped grayfaced to join him on the flagstones. The court watched silently. No breath stirred the humid air.

Time passed 'till I laughed derisively and shouted, "A sand-clock for our wizard! How long will he take? A minute? Five? Ten?" I put my hand to my hips and played the joyous clown, even signalled Rawl to toss me his skin of precious sviss, drank deep and tossed it back. . . .

"Hey now!" I exclaimed to the petrified audience, "Look on him." I pointed to the bulging eyes, the rapidly bluing face. "Is *this* the thing that's held you all in thrall? His power's gone, destroyed. . . ."

With this last jibe, however, he could stand it no longer. His eyes rolled. White spittle damped the air around him. He seized the black disc which hung at his throat, howled gibberish to his followers. They moved to form a line of bared greatswords in front of him.

On cue and instantly Rawl leapt over the table to land, sword in hand, at my right side, as did Tober, Hargis, and Charney. The joy of battle shone from their eyes. Then, and light as woodnymphs in all their rainbow colors, Murie came, and Caroween; faldirks to their left hands, swords bared and gleaming.

There was a simultaneous stirring from the tables, for us! Already the miracle was happening! In ones, twos and threes, they stood up to pledge themselves, to *us*; to offer *us* the hafts of their swords in silent supplication.

Some were already moving to leap the tables. Seeing which way the wind was blowing, I shouted, "Stay, brave Omnians! Allow *us* to deal with this priest-madman. He's challenged *us*. We'll challenge *him!*"

Thus I absolved them of the peril of this new, untrodden ground, and by so doing won them all, and more! But even as I spoke the faces nearest me blanched. A rippling chorus of horror swept the hall. Turning, I saw that our wizard had broken through: The black disc no doubt. A bubble protected his head and shoulders. It expanded ever so slowly. The light within it was a hellish red, to match his crimson robe. But then it stopped, and the pall of silence returned.

Knowing then that all his magic had come a cropper, he gave up—and did the final thing. He shouted: *"Kill them!"*

Drunk with my own arrogance, my boasting, I was caught napping. The lords literally hurled themselves across the space of twenty feet. . . . The first of the screaming, yorn-like trio (he wore a birny of iron rings sewn to leather), brought his heavy blade in a sweep from across his shoulder to take my head. I moved fast to come up beneath it, intending to gut him. I slipped, and *fell!* I had time only to catch his weapon, to turn the edge, no more. The flat of it came on, grazed my head. My face was instantly awash with blood. The room grew red then black before my eyes. I awoke seconds later flat on the rush-strewn flagstones, with the clash of steel-on-steel around me. I sought instantly to rise. But my howling shield-maiden (she'd thought me dead for sure), leaped to my back, and from there still higher so's to plunge her sword in maddened fury straight through the beard-ringed teeth and skull of my supposed slayer.

"*Die*, you cursed bastard!" she screamed. "You've killed my lord! *You've killed the Collin!*" And than, as if her sword thrust were not enough, she shoved her faldirk with unbeliev-able strength right through sewn-plate and leathern hauberk to pierce the brute's heart. She was immediately drenched with pumping blood.

Not knowing, I'd braced myself, preparing once more to rise. When she disengaged from the falling body, her foot touched my shoulder so that she lost balance, fell back upon me; whereon I shouted ungraciously, "By the fiends of hell, my princess, you *do* make it difficult for my sword to reach those sons-of-bitches!" I then helped her up while she stared at me, unbelieving.

The roar of battle was hellish tight around us. Wiping blood from my eyes so I could see, I took a moment to press upon my torn scalp to stanch the flow. I could have lasered the lot of them, but I would not. To have done so would, in the long run, have cost me more than I would gain. Not a single one of my stalwarts was down; not so the others. Twelve of theirs were slain, or so sorely wounded as to be incapacitated. Evan as I watched, Rawl, with a meaty bit of bravado, plunged his greatsword to the haft through the heart of the last of the trio of giants to shout: "From bousting, sir, I've shut your mouth full up!"

Young Charney, I noted, had just completed a similar thrust. And while Hargis protected his back, he stood on the man's very feet so's to get better purchase to withdraw his sword. . . . Griswall and Tober, the both of them bleeding from sundry wounds, advanced slowly on the wizard's re-maining twenty or so who, touched with the deadly fear of death, could now scarce stand to fight. Indeed, Griswall, with a lightening play of sword and faldirk, killed two more whilst I fumbled for the ion activating stone upon my belt.

I found it. And need I say that this time my fine meshed steel shone with a brilliance to match the sainted *Galahad*?

All action stopped. My four in front, seeing the tableau of my shining self, with Murie and Caroween to either side, sim-ply made the sign of Ormon upon their breasts, and waited. I doubt not that for a single second they also thought I'd risen from the dead. . . .

Horror had swept the hall at sight of the priest-wizard's bubble. Now, at sight of me, the glowing *phoenix*, there came a not unpleasant, whispered sighing, as of some great and soothing breeze.

The priest-wizard, hearing it, screamed out, his face empurpled, maddened. He'd recognized it for what it was—a first manifestation of timid belief in their new god, Ormon. He desperately tried to save himself. . . .

"I call you now," he shouted, "to join with me in the slaying of these apostates of our Darkest Majesty. And do you *not*, I promise you such a death as will live on in the memory of men when the stones of this castle are sand 'neath the feet of all true believers!"

He would have said more had I not interrupted. I'd stepped to the fore of my stalwarts, bidding them hold while I went on. Twelve paces I took, then stood, feet planted, to stare into the eyes of the two acolytes and the ten remaining lords. I said simply, "Throw down your swords, else give your souls right now to Ormon's hell!"

Their faces drained of blood, their legs all trembling, the ten lords kept their swords, but fled behind the wizard. I let them go. Only the red-robed acolytes remained. They raised their weapons against me. But their hearts weren't in it; their faith was gone. I reluctantly killed the two of them with a whistling blow to right and left. There was then no one but the priest-wizard himself. He stood to oppose me. The bubble was still there, as a giant inverted fishbowl upon his shoulders. I sheathed my faldirk, taking the greatsword into my two hands as would a first millennia Terran Samurai. My blade, despite its weight, had a cutting edge to halve a pillow. I'd honed it to that perfection myself. The wizard screamed and whirled his greatsword clumsily . . .

And I did exactly what I'd told my stalwarts I would do. I simply stepped in, went to one knee—and laid open his middle to the very spine. In effect, I'd killed him in a way that no one who witnessed it would ever forget . . .

As he fell forward into the instant puddling of his own intestines, I sheathed my sword and held up my arms in a plea for all to watch. Upon which I lasered both the bubble and the head inside it so that all disappeared in a crackling blueness replete with an ozone smell to burn one's nostrils.

And should I say that already the laser beam seemed weaker?

The ten lords who had foolishly kept their swords were then killed by any Omnians who could get at them first;

among these our quite delighted young Sernas. Needless to say, I would not have had it so.

I'd risked the depleted laser beam for one reason only—to impress them with my magic where the Dark One's had failed. I'd already won them with the contradictory promise of power and freedom. Now they would fear me too; long enough, I hoped, for me to do what had to be done.

Around us bedlam had claimed its own. How else can one describe the effect of the destruction of the emissary of an incarnate god, evil or otherwise, upon his erstwhile worshipers?

The atmosphere was mass insanity; directionless, purposeless—dangerous. They would not cease their shouting, their paeans of praise for me and mine; nor did they cease their drinking.

We returned to our seats at the high table first to drink deeply and then to rinse our faces and hands of blood and sweat while the bloodied corpses of the wizard-priest and his supporters were being dragged from the makeshift arena. At that point Lord Akin Sernas asked me the one question I had hoped to avoid.

"My Lord," he queried bluntly, "when your princess slew Lord Gol-Tais, thinking he'd killed you, she was heard by all to shout: '*You've killed the Collin!*' What, sir, did she mean by that?"

I looked at him queruously, hoping still to put him off. "Does it really matter?"

He frowned and bowed his head obsequiously.

But a second lord intervened. He was smiling but the challenge behind his eyes was hardly veiled. He said, " 'Tis that we've heard of the Collin, sir."

A large group of the most important lords of Om had now joined us at the high table. Their splendor in dress, their poise, their demeanor, *all* suggested that here, whether I liked it or not, was the only general staff I'd have to work with in the coming hours. Sernas' question had been *their* question, actually; it demanded an answer.

I sensed my seven swords going all tense again around me. Murie'd placed her hand lightly upon my forearm. Since they were in the most part standing, we too arose.

I said, "I am also known by the name of Collin."

"What then of the other?" Sernas asked—"that you are a prince of the Selig Isles?"

I smiled. "In the Seligs, sirs, *all* men are princes."

Sernas' brow darkened. He ventured angrily, "You jest. No matter, for we've seen your power, my lord. But you should know, sir, that we've no desire to exchange one master for another. Be ye wizard, god, or devil, it is not right to cozen us."

The ring of bearded, black-browed faces nodded seriously, giving each other courage. I was reminded of an *Adjuster* axiom: that slaves, once freed, quite often attack the limited controls of their saviors with a courage never shown their true oppressors. . . .

"What would you, then?" I demanded. "Nothing's changed. The question of free trade remains—jointly administered 'twixt North and South. I can arrange it."

"And it we choose to do it on our own?"

"So be it. You'll be the loser by your stubbornness."

There was a muttering at that and they would have gone on but I continued, saying, "I think me, sirs, that there's something you've overlooked—in your greed."

They waited, an island of silence in a sea of shouting chaos.

"The Dark One still lives, sirs. And in the few hours 'twixt now and daylight he will have learned of the plea of his priest-wizard—*the aid which you denied him.* The Kaleen's the unforgiving sort, I'm told. How did your wizard say it? That you will be put to death in such a way—"

"Nay, prince." Lord Sernas raised a hand, while the others paled. "We remember it all too well. Indeed, we're not children, sir, and we know that the battle's just begun. 'Tis that we had a need to tell you what we did."

I shrugged. "Relax. I've no desire to be your master; nor would the countries of the North. A man is free who keeps his freedom—with the sword. You've yet to earn yours. In this we'll help, for 'tis in our interest to do so. After? Well, afterwards, sirs, we'll live in peace without the help of wizards. . . ."

They seemed to literally chew on that, with a sigh or two and a rustling of armor. Lord Sernas finally said, "So be it! What now, Prince of Selig?" He'd adroitly transferred responsibilty to me.

I laughed. "Prepare for battle. And you've not much time. Don't wait for the Dark One's anger. Send now for all those not yet gathered who can wield a sword. By dawn's light, sirs; no later, you should have this army already on the march to Hish. There'll be no time for drawn-out tactics and strategy. One blow will do it all—and if we lose, we lose. How many can you rally?"

"All told, in the time allotted—twenty thousand at best."

"Good. Then we have a chance. Indeed, if that were not so, *we* would not be here. But whatever the odds, they will still be based on honest battle, and if but one captain shirks his duty—"

Again there was a rustle of swords at my implication. But Sernas—he'd been staring at me as would a Loki to an Aesir—simply threw his head and laughed.

"By whatever gods you serve, my prince," he managed, when he'd wiped the tears from his bulbous eyes, "you've caught us fair. Indeed, Cares, or Collin, you've set us up. We've nowhere else to go now—save to follow *you!*"

There were lords and barons though who'd still have fought us, in anger that they'd been tricked. Some reached for their swords to do exactly that—as did my seven, to defend ourselves. But Sernas dissuaded them, roaring: "Have done with nonsense! We have to fight, no matter what. Better this prince be with us than against us. 'Tis our only chance. 'Tis also true that if we win, we win our souls, and if we lose—"

But that was *it*. A majority grasped their sword hafts and pledged themselves on the spot, followed then by the others.

We settled to the job of it. Maps were produced amid all the howling and the drinking, and couriers of the four hundred lords and barons were sent post haste through the still raging storm to every fortress, keep, or great estate, summoning all men-at-arms and warriors to rally on Castle Sernas. Each man was to be mounted. Moreover, as per my orders, all dottles penned or in the fields were to be taken along. These would be, hopefully, for my thirty thousand Marackians. When asked the reason, I answered simply— " 'Tis a surprise, sirs, for when we'll need it most."

With each order issued the battle fervor of my lordlings mounted. The promise of bloody carnage, especially its preparation, forever elicits an almost childlike enthusiasm among humanoids. The release of adrenaline brings a glint to the eye, a spring to the step—and subliminal, emotional flashes of omnipotence and righteousness. Oft' times even the most placid is metamorphosed to a raging tiger, kaati, *meeg*—all thirsting for blood.

And so it was at great Castle Sernas. I egged it on, orchestrated it, actually. Indeed, I gave a speech remembered from my studies at Foundation Center. The original was designed, as some Terran war chronicler put it, "to make the very dead fall into line." I succeeded to such a degree that I was psyched by my own rhetoric. At one point my eyes were seen to flash (contact control), my pulses rose, and my face flushed a bright red. When I finshed, to thunderous applause, Murie, o'erwhelmed with the sheer *macho* of it, seized me in her arms in an uncontrolled display of aroused passion.

Her beauty; indeed, her obvious, downright *lust*, was so apparent to all who watched that the very walls were like to split from their shouts and applause.

But then something happened to put all my panegyrics to shame. In the midst of that ongoing cacophony of six hundred shouting voices there appeared the unexpected, *the* catalyst to gel our Omnian anarchy into something manageable—*Hooli!*

He was just suddenly *there!* In the open space where we had fought. And he was accompanied by four facsimiles, one with a circle around one eye. Hooli, of course wore his tam—and a single blue bootie.

My seven exclaimed in awe; Rawl crying aloud, "By the gods, Collin, the power of Marack has come to Om. Look! Jindil is there too."

"Indeed he is," I replied dryly, "—and Pawbi, Chuuk, and Dahkti, of our northern countries of Ferlach, Great Ortmund and Kelb, respectively. . . ."

"Did you know of this?" he asked, exalted.

"No, I did not."

"Our god, sir," Griswall interposed proudly, "is truly with us."

Murie but squeezed my arm, her eyes all bright with happy tears.

I said nothing to Griswall, since there was nothing to say. I could in part explain myself and my "magick"; but the Pug Boos—never. I didn't even try.

If my seven were struck dumb with religious fervor, not so the Omnians. In them the Boos had evoked but a ripple of laughter at what they perhaps presumed was some sort of animal act. For Om was not Marack, and Pug Boos there were in no way sacred. . . .

The laughter, however, soon died; this, when it was seen that each Boo carried a small metallic object. Hooli, of the tam and bootie seated himself, cross-legged, in the ensuing silence. He placed the object to his lips and blew three soft but penetrating notes. Their effect was similar to words that trigger a post-hypnotic act—except that the notes would key an hereditary memory pattern, *dormant for five thousand years*. The very sound of those notes was sufficient to pin all

Omnians to their seats for whatever length of time that Hooli's "band" would choose to hold them.

I watched, unbelieving, though I'd seen it all before. There they sat, five fat-fannied facsimiles of a Terran koala bear with raccoon hands; all of them playing music such as those Omnians had never heard before, nor would again, except by Pug Boos, on any tape, disk, or crystal gauge. . . .

Light from the guttering candles and oil lamps seemed to leap to the sound of the music, to dance in weird shadow-shapes upon the walls and ceiling. And there was color, too. Blues. Reds. Yellows. Blazing and melding into an ever changing kaleidoscopic light show of joy or horror, depending upon one's point of view. And the sound and the colors seemed three dimensional, tangible, *palpable*. . . .

Outside, as we were told later, the storm had instantly subsided. More! The clouds had parted to allow the silvered light of small Ripple and then Capil, Fregis' two moons, to cast a sheen in their passing o'er all the great rain-sparkling meadow. And those within the tents, *all* of them, came out to stare toward the castle and to listen to the Pug Boo's music.

It was symphonic: a medley of every reed or brass or string or pipe that had ever been played *anywhere* in the Galaxy. There was no explaining it or its source. I'd seen the instruments. It was simply a hollow tube of some unknown metal upon which no one else could produce a single note. And the tube *existed*, or it *didn't*, at the Pug Boos' pleasure.

And so they listened—*we* listened, rather. And my mind was invaded with sound and mood and imagery, each facet a variation of a thousand themes, melding, expanding, to explode into great bursts of light that was not light, into a blackness of space that was not space. And through it all a thread emerged, a theme which had most likely touched upon the subconscious of northern men for all their lives upon this planet. It was a mind-story of worlds shattered and ruined in seas of rolling fission, of a holocaust beyond understanding. There was the repetitive image too, of the humanoid planet, Alpha—before the fall; a world of indescribable beauty. The events shown were of its death in the great cataclysm, and the reason. There was a hint, too, of total evil, a suggested horror so enormous as to blast the mind that sought to understand it. . . .

Yet still another thread ran through it all—a suggestion of beauty, peace, and above all, *hope*. And as I listened I knew that those around me would see what they were meant to see—the dim view of the faery world which once was theirs,

107

though they would know it not; nor would they truly remember, *after*. For the Pug Boos—and of this I was sure—sought only, as of this moment, but the vaguest of contacts between the *now* of Om and that other, far time, of Alphian ascendency. The thread, however, and its *touching*, would change them forever.—*And that was the fact and the deed of the Pug Boos' music!*

In all of Galactic history there was no counterpart, no parallel. As an *Adjuster* I could not help but be impressed. Still I was reminded of a question I'd put to Hooli immediately after the battle of Dunguring as to just who in the bloody hell he really was. He'd replied in his infuriating way that in terms of adjusting, *he* was Universal while *I* was merely Galactic. . . .

The thought had been frightening then, it remained so now. The difference between the two of us in personal, *gut* terms, was plainly obvious.

Here I was with armor and greatsword, a magick "belt" to bedazzle the natives, and a laser factor whose efficacy was wholly dependent upon a fast-waning energy pack. With this handful of trifles I'd pitted myself against an alien entity with a potential for the Fomalhaut system's destruction. Hooli and his cohorts, on the other hand, risked *nothing*! Still it was *they* who called the play, determined the scenario.

With each hard-won gain I'd made, there he'd be, ready again to press the proper button to set the stage for another victory. The clincher was that to attain it, I'd still have to fight, to risk my ass, and to lead others to do likewise in one more battle—while *he* risked *nothing*!

The true irritant, however, was my own *Adjuster* knowledge of an undeniable fact: With or without his help the course I followed was, objectively, the only logical one. A cause to wonder, perhaps, where *Alexander* really came from, and who or what were *Arthur, Mao,* or *Tengsin Pata.* . . .

As is true of all creatures the brain of a dottle serves a dottle's purpose. There is no known reason, for example, why a dottle will pace itself at exactly twenty miles per hour for any distance beyond a half a mile or so; this, when they sense or *know* that there'll be many more miles to travel. Moreover, they can keep it up without tiring for many hours. Distances on Fregis-Camelot, therefore, are reckoned in so many dottle hours . . . The area covered in our recruiting was restricted to approximately fifty miles in every direction save toward Hish. No point, we decided, in beating a kettledrum under the Dark One's very window.

The high point of Sernas' dinner had been at eight. Within but a few hours the nearest contingents of warriors had already arrived. They were hastily marshalled under certain young lords to join with the first five thousand and were thrown in a peripheral screen, or line, at about three miles from our stronghold, and in the direction of the Omnian capital.

More and more arrived; each company with an added dottle pack so that the broad fields aroung the castle soon teemed with them.

Necessity breeding simplicity, our plan was a simple one. We would advance with all speed at dawn's light. Our main force would consist of ten thousand. Flanking units would be to the amount of twenty-five hundred each. Another five thousand would be immediately to our force, ready instantly to overwhelm any opposition at front or either flank, until such time as we'd arrived at the gates of Hish, or a major battle had been enjoined.

With luck we'd be battering at the capital's walls before high noon. With more luck—plus the heaven-splitting arrival of our Marackian thirty thousand—we'd be into the city and besieging the temple itself as darkness fell.

Rawl asked and received the command of the roving five thousand. I think he wanted to fight on his own terms, to show the Omnians what a Northerner could do *without* the Collin's "aura" to protect him. I let him go. He chose Hargis, Charney, and Caroween as his body swordsmen. Young Sernas and his blooded-sybarites would be his lieutenant-captain spread out among the companies. Tober and Griswall would remain with me—to guard the lives of the Princess of Marack and myself.

In the small hours the "Collin's curse" caught up with me. I was again dead-tired, bone-weary, while the others seemed as fresh as kiddies at a birthday party. I begged leave to sleep the last few hours 'til dawn.

What I'd guessed, indeed, had hoped would also happen—did. I'd hardly closed my eyes after first assuring myself that Murie was asleep—in her innocence, her Fregisian head had but to touch a pillow—when Hooli came, with his companions.

They sat in mid-air, limned by blue lightning from beyond the windows—and I saw all this through tight-shut eyes. They sat and stared, with kneeless legs flat out, sedately folded paws on furry tummies. Hooli was in the center, flanked on either side by two of the four. He'd found his missing bootie, too.

The five of them spoke with a single voice, inside my head. The communal delivery was straight; no attempt at the ancient Terran idiom that Hooli used.

"Collin!" they announced solemnly, "The peril mounts, comes closer. We know the time now of the Dark One's effort, the exact minute when he'll make his attempt. There are less hours than we'd hoped for."

I mentally yawned, for I was tired. I groaned, too, mentally. "All right. So how long *do* we have?"

"Dawn breaks in three hours. There will be fourteen hours of daylight and four of darkness. The Dark One had set his mechanism to function coinciding with an exact alignment of the north-south magnetic lines of Fregis, the pyramid, and the two moons, Capil and Ripple. The conjunction of all factors will provide for but a slight additional surge of energy. But apparently he needs it."

"Eighteen hours?"

"That's right. The risk is great; too great, in fact. We would therefore now suggest that you change your plans."

"To what?"

"That you alone attack—with your ship. You know the place of the mechanism, the sky-room of the pyramid. *Destroy it with the ship.*"

"Destroy? How? The scoutship's unarmed. The only weapon I have is the laser, and the energy pack's near dead on that."

"*Ram it!*"

"Ram it?" I repeated incredulously. "Ram the pyramid? Are you out of your pea-brain skulls?"

They said nothing, just sat there watching me sadly.

I took a deep breath, said softly, "You really mean it. . . . You're really asking me to kill myself."

"Better you, Collin, than all this beauteous world."

"Dammmmmnnnn!"

"You might survive." Their collective voice was frightening.

"*I*—might survive?" I breathed. "Well, screw you, you little brown-bag sons-of-bitches. Why don't you do it? Yeah! Why don't *you*? It's you who have the power. You're the real 'games players.' The way I see it, the five of you could make a *nova* of both Fomalhauts in the time it takes me to say it."

110

And then I yelled, mentally, in petulant, driven anger. "To hell with the lot of you. *I've had it*!"

"Collin. We cannot do it."

"Gog shit!"

"We are not permitted."

"Really? And who or what exists in all this universe to deny *you* permission?"

The collective hesitated. Time passed. They finally said, "We are not programmed for the destruction of life—"

I interrupted: "What about the sterilization job you did on Alpha?"

"—above a class 'C' category."

"Class 'C'?"

"Mollusks. Anemones."

It suddenly reached me. "Not *programmed*? Are you telling me that you're a bunch of damned computers? If that's so, gentlemen, I'll bow out right now and to hell with your lousy games. I've walked knee-deep in blood on this damned planet—for you. And now you're telling me to cancel myself out so you can win *your* game! Unh-uh! Nyet! I'll blank you out, kiddies. Whatever's done from here on in, I'll do it. And I'll do it *my* way!"

"If you do, Mack," an intruding voice insinuated; and it was no longer that of the collective, "If you do, you're a dead monkey. Without us, Ace, you couldn't win a stud hand with a royal flush!"

"Is that you, Hooli?"

"Who else, butter brain?"

I sighed deeply. "All right. In one word, Hooli: Are you a machine?"

"Nope."

"Well? Go on . . ."

"That's all."

"No way.—Prove it."

"I love you, Collin," Hooli said.

"And I love you. But in my quarters at Foundation H.Q. I've got an eight-hundred-year-old koala-bear bank, which I also love. It looks like you. It rolls its eyes, waves its fanny, and squeaks when I put a facsimile, England Isle, 'shilling' in it.

"We are not computers."

"*Prove it.*"

"All right! You asked for it! I'm going to give you one peek, just a flash, baby, at what I look like. And you know what's going to happen? You're going to *implode*. That's how

111

bad it will be. . . . Are you ready for that? Just brace yourself and let me know."

I hesitated. I had good reason to. As an *Adjuster*, I've seen a lot of life forms; some that humanoids were simply not meant to see. Just the thought of what Hooli *might* look like scared the hell out of me. And, too, I knew he wasn't a robot. *Adjuster* training can spot a sentient, occupied—or in occupation! Actually, I'd thought to rattle them with my accusation. I shrugged, grinned, mentally, saying, "Forget it. I'll have a look at you after—maybe."

"Then you'll do it? Hit the pyramid with the scoutship?"

"*I sure as hell won't!*"

He leaned forward until his little wet nose touched mine. His beady eyes blinked. "You'd risk Fregis, Marack—the Princess?"

"Not exactly. Like I said, I'll do it my way."

"You'll let it all die?" he insisted, "just like that?" He snapped two furry fingers; the ensuing sound being like the Zen clap of a single hand.

I sighed. "Get off my back. In my book you guys are cop-out, rat-finks; which goes with that scared homily you implanted in all Northern heads, that 'gentle Pug Boos never go to war.' In a couple of hours, bag-belly, I'll be marching out to take on the Dark One. The five of you can help, and take your chances like the rest of us, or you can sit on your little fat asses and watch all Fregis atomized—if we lose."

Hooli said solemnly, "You're a hard man, Magee."

There was a deliberate twinkle in his eyes which I didn't like.

"What's it going to be?"

"We'll have to think about it."

"Sheeeee!" I sighed again.

The five of them still sat serene, their fluffy bodies glowing in my mind's eye.

"Collin?" It was the collective voice again.

"Yeah?"

"You must make no attempt to contact the Deneb-3."

"How can I? If I do, with the 'null' screen down, there goes the game."

"Just the same, you could be tempted."

"So? I'm tempted." Then I took a page from their book, saying coyly—"I'll have to think about it."

At which their extremities lit up, kyrilian style, a signal that they were cutting out. The collective voice said, "Kyrie Fern. We'll help you, but you might not like it."

112

"Just what the hell does that mean?"

"We'll sound three notes at the key intervals, connecting their subconscious to their past. The effect will be less fear and, conversely, more overt objectivity. That should be worth a few battalions."

"Fine. But what is it that I might not like?"

"We'll see."

I said, "You bastards!" And with that they faded into the darkness of my mind, though I could still hear a faint singing—Hooli's voice. The words of the ditty were, as usual, from the archaic. Hooli sang: *"C'est la lutte finale/ Groupons-nous a demain."*

And when you think about it, how better to distinguish a sentient from a non-sentient than with the use of humor—even the slightly perverted cutting edge that Hooli used.

The Dark One was stirring!

I knew it the moment I opened my eyes. Despite all efforts to mentally prepare myself for the shock of *his* knowledge of *me*, the effect of it was as a sword's blade along the length of my spine.

How did I know it? Well there was a tingling at the base of my skull and a far off humming from the direction of Hish, no more. The damn thing was scanning. It had touched upon the imbedded node. And then it was gone. Thank Ormon for the scout-ship, or whatever. We donned full armor, dressing each other, Murie and I. Then we joined Lord Sernas, staff and Rawl and Caroween, and Griswall and our stalwarts for a hearty breakfast of black bread, gog-meat and milk; the last being laced with a potent facsimile of Omnian rum to drive off the dawn's chill. I took a second tankard.

"The master knows!" had been the first words Sernas said to me, thus substantiating my own precognition. I ignored his remark, discussing instead the condition and deployment of the warrior companies.

Outside on the meadow the long ghostly lines of mounted, waiting men seemed as so many *menhir dolmens* in the lifting mists. The herds of dottles also waited. They would follow our progress at a distance of two miles; my orders. No use subjecting them to unwarranted peril. Bad enough that unlike in the north, whereat *all* fighting, excepting tournaments and the like, was done on foot so as not to endanger gentle dottles, here it would be otherwise.

Still, unlike the previous days, the dottles were no longer

sad. Indeed, they were happy; frisky, even. They had obviously drawn some benefit from the spread of Pug Boo "goodness". Even as I watched one of them gave a wet and slobbery kiss to a young dottle-warden who then leapt grinning into his saddle, unaccustomed and somewhat embarrassed by the dottle's loving gesture.

And need I say that I too was aware of the Pug Boo's ongoing, sub-audible music?

For it *was* there. Obtrusive. Insistent. There'd be a minute of it, then nothing. And then, a half hour later, perhaps three minutes, and like that. As stated, you couldn't *really* hear it. It was more an internal thing, like the silent view of wind gusts in the branches of great trees—a soughing, whispering, unheard, but *felt*. One could see the effect, however, in the rapt faces that gazed toward the Omnian capital with an almost exalted composure. I was quite sure of one thing. There was hard determination there. They would fight and fight well . . .

The thirty miles to Hish consisted of rolling country, forests, fields and fast-flowing streams. The streams were small since it was late summer and, too, the area was more or less highlands with an altitude of three thousand feet or more. The forests and fields gave way to open farmland, broad meadows and villages in the final fifteen miles.

According to limited maps shown me by Sernas there would be three areas where the Dark One would most likely attempt to stop us. The first was a deep north-south gorge at the bottom of which was a white water stream. There being two parallel roads to the main one which we would follow, there were, therefore, three suspension bridges, each consisting of four link chains tied with ropes and with a planked bottom so's to create a narrow road. The gorge was at a distance of about eight miles. Orders sent out the previous night had directed certain companies of ours to advance and seize the bridges at dawn's light.

The second area, perfect for battle, was a broad valley of some fifteen miles toward the Omnian capital. One would come into it from a line of forested hills. Beyond the valley was another range of hills, opening finally to the great plain surrounding Hish.

The last area would be about six miles from Hish, itself— an indentation in the plain made by a wide but exceedingly shallow river. . . .

We had hardly set the main bodies of warriors in motion when a covey of riders, coming at full gallop, shouted that whereas the flanking bridges had been saved, the main bridge had been taken by the enemy.

Rawl, shouting command orders, saluted Sernas and myself, and with Caroween, Tober, and Charney, led his five thousand instantly in a wild dash to take it back. We sent quick orders for the flanking units to drive full speed across their bridges and to set up immediate liaison on the far side with each other and ourselves. We then drove straight ahead in Rawl's wake—at our dottle's pace of twenty miles per hour.

I rode with Sernas and the Lord Gol-Stils. Murie was to my left side; a proper spot for a shield-maiden. Griswall and Hargis rode to our rear. The Pug Boos, Murie told me, had each been put upon a separate dottle and had been given a heavy guard for protection. They were following on in the midst of the dottle herd. As we rode, I had time to wonder at the instant acceptance of the Boos by everyone. It was not that Omnians had suddenly recognized them as something to worship, as did Marackians, but rather that they were seen as something different, to be wondered at and protected— *though they knew not why*!

Om was in every way as colorful as Marack. Indeed, more so! The household banners of this lord or that were a sight to see in wind-blown silk or satin. And the emblazoned surcoats of even the men-at-arms displayed the wealth of five thousand years of total exploitation without the ruin of havoc and pillage. I'd thought to mute the cry of horns and the thundering beat of the kettledrums—to no avail! They'd have none of it.

"If we're to die, Prince Cares," Sernas informed me, reverting to my Seligian title, "we'll do it, sir, as men who for the first time are allowed to *act as men*!" And whereas there still were those who'd disagree with him, he generally spoke for all.

We thundered past the hidden scoutship. I'd dismissed any thought of contacting the Deneb-3. There was simply no way to do it without negating the "null" effect, and thus alerting the Dark One to its presence. Still, I'd eventually have to get back to it, and before the final attack, too, to *move it*, advance it to Hish's environs, else the protection it afforded us—diminishing considerably at twenty miles—would be useless against the Kaleen's wrath.

Which had, as of that very moment, become visible, palpable; substantially real!

Like the two previous mornings, we had awakened to clouds ringing us round on all the surrounding horizons: clinging fast to the edge of the great tableland upon which was the centered Omnian capital. . . . Now, however, they were encroaching rapidly, driven, I knew, by an unseen hand. Great thunderheads arose above them, and even as I looked, took on the fleeting casts of sorcery, of writhing tortured faces, tentacular arms—reaching, grasping. There was then a veritable spate of sheets and angry spears of lightning. Great thunder crashed from all sides. And, as we mounted a ridge and poured down its far side, we saw ahead the first fingers of a great miasmic fog, brackish yellows and browns all roiling and boiling upon itself as if it were alive—had thought and purpose.

It moved rapidly over fields which, Sernas told me, led to the deep gorge and the bridge. And then—even as we watched, the fog was halted, dispersed by some unknown hand to reveal a large body of men, mounted and afoot, being driven back across the narrow bridge by hard-fighting swordsmen of Rawl's five thousand. More! At that very instant, I saw my shieldman's colors, followed by a few hundred of Sernas' best, smash into the fleeing flank of the Dark One's warriors, hitting them hard at the very edge of the bridge. Then, having freed the span's entry, he swung to lead his men directly out upon that swaying bit of iron and rope, slaying and literally *hurling* all those who dared oppose him down to the waters far below.

On the far side he directed his men to right and left, against those of the Dark One's men who'd been poised to cut the ropes and chains if the bridge was lost. They'd no time to wield a single axe. He cut them down, and drove again into the mass of Hishian soldiery, so that we saw his and the various banners of certain lords and captains who'd dined with us the previous night all tossing and waving alongside raised swords, axes, and the bloodied weight of mace and hammer.

It lasted but seconds. Rawl's remaining thousands, led by young Sernas, then went thundering over the narrow way to shatter, ruin, and then pursue all that was left of those Hishians who'd thought to hold the bridge.

A cheer went up from all who watched, including us, such as I'm sure that none in Om had ever heard before. The first skirmish. And the first victory! The sound of their cries of joy wafted up to us as we too poured down upon the bridge.

And the Dark One moved again!

Intent upon the fighting, I'd not noticed the approach of the clouds. A gigantic thunderhead, a wind-driven battleship of tremendous size now hung directly above us. It covered at least a mile of front. From it there came a crashing bolt of lightning such as I had never seen before. But then I'd never been that close to a bolt of lightning either. It was directed at the bridge. It missed! Another came—and missed! And still another—and it, too, *missed*! I stared in awe. There was simply no *way* he could have missed—except? A last bolt came to join its light with the mighty thunder of the previous blasts. I'd set myself to watch it closely. It was not directed at the bridge—but at *me*! And it, too, *missed*! Or rather, it was *deflected*. And that, for the moment, was it. The cloud, diminished by its loss of energies, broke up, was wafted away by puffs of wind from the final ensuing thunder. The crackling stench of ozone was sufficient to make our dottles cry.

How had the little bastards said it? "We'll help you, but you might not like it—" And so they would. And the Dark One, seeing, would lay the blame for the power all on *me*. I sighed. From here on in, when the Dark One sought to work his will, he'd be singling me out as the prime target. By all gods, they were *so* right! I *didn't* like it!

Still, gazing at the blasted boulders in the stream below, and at all the burning earth around us, I couldn't help but smile. I then looked up to see Murie, Hargis, and Griswall all gazing at me proudly, whilst Sernas and a dozen great lords and barons were ogling me in awe. I frowned at their misplaced belief, then thought better of it and *winked;* which I shouldn't have done. For from now on, too, in a tight spot, they'd expect the same—and I damn well couldn't deliver. Those little bastards had me again, and this time by the short hairs!

"My Prince," Lord Sernas said slowly, for he had to say something, if for no other reason than that the others would expect it of him, "you do ease the hearts of all of us. I must confess, I had not thought there was a chance. Now I know better. Indeed, though we still might die to the last man—we and our twenty thousand—I know that a final victory will be ours."

I answered just as slowly, sternly: "My thanks to you. But I adjure you now to erase all thoughts of *not* winning. For hear me"— and I arose in my stirrups to address them all. "If

117

we do *not* win *today*—we will have lost our chance forever! And it's because of this fact that I'll now disclose to you that you are not alone. Indeed, know this—and pass the word—before three hours past high noon you'll be joined by thirty thousand of the finest warriors of all the north. And sirs, m'lords, despite small victories, by that time we'll sorely need them."

As we neared the bridge we saw the headless bodies of the original defenders, warriors of the house of the Lord, Gol-Stils. . . . Others of his men, attached to Rawl, were taking their vengeance among those of the Dark One's levies still alive on our side of the gorge. One group of fifty or so Yorns now stood at bay. I recognized the leader. Strange, I thought, that I should meet him again and in almost the same circumstances. Perhaps it was an omen. I broke from Sernas' troupe and rode to where I could put my dottle between the Yorns and their attackers. "Down swords!" I shouted, and raised a gauntleted fist for emphasis. To the Yorn leader, I cried, "Well! So we meet again, warrior of Yurnal. But why do you now fight on the side of the Dark Kaleen? Did you not tell me that you were of the pack of Twill, enthralled to our Lord of Haken?"

"I know you, lord!" he called back. "And so it was. But we'd been beaten, which meant our death anyway. So I took those of the pack who would follow me to seek the protection of the Dark One."

"Would you fight for me now?"

"What is the difference?"

"Would you fight for me—to win your freedom?"

"What is freedom?"

"To live as men, in Om."

"Who but the Dark One could grant such a gift?"

"Which he will never do. Fight for me—all you and yours. You'll win your freedom under a just god whose name is Ormon. . . . I promise you!"

"How can we trust you?"

"As you did before. But if you stay with me, then will I ask you to beseech all Yorns whom you meet in battle to turn their swords against the Dark One—and to join with us. What say you?" I grew impatient.

Their communal thinking took but seconds. The leader said aloud, "My name is Unghist, and I am chief of these. We will fight for you."

The whole thing had taken but three minutes. I sent Hargis

to see that they were given mounts and then to catch up with us.

I said not a word to Sernas' raised eyebrow, nor to the perturbed looks of the other lords of our privy council—nor to Murie either. For it was a most natural thing for all those descended from Alphians to detest Yorns. For they knew instinctively that Yorns were what they could have been, had they been born deformed, twisted, grotesque, touched with the Dark One's curse. 'Tis a standard humanoid reaction everywhere.—Kill the deformed!

We drove on!

The black clouds came streaming in again from all the compass points. Thunder and lightning were everywhere, blasting the darkness the clouds had brought with a blue-white brilliance. Hard rains lashed the forest to the south—then stopped as quickly as they began.

What, I wondered, would the Dark One do now? What *could* he do? I was reminded of Hooli's statement: "He can throw rocks. He can rain on you. He can zap you with lightning bolts." That's what he'd said. But surely the Dark One could do more. . . . A mind seizure perhaps, despite the scoutship's "null" effect, and wherein half our men would fight the other half—*to the death*? Nyet! No way! "Null," or the strengthening of all magnetic lines of force so as to put them beyond the use of sentients in the one area—for the control of other sentients—*did* exist! We *were*, in part, protected. And, too, the Kaleen was in no position now to give full attention to this Omnian rebellion; even with the peril of its ultimate meaning. . . . Still, I could scarcely believe that he would allow us to attack—and just send humanoids and Yorns against us.

On we went at the dottle's mile-eating pace. Cloudbursts nearly drowned us. Bolt lightning came again. And we lost men, too, for not every bolt was deflected. At a number of points flanking squadrons of the Dark One's gathering hosts who'd filtered through our advance companies, drove into us. They were led by cowled warrior-priests in flaming red or black. I was glad of the attacks. For I knew what the Kaleen didn't know, that our men were spirted, ready; that man for man we'd win. And there's nothing quite like victory—a blooding of your own—to set the heart to racing and the hopes to rise. Each time they came at us, Sernas detached an equal number of ours to meet them under the command of this lord or that baron. The enemy fought poorly. Indeed, with but few losses to ourselves, we cut them down like so many gogs to the slaughter.

The cheers of our warriors who watched these small victories, and the difficulty our captains had in keeping rein on those who wished for a part of the glory, *now*, was real indeed.

And then—and then—ahead of us the sky began to glow a hellish red from beyond a low range of hills to our front. It was the second spot, the area of the valley where the first real battle might be expected. I had not thought we'd reach it so soon.

Rawl's five thousand, advancing ahead of us, rode up through the forest to show themselves upon the skyline. To the left and right our flanking thousands did likewise—but drew in upon the center. And on the hot winds that seemed to come now from that valley there was also some kind of vagrant, far-off howling. . . .

"My lords," I said to Sernas and the others, "It would appear that Sir Fergis does not go on, which means that we must go full speed to him." And we did it, to a tattoo of kettledrums and a skirl of pipes. The howling grew, matched by a shrieking wind that suddenly raged around us. We burst out upon the grass-grown upper slopes and raced toward the cleft of the road where our barons and lords joined quickly with Rawl's command. Below we saw the source of the howling.

How the valley must have looked to an Omnian is one thing. To a Terran, steeped in the history of a beauteous world and its varied religions, the scene was "inferno," a steel-point from the ancient Dante. I had ridden twice through the area. It was now unrecognizable. From the small dam to the north, to the encroaching forests to the south where the valley narrowed, all was a desert. Gone were the green fields, all burning now with the fires of hell. Gone, too, was a small, remembered village, reduced to blackened stones amid the ashes of its surrounding groves of fruit and nut trees. All now was but a red-fogged, blasted earth upon which, on the slopes of the farm hills, there awaited the massed host of the Dark One.

Young Sernas had told us that even on short notice the Kaleen could easily count upon a minimum of twenty-five thousand warriors. Well there they were! And something else had been added, too. For spaced between the companies of warriors and knights, and dark cowled priest-wizards, were a hundred great kaatis, at least a dozen *meegs*—and another

120

creature: the only thing in all of Fregis-Camelot, except a Vuun, that could kill a *meeg*. . . .

It had been placed in the very center of the Dark One's host. The howling came for *it*, amplified you can bet, from where *it* now seemingly crouched in the spring. It was called a skaiding by the Vuuns, for neither Omnian nor Marackian had ever seen its like before. It was a plated and scaled, meat-eating dinosaur. Its thirty-five foot body, inclusive of a horned tail of twenty feet, swayed heavily upon four monstrous legs. Extending from its front was a thick neck rising some ten feet from the torso. At the base of the neck were two more legs, or arms, with taloned extremities for the grasping of its prey. But the true horror was its head. The only parallel would be the Terran *Tyrannosaurus Rex*!

We stared, transfixed, at what could only mean our death. At that very instant the warm earth shook beneath us. Noxious gases arose from newly opened cracks in the ground and the stench of brimstone was everywhere. I had time to wonder what the Dark One would do next. But looking again at the skaiding, I doubted he could top it.

Whatever. The issue would soon be decided. For but *fifteen* hours remained for us and him!

From our ranks there arose another howling to match the one across the way. Our dottles had seen the skaiding. Their moans and cries were a cacophony of terror.

The lords, Gol-Stils and Gol-Tabus had ordered our lightly armed archers forward to screen our front against any untoward advance of the Kaleen's host—this, while we discussed what to do. "It appears to me," I told them all, "that though they possess superior force, they'll still wait for us to attack them. The Dark One has but to bar our way for his plan to succeed, whereas we must hack our way through all that mess over there just to get at him."

"The more reason, sir," Gol-Tabus said pompously, "for us to begin right now. Allow me to inform you, Prince Cares, that I've killed many a kaatl in my day, and I doubt me, sir that yon other strange beasties have charms against our spears."

Young Sernas interrupted. He'd ridden up from the liaison with the units of the left flank. "That dam up there's a peril," he said calmly. He doffed his helm to wipe streaming sweat from his face. "We must seize it afore they do, else they'll free the waters—to drown us all."

His father grunted. "The *peril's* sharpened your wits. Seize it! Take whom you need!"

121

Young Sernas instantly whirled his dottle—shouted back over his shoulder: "Ten minutes, Sire, and it's ours." And off he rode in a thunder of red dust, trailed by his blithe companions.

Interesting, I thought. There was a certain stiffness to his spine and a pride to his voice unnoticeable 'til now. I asked then that we quickly advance our warriors to just this side of the stream. "In that way," I said, "his maneuver will seem but a part of ours. But—unless the dam is opened—we will stay and he'll attack. And that way we'll see the 'way' of it."

I marvelled that they, who just short hours before had bowed so obsequiously to the Dark One's every wish, could now show such calm: considering that any advance at all on our part would be into the very jaws of hell itself. A plaguing thought touched me. Did they rely on me too heavily because of the Pug Boo's counteraction at the bridge? I shrugged. What difference now?

"We'll see two things," he was saying. "How our enemy fights, and how those horned things with stings do answer our Dark One's call. . . ."

I inwardly shuddered. For I knew right then that my Omnians had never seen a *meeg* either. . . .

The sun broke through again to change the reddish hell to a bronze-gold hell instead. Hooli? We rode down over the still burning earth. Bodies were everywhere in the destroyed huts of the village. Those who'd had no time to flee had simply been butchered. And so it was on all the farmsteads, too. We passed great cracks in the rived earth; saw them for the first time. some were as much as a foot in width, with flames and gases still ensuing from their depths.

Despite the heat we were forced to protect our faces with a section of our cloaks, wet with water. Our poor dottles suffered.

We halted in the burnt fields on a line some hundred yards from the meager stream. The Dark One's host was at another hundred yards on the farther side. They were motionless then, drums and horns quiet. Indeed, all was silent—excepting sporadic howls from the awesome skaiding. Cowled wizards—as opposed to priest-warriors—and I counted twelve of them, sat their mounts before solid companies of knights and spearmen. Each one was protected by a half-dozen great Yorns in bronzed armor. Noting this, I sent Tober to quick collect my fifty with their leader, Unghist. "I've a trick," I

122

told the frowning Sernas. "We'll fight the Kaleen's 'Cowls' with *Ormon's fire*."

To Unghist I said, "You and yours will stay with me wherever I will go. And thus will you earn your freedom."

At which Rawl shouted fiercely, disclosing his own unreasonable hatred of Yorns—"And since where he goes, 'all trouble comes,' you can damn well prepare to die!"

Unghist said nothing, simply nodded. I glanced hard at the others. They nodded too. And that was that.

The dam—we were looking upstream toward it—was still visible in the haze. We therefore witnessed young Sernas' attack. He and his cohorts were obviously anxious to prove themselves—thought, too, I'm sure, that if things went awry, I'd rescue them with my *magick*. This is not to say that they lacked in courage, but rather to suggest a certain, lingering opportunism. For they *were* Omnians. And character had in no way been a part of the Dark One's curricula.

The cowled wizards, seeing Sernas' advance, moved to counter him. Driving hard along the dam's top, he met them three-quarters of the way across. The height of the earthern structure was fifty feet. Dottles and riders alike were literally hurled from it to fall like rain upon an equally vicious *melee* at the dam's bottom. It was a sight to see. Sernas' sybarites led their men bravely, fought recklessly, and for the sheer joy of winning. The Dark One's warriors fought because they had to. And, in the doing, found they could retreat with little or no risk from their master. Upon which they retreated still further, and faster. A disastrous error, really. Sernas' warriors simply drove into their undefended backs with fighting spear and sword.

It was a massacre!

Until the Dark One unleashed the first of two gigantic *meegs*. I say "unleashed," for it had obviously been held in check until that moment. But the Dark One, ever stupid in the area of detail, had simply overlooked the fact that to a *meeg*, meat was meat. The living prey was anything he could get his sting into and clutch in his ghastly claws.

In effect, finding that he could move again—and he could just as easily have leapt backward—the thing jumped ahead one hundred feet to land in the midst of a group of the Kaleen's fleeing warriors. His great body crushed a number of them; his sting jabbed in lightning-like rapier thrusts in all directions and his claws seized instantly upon those he would kill and eat, for he was ravenous. . . . The sight produced a wave of horror in the ranks of both armies. Young Sernas, now in possession of the dam, top and bottom, understandably made no move to advance any farther.

"So *that* is a *meeg*," my princess said.

I patted her arm while Rawl answered for me, saying, "Indeed, it is! The very reason we'd not be here if there'd been no ice and snow in Marack. . . ."

Why the Dark One failed to advance his monster farther, I could only guess; the first guess being that perhaps the horror could not be forced from the feeding—even by the Kaleen. The one thing I did know now—it would be of little use to him in the long run. For, as we'd seen, it attacked *all* living things, *indiscriminately*. This was not true of the kaati's though, the Fregisian grizzlies. With them there was a certain control. As for the skaiding? Well, there was but one of those.

We'd have to kill it!

Great Fomalhaut mounted higher in the eastern sky. The rising heat of it—or mayhap some other power?—fought the Dark One's clouds, forced them away, only to have them return again. There was no point in waiting. Time was running out.

Our realignment was made quickly and in the face of flights of arrows sent against us. The distance being too great, they did little damage. Rawl's five thousand split to join with the twenty-five hundred at either flank. Young Sernas, after leaving five hundred at the dam, took over the left flank with his blooded captains who were now quite proud of themselves—ignoring, of course, the reality of the *meeg*, against which they had dared not advance.

The Barons, Gol-Tabus and Gol-Tairs, moved off to command the right flank. Myself, Lord Akin Sernas and Lord Gol-Spils, would command the center. Three thousand of our best were placed under the command of Lord Hakem and Rawl to act as a reserve . . .

We did the one thing needed then, by the Omnians, though I thought it a waste of time. We ceremoniously rode down our length of front to show the colors of all those in rebellion against the Dark One. We did it twice, back and forth; with a dropping of the various commanders to the front of their respective units. At the second pass we were joined by five dottles, led by Hargis, who flew my twin banners. Riding the dottles were Hooli, Pawbi, Jindil, Chuuk, and Dahkti, of the five kingdoms of the North.

I explained this to Sernas and the others. It meant nothing to them. Though the effect of the music of the previous night remained (along with the ongoing, keying of the notes of today) any memory they might have had of the Pug Boos actually playing their instruments had fast faded—a part of the built-in package. So they remained in Omnian eyes what they had always been: mangy little leaf-eaters who were good for nothing at all. They even tasted bad, Lord Gol-Stils told me. Fortunately he did this out of the hearing of Murie and my stalwarts, else they'd had his liver then and there.

Still, the presence of the Boos did seem to add the lusty cheers and hoorahs that greeted us all down the line. Strange that they had that faculty—to be able to shout, even boast, in the face of the horrors across the stream. In a way, though they knew it not, they *were* changing. I even sensed a wave of tingling euphoria from all of them. Its origin most certainly lay in Pug Boo "goodness."

The drums were now going at a hellish rate on the other side. A myriad of great horns were also blasting out. They sounded like great gerds in challenge. As we neared the center again, I ordered Hargis to conduct the Boos to the rear. . . .

—Upon which, Hooli's voice, loud enough to crack a mastoid, sounded off. "Collin-Kyrie, you've one job to do before you get this mass of meat in motion. Unless you kill that goddamn lizard, baby, they won't make it."

"Whaddaya mean. . . ? Check that enthusiasm, man! They're *ready*!"

"They'll fall apart. Don't you understand? The skaiding's controlled, by *himself*!"

"The Kaleen?" Even inside my own head, I could hardly hear my voice.

"That's right."

I breathed deeply. "And if I don't choose to fight it?"

"How can you not—*Collin*?"

"Even if I killed it—" I became evasive in my sudden fear—"What's to prevent another from showing up immediately?"

"That will not happen."

"*I* don't know that."

"*I'm* telling you."

"Damn you, Hooli! The Omnians will kill the skaiding. They're ready for it—*psyched* for it. . . ."

"Kyrie—they know not what they do! They are true Alphi-

125

ans, born with the curse and the *courage* of that dead planet. They will ignore what they cannot *stand* to think of."

"*No!*" I said.

"What will you do then? lead these poor bastards to their death. Better you crashed your scoutship against the pyramid, *Adjuster* Kyrie Fern, than to mindlessly attack the skaiding."

"How in the name of your bloody Dark One am *I* supposed to kill the skaiding?"

"You did not destroy the pyramid. The skaiding is therefore your problem. If you cannot kill it, certainly none of *these* can."

"Even if I did, what of the *meegs*, Hooli? A skaiding can kill a *meeg*. But a meeg *can* and *will* kill ten times the men a skaiding will—for the sheer pleasure of it."

"Just kill the skaiding, Kyrie. No one can help you. Just kill it, *now!*"

And he was gone. And the others watched me strangely, as if I had been away and had just returned.

I breathed deeply and looked across at the Hishian host and wondered how, even with skaiding dead, we could defeat that mass of warriors. Our Marackians had yet to arrive, and across that stream were now at least thirty thousand of the foe. I breathed deeply again. They were waiting for my signal.

Rawl bent close from his mount. "My lord. Is aught amiss? You're acting strange."

I said softly, "Shieldman, brother. 'Tis that I must first fight that goddamned thing alone."

His eyes blazed in both anger and fear for me. He shouted, "By Ormon, Collin, and do you do it *alone*, I'll never call you friend again."

The lords around us all drew back not knowing why Rawl said what he did, or what he meant.

"Do you think," I said harshly, "that I make this choice myself? Nay, swordsmen. Not this time. My word, sir. If I'd a choice, I'd let *you* do it ten times over. . . ."

"*Now hear me, all!*" I cried aloud, rising in my stirrups. "It is written, sirs, on the palm of my hands that 'the Collin' must fight that dread beast yonder. Therefore I ask that no man bar my way, nor seek to join me in what I have to do, for his honor's sake. Only these Yorns will I take with me, and my swordsmen Griswall and Hargis. . . .

"My Prince Til-Keeves, who is the true Lord Rawl Fergis of Marack, nephew to Marack's queen, will command in my absence. *Is it agreed?*"

And they, expecting miracles, cheered. And why should they not agree?

But my Princess, sensing something rotten in the state of Om, seized a skin of small javelins from the nearest warrior and said strongly to me, "I go to live or die with you, my lord, for yon 'beast' is not Gol-Bades, nor is it a frozen *meeg*. And if you try to stop me, sir, I'll draw first blood from *you*. So speaks your Queen. Now lead, and I will follow."

I swallowed hard and nodded, bade the three of them to ride close on my dottle's rump.

At the stream's edge I called the Yorns to me. "There are twelve wizards over there," I nodded, "and fifty of you. Each wizard is guarded by many Yorns. Do you stay to the rear of us. If a wizard approaches, send some of yours to stop him. They must speak with the wizard's guards; tell them that I and this new Omnian army bring them their freedom to live as men; that they must *not* defend the wizard."

"Must we then attack the wizards?" Unghist and the others asked in awe.

Without your fellows there's nought to attack," I said bluntly. "Strike at the cowls. You'll find them empty, filled only with the Dark One's voice."

Unghist, hesitating, looked to the others. They nodded. He said, "We will do it, Lord."

"You will do more than that," I snapped. "For if this princess, my companion, is attacked, you will defend her to the death. Is that understood?"

"It is."

"Good!"

I turned then toward the Hishian host, my spear above my head, and shouted in an amplified roar to be heard in all directions:

"HEAR ME NOW! I AM THE PRINCE TIL-CARES OF THE SELIG ISLES: HE WHO IN THE NORTH IS KNOWN AS THE 'COLLIN' OF MARACK! I WILL SEEK NOW IN SINGLE COMBAT TO TEST YOUR MONSTER, THE DARK ONE'S IMAGE, ON THE FIELD OF BATTLE. . . . DO YOU HEAR ME, FIEND OF DARKNESS?" I roared dramatically to the skies. "I COME TO KILL YOUR SKAIDING! DARE TO SEND HIM FROM YOUR RANKS, *NOW*!"

And I sent my mount, an aging but heavily muscled dottle, to dash through the knee-deep stream in a froth of spume and water.

As the others plunged in after me the very earth around us shook again. The Dark One's answer?

The Hishian kettle-drums began anew. I rode arrogantly toward their mounting roar; headed directly to where the great standards of this lord and that hung limply in the heated air. Some pranced their mounts and made as if to charge us. Two did, ponderous in their armor. They rode full at us, spears crouched, each twelve foot shaft tipped with a full two feet of fine-honed steel.

Hargis and Griswall rode instantly against them, the red burnt earth a cloud of dust around their pounding dottle paws.

Griswall, whose every move was completely professional, was a delight to watch; that is, if you like that sort of thing. With this inept opponent, he simply rose in his stirrups, whirled the great spear's blade this way and that, dodged his adversaries' points—then took the man's head with the tip of his spear alone.

Young Hargis—he'd left his shield to his back—also whirled his spear, disdaining the thrust. He knocked his man's shaft to one side, then, as the fellow rode by, whacked the back of his helm with his spear's butt. The helm flew off. The skull was crushed. A spatter of brains flew out to damp the dust.

A roar of shouts and applause went up from our sharp-eyed Omnian army. . . . An interesting thing happened then. The two dottles, freed of their enemy riders, did not turn back to the ranks of Hish, but ran instead, moaning and crying, to the ranks of our own host on the far side of the stream. . . .

I halted within a hundred paces of the skaiding where I raised my arms again for their attention. "Stand clear!" I shouted. "My battle's with your Dark One's image—that great and wiggly lizard. Send him out, if you dare. I await him here."

But there was little need to force the skaiding. Indeed, it *came* out, propelled, I knew—and instantly—as if Hooli himself, had put the thought in my head, by the very intellect I'd claimed in sarcasm. The sure knowledge that in part I now faced the Kaleen himself, sent a chill of absolute dread to weaken all my limbs.

And the horror, at *my* call, moved ponderously toward me. Six months before, when I'd scanned it aboard the Deneb-3, I'd thought it unimportant. For its habitat was limited to but

128

a few hundreds of square miles of jungle where no Fregisian ever ventured.

I now knew different. It moved slowly, a veritable armored tank, impregnable to any Fregisian weapon, sword, spear, or mace. I'd thought, in my arrogance, even as I'd argued with Hooli, that I could still take it if I had to; that I could find some obvious flaw in the beast's defenses. . . .

I saw now that it had none!

Those monstrous, taloned "hands." That great head. The blazing, nightmare eyes, horned crest, and a mouth to engorge a gog-calf whole—all coupled with the Dark One's presence—had finally reached me!

And a sly and pervasive knowledge crept into my thinking: that the thing was without speed to catch me, if I fled! The thought blanked out all else. Even the fact that for me to flee was to lose the battle; for if *I* ran, *so would Sernas' army!*

And Hooli had known this, had somehow guessed that I'd never really *seen* a skaiding: and guessed, too, that I'd choose to run—and lose the battle. Therefore the alternative—to ram the pyramid with the scoutship. Now he could but hope that I wouldn't run; that somehow I'd find a way. . . .

But for the first time he was wrong. *There was no way!* And knowing this, I knew, too, that as sure as a dottle has six legs, the skaiding would surely kill me. In effect, I truly *saw* my death!

My body became all damp with the cloying sweat of animal fear. I could smell it, pungent, sharp! My poor dottle smelled it too. Indeed, he shied, slowed his pace instantly to look back to me who forced him on with trembling knees. Stark terror shone in the dottle's blue eyes. The trembling of my knees became a quaking of my entire body. The dottle slowed. I made no move to force it further. Two wizards with Yorn guards rode out to either side. And from the corners of my eyes I saw two groups of my own Yorns ride to confront them—a thing no Yorn had ever done before.

Their very act, their trust in *me*, should have given me courage. It didn't. My mind was sickened with but a single thought: my *death*! Here dies Kyrie Fern, the "Collin"; just here in this stupid, magicked valley, on this crazy, beautiful, miserable planet, and at the hands of some weird alien who's using the body of a Mesozoic-Fregisian misfit, already on its way to extinction. . . .

But what in the bloody, Christian hell was I to do? Even at full strength, I doubted that the laser could take it. Still, if it was a question of *my* life, I'd use it anyway. And bedamned to the fact that once the laser was gone there'd be no way to blast the Dark One . . . So? To hell with it! I'd use the laser. And after that? Well maybe a ride for the scoutship, with Murie and the rest. After all, my terrified mind suggested, enough was enough, The "contract" had never called for suicide.

I reached for my belt, my gauntleted hand fumbling so that I failed to distinguish one stone from another. At that precise moment a great voice spoke in galactic-vulgate— "*Aaaaaaaaa—Collin. Kyrie . . .*" it seemed to whisper; though the sound was that of a soughing wind. "*Doooo what you must—and—leeeave . . . !*"

I *knew* from whence the voice came. Still my trembling hand sought the laser stone—to end it all in a victory for the Dark One. I looked down to guide my trembling fingers—and saw, from the corner of an eye that Murie and Hargis were watching me; that their faces were pale, their eyes staring; their very souls shattered by the sight of the "Collin's" *fear*! I tried to control my hands. I couldn't!

Hargis, a true *Alphian*, then did what he had to do. He squared his shoulders, saluted me, said briskly: "Well, now, my lord. I'll test the bastard first. We'll find his weak point. . . ." And he rode off to face that thing that was now within but a hundred feet of us.

And did I not hear some strange and awful laughter to match the rising thunder of the drums? Still I could not move; nor, with Murie watching, could I any longer search for the correct stone at my belt.

Then Murie dashed to the front of me, as if to protect me, and then rode back; to the fore again to turn and stare right at me. Alarm was in her every movement; fear, too, for *me*. For my fear was visibly the kind that causes paralysis.

"My Lord," she cried, when she could no longer stand the sight of my abject cowardice, "My Love. You must allow us to attack it. There's hope—some way—"

Then a roar rose from the ranks of both sides. I focused my unseeing eyes. Brave Hargis—he had but nineteen years—had driven three feet of heavy spear into the monster's left nostril. Only to be instantly seized in the grasping talons of those quick and deadly forefeet. He screamed his death cry, his ribcage crushed. And even as I watched, the skaiding took both head and shoulders into its gaping tunnel of a mouth and *halved* him—bit through hauberk, plate, and steel to do it.

And, even as I watched, Murie, too, rode forth, despite the

piteous screams of her dottle, to place herself exactly beneath the beast and to hurl with unerring aim two small javelins to pierce its great right eye. Green juices poured from the eye, horrendous howls of rage from the depths of its being. The skaiding hurled Hargis' remains away, turned slightly—and with one sweep of its mighty tail dashed her and her dottle to the ground.

But the spell had been broken!

Indeed, I'd been moving forward with Hargis' scream, snapped from my paralysis by his death, and the fact that most likely Murie, too, was now dead—because of me. . . . Griswall was already ahead of me, since he'd moved to follow Murie in the first instance of her challenge. Now he leapt from his dottle to stand also before the monster. At that moment I joined him, he'd hurled his twelve foot war spear toward the one remaining eye—and missed!

"Griswall!" I shouted. "To your princess, sir! She's not dead. If you're going to die, 'twill be protecting *her*!"

Whether he dropped back at that precise moment or not, I don't remember. Still, my head had cleared completely of the Dark One's intrusion. The fear was gone. Cold logic took its place, touched my heart and slowed its pounding. A tenth of a second's scan showed me the field in photo-image. Two groups of Yorns, mine, were larger now by the addition of a number of enemy Yorns who had joined them. Two black cowls waving on gleaming spear tips brought scattered cheers from our ranks. To the left a faint shimmering denoted something, too. It came from a crouching *meeg*. I knew, and *instantly*, that that *meeg*—and most likely all of them—was encapsulated in a below-zero air pocket.

In effect, not a single *meeg* would ever move again!

"Well, why not the skaiding, too?" I howled mentally. For I also knew just who had tinkered with the *meegs*. But no way—if I'd done what they'd asked me—crashed the pyramid it would all be over now. But I hadn't. So. Whatever the reasons, the skaiding was mine alone.

He'd swiped at me and missed—and given me the single idea I'd had so far to take him. At the next swipe, I leapt to the taloned, grasping foreleg, seized upon it, straddled it, riding its wrist. The dullness of its brain assured me there'd be no nerve ends sufficient to detect my presence. The arm was on his blinded side, preventing him from knowing where I'd gone. Then the monstrous tail came around to slash the air. It turned its head to look; saw nothing! The tail came whistling back, dug a trench in the earth. Nothing!

By then I'd hauled my shield from off my back, grasping the handholds of its three-pointed rectangle firmly—*but upside down.* My greatsword was a simple extension of my right arm. The creature had never ceased to howl from the pain in its blasted eye. Except for that, as a distraction, I think he would have known where I hid. Now that I *wanted* him to know of my presence, I had actually to pry at a scale to attract his attention.

He brought his foreleg up to his remaining, slitted orb—and saw me! He then did one thing that could bring his death, the thing I'd counted on. *He opened his mouth to take my body.* . . .

I met the gigantic head direct; dived straight into that cavernous maw. My legs were caught on the front teeth. But I had time to wedge the shield, flat-top down, and with the point to the roof of the mouth, to protect them, while simultaneously thrusting the greatsword forward so that its point pierced the monster's palate. The haft was then firmly anchored in the scarlet flesh of the tongue.

The sword was twice the shield's length. Therefore, with the instantaneous snap of his great jaws, at least three feet of the blade was imbedded in the palate below the brain before the front of the mouth touched the shield. To open his mouth again was to free me, which he would not do. Indeed, I would have died anyway and in short order, had it not followed its natural instincts—and bitten down still harder in its rage . . .

The sword's tip was driven still further up, piercing the tiny brain. And so it died. . . . In reflex action the great head shook, the mouth opened, hurling me from it. To save myself I clung to the horror's teeth, breaking my fall, so that when the scaled head fell earthward, I was able to leap free.

In life-and-death combat most things take place in seconds. And so it had been with myself and the skaiding. Even as I hit the ground, I was up again to snatch Hargis' broken spear from the monster's nose and to climb its horned neck for the platform of its still quaking shoulders. Murie and Griswall raced to join me. My Yorns came streaming to surround the body of the skaiding to defend the three of us from the yelling, screaming Hishian host, a part of whose line was moving forward while the greater part held back.

I yelled with all the strength of my lungs and waved Hargis' spear—"OM! MARACK! OM! MARACK!" I shouted. But there was little need to. . . .

Indeed the Omnian wave of Sernas' army was already at

the charge, kettledrums thumping, fighting spears couched. It was a sight to see. Sir Rawl, at the very moment I'd dived into the skaiding's mouth, had led them out. As he told me later, he figured to do or die right then and there, as any true Marackian would. At the river's edge however, they'd seen the creature die, and me emerge—at which point the roar of Sernas' twenty thousand was then sufficient to raise the dead of all Om's five thousand years of servitude. . . .

Those of the bravest of the Hishians who had dared attack the Yorns protecting us were almost instantly engulfed in the first wave of Rawl's bloodthirsty thousands.

Victory's a heady thing. Defeat's disaster. And so it was with the Dark One's host as it fell back before the Omnian onslaught. Only the Kaleen's control saved them from the complete rout. Winds came; a howling gale to instantly whip the dust into clouds, blinding attacker and attacked alike.

We still forged ahead, driving them over the range of hills and beyond. The vicious, running battle was not without casualties for us, too. For here and there a Hishian lord would stand to fight to the death—for his honor and his god. And, being an Alphian first, he'd make that battle a thing to remember. . . .

Clouds came, and more rain to wash the dust away. And I couldn't tell what was Pug Boo sponsored and what was not. But when the dust was laid the pyrotechnics returned so that more of ours were lost to great bolts and sheets of lightning that shattered all the valley. Innumerable fires were also set. Peasant homes, barns, whole villages and entire forests went up in flames.

I halted my little group and our remaining Yorns—they'd lost a dozen or so in our defense—beyond the first range of hills. Actually, I could go no farther. My left leg had been deeply slashed by the monster's teeth. It was partially paralyzed. We were also moving beyond the protection of the scoutship. Somehow I'd have to get back to it and take it forward.

It was exactly then that Hooli chose to play "knock, knock." He said sharply inside my head, "You've got to bring your ship up, Collin."

"I *know* that," I answered in exasperation—my forced *mano-a-mano* with the skaiding had in no way endeared him to me—"In the meantime, I'd suggest that you and yours go on ahead—hold off the Dark One. Play some tricks. Give *him* a bolt or two."

"Not without you. He must not 'see' *us*, Collin."

133

"Bloody Ormon! Hasn't he 'seen' you yet?"

"Only you, Buby. He think's it all from *you*."

"You little bastards. I'd guessed as much. But what the hell difference does it make *now* if he does 'see' you?"

"Then all would be lost, whatever *you* would do."

"Gerd tits!" I exclaimed. "Look! I suffered some hurt in that damned thing's mouth. I need your healing touch, now!"

He didn't answer.

They laid me out on an unburnt grassy slope, against a granite boulder. Murie and Griswall undressed me. Water was brought, and sviss. I drank copious draughts of both while the sviss was poured directly onto the gashes left by the teeth of the monster. The fluids of its mouth had undoubtedly contained some kind of poison, for I was fast losing any feeling in the leg.

Murie held my head in her lap, protectively. Griswall stood by, leaned heavily on his sword. Lord Sernas and a handful of his officers had held back briefly to see the nature and the extent of my wounds. They were visibly concerned.

Sernas said, with an attempt at humor, "One would hope that with such power as you've displayed, my lord, those wounds would fast be healed."

"Mayhap they will be," I replied. I told no one of the paralysis. "The flow of blood's been stanched. I'll need but a few minutes' rest, then I'll follow on . . . Be assured, sirs."

He took that as an order and he and his entourage saluted and moved off to join the pursuit. We were at about fourteen miles from Sernas Castle now—halfway to Hish! The power of the scoutship waned considerably with each mile's distance. To assure our Omnians of even its limited protection, I'd have to move it and quick. I called to Unghist. He came, huge, bloodied and serious. As ugly as he was, I was beginning to like him. He'd proven one thing: he *could* be trusted. I focused my contacts to ten mags, stared over the plain. I chose my site. "Look there," I told him. "You see that clump of trees on that third small hillock next that peasant wattle hut and barn?"

He said he did.

"Find a half-dozen additional dottles and hold them there for us. Do not leave that spot. We'll join you shortly. Go, now. . . ."

He stared soberly at the mounts we already had. Then, without a word, he saluted and left.

Good boy! I was *really* beginning to appreciate him.

Turning again to the others, I saw that Murie, sore bruised

134

herself, *was cuddling Hooli* who, as always, had appeared from nowhere.

"So you've come!" I said from inside my head. "Good! Now fix me so I can ride, you miserable damned rodent."

He scrambled from Murie's arms and climbed upon my belly as would a questing squirrel or honey bear. He padded up to peer into my eyes. He said, "Gawd, you're ugly. Repeat after me— There's no place like home! There's no place like home!—"

I said, "Stop the shit, Hooli!" The pain was beginning to reach me. "*Do it!*"

He turned, padded back again, took one of my toes between his teeth as if to gnaw it, seemingly thought better of it, climbed down—and returned to Murie and cuddled in her lap.

And I was cured!

A laying of hands? Call it what you will. There were no longer any gashes upon my legs, no open wounds upon my back. More! There was a surge of energy, of *goodness* throughout my body so as to make me think I could challenge a dozen skaidings . . .

I sat up, got to my feet, saying the while, "Ride with us, Hooli. Rejoin your friends." To Murie and Griswall, I said, "Let's to the ship, quick! The farther these Omnians advance, the greater their peril."

I dressed and we mounted up—and without a word being said about my recovery. Indeed, I sensed the same physical euphoria in the both of them that I felt. Hooli's touch had the Midas quality. . . .

We rode hard, passed the great dottle herd some two miles to the rear where we gave Mr. "tam" and "bootie" into the company of his companions.

As we drove on. Murie said cautiously at my side, "My lord. I feared for you when first we fought the skaiding."

I laughed. "And with good reason. For I too 'feared for *me.*'"

"He had you, didn't he—the Dark One?"

I smiled. I had wondered how she would rationalize my cowardice. True. The Dark One's presence within the skaiding *did* have something to do with it—but not all that much. I said softly, "Nay, love. What possessed me is the thing that possesses all men at one time or other. The Dark One was in the skaiding, true—until you dared sink your shafts into its eye. Its pain was sufficient then to drive the Dark One out— else, my dear, we'd all be dead right now. . . ."

"Still, in the end you were wondrous brave, my lord." She leaned across to kiss me. And I sensed as she did it that she had really known quite well that her Kyrie Fern had almost died back there—of bloody fear.

At the ship's site, I phased it in and within seconds we had lifted above the now war-torn land and were headed toward the grove of trees guarded by our Yorns.

Beyond, the pursuit continued, but slower now as additional Hishian contingents moved into the fray. They came direct from the city, along all the side roads from north, east and south. Lors Sernas had suggested the Dark One's amassing of some twenty-five thousand in a few hours. It was visibly obvious that he could get three times that many in twelve.

I took the scoutship lower, risked everything for a look ahead. I had to know what awaited us between Rawl's advancing warriors and the city. The ship—in "null" plus five—had a distortion factor sufficient for invisibility. This of course would not apply to the Kaleen, should he be scanning.

At a halfway point beyond our advancing front, and at just five miles from Hish itself was the river, Kiis. It was wide and shallow, at about five hundred yards and with many sand flats. The flat stretches of slow moving water was at best a foot or two in depth. The river itself presented no obstacle. But the banks to either side, did. The far bank was a sharply sloping bluff of some thirty feet in height. And on that bluff was ranged as many as five thousand archers. They screened an additional force of thirty thousand lords, barons, and warriers; all being rapidly supplemented by the remnants of the thirty thousand who had fled before us . . . The Dark One had truly drained all the land around.

He fought for time, obviously. He had no choice, or so it seemed. He could stop what he was doing and concentrate on us—or he could continue, hoping to hold us 'til the gateway was completed, when he'd have all the power he needed to do what he wanted. Still, I wondered: Why the urgency? Was there something we didn't know? A reason, linked perhaps with the exact alignment of Capil and Ripple? I'd not discussed it with Hooli. Indeed Hooli'd not discussed it with me. . . .

Whatever. We had arrived on the scene at precisely the moment when he needed to focus all of his energies upon the creation of the gateway. We were forcing him to draw upon those energies now—to prevent us from bringing the whole thing down!

His major effort, I concluded, would have to be made at that river and along that line above the bluff. . . .

At the grove of trees I selected a small vale hidden from the road, and decked the ship. The "null" factor had never ceased at full. Its controls now extended to Hish and beyond.

We stepped out of the grove and to the rear of our Yorns. Their stoicism, at sight of our mysterious reappearance, remained unshaken. "Unghist!" I called. "We are here. Bring us our mounts, for we would join the center command."

Stoicism aside, their attitude toward us was still nothing short of awe.

Our twenty thousand had pushed to within two miles of the Kiist River. We caught up with the main body as it drove inexorably through a final burning village. Seeing the approach of my double standard—the "Collins's" sprig of violets and the three golden dolphins against a black wave's curl—Lord Akin Sernas called out: "Well, sir, I've never seen the like of your recovery. Would to whatever gods that we'll now pray to, and to this *Ormon* most certainly, that all in the world who are ill of wounds will recover likewise."

There were cheers all around; especially so since most of them had thought to be dead by now and instead found themselves riding as victors. And to "victors" the leader of the victory can do no wrong. Rawl came up with Caroween, Charney, and Tober. The lithesome, beauteous redhead, her surcoat and hauberk all bloodied, for she'd truly been Rawl's shield-maiden, took Murie in her arms. . . .

The ebullient Rawl, seeing my condition, said happily, "By the gods, Collin, you've more lives than a Gheesian louse. While you've been resting," he boasted, "we've killed full half their army."

I smiled in the knowledge that he knew well—since his eyesight was as keen as a marsh eagle's—that the main battle had yet to be fought. Though the plain of meadow and farmland was now generally flat, there was a slight sloping toward the river so that the far bluff could be seen—and along with it the monstrous array of spears and banners. "There's still another army, though methinks 'twill be their last."

And have I said that the sun, great Fomalhaut, was now approaching noon?

All opposition had ceased. Indeed, even as we rode on, the last of the fleeing enemy was racing across the shallow waters

137

to join their Hishian brothers. I decided then to risk the telling of Marack's arrival. . . .

We halted at the far end of the ruined village. Sernas, when I told him that I would have council, made as if to call in all his captains. But I warned against it, saying, "What must be said should be told to a handful first. The information can then be passed along. For the Dark One, sirs, would dearly love to catch us in one great meeting and there's no way to abort the lightning he can launch if he's a mind to. Now, within but a few hours," I told them soberly, "and as previously stated, there will arrive on your Omnian soil, and at precisely the site of your dottle herds, thirty thousand Marackian warriors—all led by Marack's greatest generals. They come either to win with you or to die with you. For such is the peril of our world. 'Tis said, and true, however, that nothing works as we would like it to.—In effect there may be delay, treason; whatever! Anything can happen. Therefore I adjure you that though we must believe in Marack's coming, still must we advance to slay these minions of the Dark One as if Marack were never coming. If she comes in time, she'll share your glory; if she comes too late—she'll avenge you, though mayhap, too, she will die herself in the doing of the deed . . ."

They listened quietly, in deep thought.

"How," Lord Gol-Tares asked, "will they get from there to here?"

"I cannot tell you that," I said, " 'til after."

Lord Sernas chose to ask the obvious question: "How long will Marack stay in Om?"

"Until the Dark One is no more—no longer."

"We have your word?"

"Yes—as you will have the word of the Lords of the North."

"Then so be it. How many," he changed the subject, "would you say confront us now, beyond the Kiis?"

"With the remnants of the first army enjoined with the second, perhaps 50,000; mayhap with more kaatis and such."

"No more skaidings? no *meegs*?"

"I doubt it. The Dark One grows more limited, sirs. He dares not waste his energies, which he must save for the thing he must do. But there might be other things . . ."

"Such as?"

"I do not know. But I do assure you, his greatest power lies in the sword arms that still support him."

138

The beatle-browed Gol-Stils said peremptorily, he'd been watching the far bluff with steely eyes, "Let's to it then. With or without Marack; with or without your magic, Collin, I've a mind to test those sword arms you speak of. It just might be, sir, that all that is best in Om can do the job itself—without your help."

"I pray it will be so," I answered simply. "Indeed, we'll help you do it; me and my remaining swords."

Upon which he took my hand and begged my pardon, not out of fear, but for the slight he knew he'd given. . . . I thought then that the Boo's music had made—was still making—true Alphians of them all in ways of courtesy as well as battle.

Throughout our talk Rawl's hand was strong upon my shoulder. He now asked, smiling, "My Lord, Collin, what of yon host? How would you go about it?"

"Why," I said blithely, "let's ride up to it first and have a look. I'd caution all, however," my voice rose, "to spread out; to keep a measured pace. That way, should lightning come, we'll lose fewer swords. Once joined in battle, 'twill be the opposite. For where we're locked with the Dark One's men, no bolts, or such, is possible."

But when we came to the river's west bank we found a thing we'd not seen on the approach. The bank was diked. Apparently, at flood season the waters could otherwise quite easily inundate the western area for a mile or two of excellent bottom land. . . . The dike rose some twenty feet in a gentle slope from the fields and sharply for a last twelve feet. The top of the dike was as much as fifty feet across, whereupon the bank then gently sloped into the wide flat river. No wonder then that I'd not seen it from the skies either.

We halted at the exact spot where, when we came up the slope, our heads first cleared the dike's top. From there we could see all we had to see, whereas the Dark One's host could see nought but our heads and banners. The Lord Sernas sent word down the line to rest our forces 'til we had determined what to do.

Young Sernas, riding up, shouted with new respect to his father, "Sire! Methinks this bridge, too, should be seized, at both ends, and instantly."

His father smiled. His reply held a like respect for his son which, I warrant, had never been granted him before. "No need," he said calmly. "The water's shallow. The bridge leads to but a single cleft in the bluff among many."

"Ah!" young Sernas exclaimed, "I see your point, pod."

139

"At least you're learning, you copulating rapist," Lord Haken yelled—he'd conducted himself quite bravely in the burning valley . . .

"When we attack," Rawl Fergis mused from the saddle, "they will most certainly have amassed their very best at each cleft top. 'Twill be to our disadvantage. . . ."

"Let's lure 'em out," young Sernas said, "then follow *them* back up. The confusion should even the odds somewhat."

Lord Sernas said thoughtfully, "Mayhap we can surprise them, seize but one cleft with picked men; expand from there?"

I said to Akin Sernas, "My Lord, I think your son may have something. So far we've found the Dark One to be lacking in detailed planning. Why this should be, I cannot say. But it is so. You can trust him, therefore, to do the obvious. Example: Their troops, outnumbering us, await us on the bluff. When we attempt the river there'll be more lightning bolts—mayhap a hurling of stones. The thing is: what would the Dark One do if in mid-river we panicked and ran?"

"But we will not panic, sir!" Gol-Stils shouted.

"Nor will we run!" the doughty Haken roared.

"You miss the point," I said. "The question is: what will *he* do if *we* panic and run?"

"Why, Sir Collin—" Lord Sernas entered the fray—"they'll follow on, the bastards. They'll think to take us as cowards—in the back."

"As we took them this morning," his son interjected.

"And if, as your son suggests, our panic is but a ruse—what then?"

"Why!" Gol-Pares cried, "We'd turn on 'em, drive 'em right back up through those clefts."

"Except," Rawl said, his eyes all twinkling, "they'd be disorganized somewhat."

"Hah!" Lord Sernas said.

And "Hah!" the barons Gol-Spils and Pares said in unison, while Haken roared with laughter and young Sernas pranced his dottle as if to draw them down himself.

"Fine," I grunted. "But let's just select three clefts from which to expand. In that way our archers will be more effective. Now, do you," I addressed them all bluntly, "have true confidence in your control over your men? In effect, can you actually, in such circumstances, force them to retreat against their will, when all their thoughts will be to get their swords to the throats of the perpetrators of their hurt?"

"Sir Collin," Lord Sernas advised me haughtily, "our warriors are neither imbeciles, nor rogues. They will do as our captains tell them."

"Then let's to it," Rawl exclaimed impatiently. "As our Collin has said—time's running out!"

At Lord Sernas' orders the captains withdrew to advance half of our flanking units toward the enemy. They would be sent, straggling, to disguise the fact that a full half remained behind the dike. Rawl, likewise, would lead but three thousand of the center. But behind him, and also moving forward, would be our three thousand archers.

We'd decided that the three cleft-ravines to be seized would be the bridge and the two to the left of it—"Upon which," Rawl had explained, "we'll quick throw the archers along the crests to feather all who attack us, until you, sir," he said to Sernas, "come to our aid with your seven thousand." He laughed. "I doubt not but that we'll need them at that point . . ."

And so it was decided.

With proper leadership true Alphians simply cannot think in terms of defeat. A fact which has both its good implications and its bad. . . .

I naturally rode with Rawl. Young Sernas and his jolly captains, well blooded now, led the left and Gol-Tares the right. The maneuver went as planned. But just why in the bloody, Ghastian hell we thought we could take that bluff with but twenty thousand against fifty, I'll never know. *Most surely there was Pug Boo influence at work*! They were more conscious of the time factor than I; more knowledgeable of the total picture. . . .

Clouds gathered again, great whopping thunderheads. Rain, hail, and shards of ice stormed down upon us as our companies mounted the dike's top couched spears and went trotting down the slope and out upon the flat sands. The river's five hundred yards of width was but a meandering of many streams of water, really; each but a foot or so deep. We dashed across it, picking up speed.

Above us the roiling clouds all suddenly took forms, became monstrous, darksome gerds, *meegs*, skaidings, and other horrors. And they roared! And brilliant lightning came direct from *them*. Those of ours who slowed to stare at this awesome phenomenon were hit by great swaths and pillars of blue fire. Whole squadrons were flattened, destroyed instantly. The mad cacophony of the drums from the opposite ridge were then enjoined by the screams and cheers of fifty thousand Hishians—all amplified to one continuous, hellish bedlam, by the cowled wizards.

Still, we went on. In the hopes of drawing some of the pyrotechnics to me (with the added hope that the Boos would intervene to deflect them), I turned up the ion effect so that I and all others around me glowed like so many luminescent suns upon the fast darkening field. And it *did* happen! And the bolts *were* deflected! The diversion, however, was lost in the continuing rain, hail, and shattering sheet lightning which took its toll. And, too, our charging ranks had come under the first flights of Hishian arrows. Again, many of ours went down.

Sir Rawl Fergis—he was but a few yards to my front—then shouted suddenly, "NOW!" Upon which, those who carried our banners reared their dottles, waved the standards wildly, and halted. I rose in my saddle, quick-focused right and left through the pouring rain. The nearest captains had seen the signal, were passing it on. The line hesitated, slowed, *halted*. We then began a great milling about, as if undecided to continue. The thing was, would *they* see our indecision, seek to take advantage of it? As we milled about on the river plain, they did the same on the bluff. Their forward line grew thicker, bulged in spots so that some riders were actually forced over the bluff whether they liked it or no. . . . And then, amidst a bloody howling to shiver the spines of weaklings and a sound of drums to drown the thunder, they could stand it no longer. They came boiling down those ravine-clefts and off that bluff like a stream of molten steel.

The fact that we'd turned to flee had been the final straw. Then, with our backs to them, we rode for our very lives! We bunched, as planned: two center groupings and a group on each flank, with a wide space in between.

But we'd been a mite too slow. A glance over my shoulder revealed a sight to chill the marrow of the heartiest warrior's spine. Their first spear ranks—a seething mass of Hishian soldiery—was but a hundred feet to our rear. The rain had lessened; not so the pyrotechnics. And if there was no sun to light the face of doom the blue-white brilliance of the shattering bolts continued—strobe flashing the entire river's breadth with the true light of hell itself.

The dike loomed but seconds away. We'd reached the point where we had to turn to receive the shock, the weight of their steel. We'd timed it wrong by seconds. Indeed, Sernas, too, should have charged while we were still in mid-

142

stream. At that distance he would have had the momentum to stun them, *stop* them.

He was charging now, but again was seconds late. Even as we turned he smashed through the gaps between our groups, drove hard into the Hishian ranks. But they were not stopped; or rather only those were stopped before *his* spears —the remaining mass hit us—drove into *us!*

The only thing to hold true in the ensuing melee of whirling spears, axes, and swords, plus the flights of arrows from our own who'd made it to the dike's top, was that the Dark One could no longer wreak a personal victory. We were totally enjoined. All lightning bolts now would do more damage to his side than to ours, for his numbers were greater. . . .

With my own spear's blade I took the screaming, bearded head of a great bejeweled lord—and in quick succession two more; both blinded by his spurting blood. But there was little room for spear work. Were we the better? Indeed we were! Griswold, Rawl, myself, Tober, and Charney. We killed 'til our arms were leaden, 'til our hauberks were puddled with the sweat of it, and the blood, *our* blood, that seeped from a hundred wounds—*our* wounds! Murie—and she was ever at my back or to one side or the other—had long thrown her last javelin, had become like us, blood-bathed from head to foot, her sword wet to the hand-haft with the stuff. More! The no-quarter fighting was terrible. The very air was a spindrift of red-blood to mingle with the rain and to bring an encarmined, clotted froth to the shallow waters of the river.

Everywhere it was the same. We carved a space around us, kept it open—except for the direction wherein we charged. To our right I saw the tattered banners of Lord Sernas holding strong within the very mass of the foe, where he'd driven his thousands. So was this true of all our attacking units. The banners of young Sernas and his captains still flew; indeed, moved this way and that as *they* so chose. To our left-front Gol-Stils likewise held his own. Only Gol-Tares had gone down, pinned to the bridge abutments by ten thousand howling Hishians and Yorns. Most of his men still lived. I quick sent to our archers to concentrate their arrows upon the enemy around the body of Gol-Tares, and myself led a charge toward our remaining warriors there. My poor dottle was instantly killed beneath me, the second to die thusly. I slew a Hishian baron and seized his mount and went on. . . .

We then burst through a thousand attackers of some Hishian lord whose standard depicted a crucifixion of four men. Rawl slew him, wielding both axe and sword in either hand. I halved the Hishian's sword-companion with one sweep of my blade, and those around him fell back in terror. The more so, too, because Rawl, angry at the screaming taunts of another of the lord's companions, a captain of great girth and strength, ran his great sword right through him to the haft—and lifted him from off his saddle to hurl him down to the bloodied mud. . . .

We then took our rescued warriors and drove toward Sernas' center. This time our Griswall was at point with my two stalwarts, Tober and Charney. The three of them were veritable killing machines, for he had taught his students well. I had time to marvel even then at what they'd learned in one short year.

And finally our disparate units were one again: flanks and center; excepting that now we were but ten thousand. We'd been driven back a hundred yards or so, no more. And on their part, they'd even withdrawn a bit, to catch their breath and lick their wounds.

We, too, were sorely tired. But the fact remained that whereas they could take their rest; indeed, take time for sup if need be, time, for us, was still running out. Consulting quickly with a bloodied and badly wounded Lord Sernas and his captains, I suggested that we form a single, hollow diamond, and that we drive it through them to the bridge cleft. We would then, if we managed to reach the bluff's top, race on to Hish.

It was as good a plan as any, considering. And they agreed and instantly began to dress their ranks so as to begin the movement. And while the shift of companies took place around us, I noted curiously that of those who still lived, Lord Akin Sernas, his son, Lors Sernas; Lord Haken—he'd lost an arm, but still fought on, and Gol-Stils and many others; in all of them there'd been a change. Perhaps it was just my imagination. But somehow, subtly, where before there'd been a loose-lipped cynicism, a certain brutishness; indeed, a cruel selfishness, there was now a difference. Not much, to be sure, and mayhap even that was illusion, wishful thinking. But now it seemed there were more smiles here and there; firm jaws; blue-purple eyes alight with pride in self, and an open respect for others and what they too had done and were prepared to do—the ultimate in selflessness.

I'd not forget it!

And then—well, it was sort of like the "light at the end of the tunnel" when you'd just decided you'd made a wrong turn right back into the heart of the mountain. . . .

This time his words burst inside my head to almost dim my vision: proving that even Hooli could get excited. "Collin!" he called. "Hear me, Collin! 'D Day!' 'D Day!' A 'loverly bunch of Coconuts.' The Vuuns have landed, Collin. The Marackians are all mounted! They're coming, now, Collin! All you've got to do is *hold!*"

Instant tears streamed down my face. Murie, seeing—she kept an eye on my every movement—put up a small and bloodied gauntlet to touch them. Her own eyes were tearing too, though I'm sure she didn't know why. Rawl stared in awe. Caroween, displaying a surcoat and hauberk long soaked with the ichor of at least a dozen Hishians, wrinkled her dainty brow and sniffed in sympathy.

"Nay," I said softly. I brought Murie's hand to my lips as I reached to touch an errant tear on Caroween's cheek. " 'Tis that our Lord of Durst, your father—" I nodded to Caroween—"has landed. Marack is coming! All is not lost. *All will be saved!*"

They looked at me as if I'd gone mad. I realized then that despite all we had done, despite everything, not a one of them had really believed that Marack's thirty thousand could ever come to Om to aid us. Or shall I say they believed, yet did not believe. I could even understand the contradiction. For to those who live with "magick," the act is *believed* as it happens. But that it will happen again in the way proscribed, well that's always something else—in no way certain.

Hooli's voice, faint because of my own intruding thoughts, came through again. . . . "Collin! You're but to hold right where you are. The Marackians are already on the road."

"We cannot," I informed him. "Our only protection from the lightning is that we attack, join with them, body to body. Apart, we're in deadly peril."

"Lightning needs clouds, *Adjuster* Kyrie. Look up, above you!"

I did, and saw them being wafted, blown quickly away. I then asked in choked mental anger—"Why not before, Hooli, when we were dying, when we needed it most?" I'd guessed the obvious reason, that he could control them, *even against the Dark One's wishes*.

"Without the protection of those clouds, Great Ap would not land his Vuuns. The same thunderheads that dealt destruction to your own provided the screen for Marack's

145

landing. Have done, Collin! There's no time for recriminations. The thing shows fear, and such fear is perilous indeed. You must wait for nothing now—but drive straight through—to Hish!"

He was gone again and I shook my head against the cobwebs. The faces around me still stared, waiting for they knew not what.

Rawl, seeing a well-known expression on my face, tossed me his leathern sviss bottle. I almost drained it before I tossed it back. Then I climbed deliberately to stand upon my saddle and shout: "NOW HEAR ME ALL! WE HAVE BUT TO STAND AND FIGHT WHERE WE ARE. FOR WE HAVE WON! LOOK YE BACK TO THOSE SMALL HILLS! SEE THEM POURING ACROSS THE CREST? 'TIS MARACK! MARACK AND ITS THIRTY THOUSAND WARRIORS. WE'VE BUT TO HOLD AGAINST THIS PEWLING SCUM AND THE DAY IS OURS! HAIL MARACK! HAIL OM! DEATH TO THE DARK ONE! *DEATH TO THE DARK KALEEN!*"

And they did look back, in awe. And almost at that precise moment the banners of Marack *did* burst over the hills, and thirty thousand of the finest warriors in all of Fregis-Camelot came pounding across the intervening few miles, banners waving, trumpets blowing—and with a howling of kettledrums to shiver the very souls of those who opposed us.

There was then a rolling cheer from our depleted, tired, and battered ranks. "The orders are changed," I told Sernas. "Right here we stand to fight, 'til our friends from Marack join us."

But the Hishians saw their doom. They drew back as if to flee, then changed their minds. After all, their force still equaled ours, or so they must have thought. They charged, therefore, drove into us in one last effort to destroy us before support could arrive. They charged over the sandy loam all thickly carpeted with many thousands of bodies, ours and theirs, and those of the poor dottles, too. Many of the dottles were wounded and they cried and moaned quite piteously . . .

Again we were locked in hellish battle, mindless battle. Again we killed, more now to save ourselves, I think. There was little glory to it, even for Alphians. . . .

And then there seemed a lessening of the pressure, a fading away of the swords that were raised against us. A new roar of battle cries swept like a wave around us, beyond us, and on toward the bluff we had failed to take.

146

And it was over!

There was no stopping the warriors of Fel-Holdt and Hoggle-Fitz until the entire bluff was taken; nor did they halt there! The pursuit, swift, inexorable, went on apace, with ourselves joining the Marackians to direct it properly.

We caught up with them a mile or so beyond the bridge. The great city itself shone in the now brilliant sunlight at about four miles distant. Time had truly flown for, I noted wryly, it was now 17:00 hours Greenwich. Fel-Holdt, Hoggle-Fitz, and a covey of young captains had halted at the roadside, next to a small orchard to await us. They looked warily at our Omnians as we rode up; our Omnians looked warily at them.

Upon seeing his daughter, bloodied and tattered, Breen Hoggle-Fitz, Lord of Durst, and soon to be king in Great Ortmund, plucked her from the saddle to engulf her strongly in his arms. He then began a paean of thanks in stentorian shouts to Ormon, Wimbily, and Harris; this, while a flood of tears wet his mustaches, beard and collar above his neck-piece. He in this way managed to ignore the most momentous event in all of Fregis' history—the meeting of North and South.

Caroween also cried, and Murie, too. Fel-Holdt and his captains, dismounting, were already bending the knee to her. Arrow-straight again, Fel-Holdt addressed her calmly: "My Princess," he said, "we have come, as 'twas ordained by our Collin. And if yon city is the pearl of Om, well, you'll wear it in your crown this very night—I promise you!"

There was an instant muttering among my Omnians and a reaching for bloodied sword hafts. I moved quickly between them crying, "Nay! Good Fel-Holdt! These men who ride with us *are* Om!" I indicated Lord Sernas and his staff. "The city's theirs, sir, bought with their blood and the lives of their heroes—all those who dared to rise, at *Ormon's* call—against the Dark One, and when nought awaited them for the deed but death itself. . . .

"They are now our friends, sirs." My voice rose and I spoke to all the Marackians. "They're our 'blood-brothers.' I adjure you therefore to take their hands. For without your love, one to the other, there will be no final victory here, nor any peace in all the world hereafter. . . ."

Lord Fel-Holdt, his tall resplendent figure dominating the Marackian group, and thus the gathering, answered gravely, saying, "I hear you, Collin. But," and he turned to Murie Nigaard, "I would also hear from Marack."

She'd doffed her helm to wipe the sweat and dirt and blood from off her face. Her hair glowed, shimmered in the sun. She said, "Good Fel-Holdt, my lord, 'tis as our Collin says: Om's enemies are ours. We'll *share* the victory in honor. But their lands and cities must belong to them, as ours belong to us. And I would remind all here," she finished softly, which was unlike her, "that *this* victory's not yet won!"

Fel-Holdt saluted solemnly, nodded to me, whereon I began to make the introductions. They still eyed each other warily, but saluted, too, touched hands, and spoke the formal words of greeting.

My sword-nicked Hoggle-Fitz—he'd been in the thick of the onslaught—oblivious to it all, as the extroverted, egocentric, lovable, courageous, braggarts of his calling usually are, had loosed his daughter to wipe his eyes and regain composure. Spotting me for the first time, he cried, "By the gods, Collin, had I known what awaited me when I promised to ride those leathern bags to hell and back for Marack, I do think me, I'd have weakened. It hailed on us, sir, and it snowed, and we fair froze our asses hanging to those body nets while the gales blew for a full twelve hours of riding through the air. When we landed, sir, we could scarce move a muscle, so frozen to the nets, we were. Indeed, without the miracle of this small bickering which has set our blood to flow again, I doubt me I'd have ever thawed at all—" He frowned suddenly, stared 'round him to ask suspiciously, "And who are all these people?"

The battered Rawl burst right out laughing. Lord Sernas, esthetically aware that he was face to face with something extraordinary, smiled, said nothing, but still held out his hand.

I said straight-faced to Hoggle, "Here, sir, are brave Omnians who fight for Ormon 'gainst the Dark One. Do you take their hands, now, and call them brother."

And he did, muttering the while and scratching his head.

We talked then, drank wine and sviss and ate of a steaming gog-stew brought forward from Sernas' castle. We didn't plan much for the simple reason that there wasn't much to plan. Our objective, to seize Hish and to advance me as close to the temple as possible, was fully understood. And even as we talked, the pyramid loomed over in our view, rising high over the great walls.

Hey! *We could see it!* What then of the bubble? It was gone, obviously. But then, what difference did it make. With the exception of myself and the crew of the Deneb-3, no one else had seen it anyway. . . .

The instinctive conclusion by all that the final scene would be *me* versus the *pyramid* should be easily understood. For who else among them had the power to challenge the Dark One in his lair? I was the proven champion, the *self-admitted*, "Collin"! I alone, in their eyes, had maneuvered the victory of the battle of Dunguring. It was me, in Om, who had deflected the Dark One's bolts—or at least *some* of them: I'd fought the skaiding, and won! 'Twas me that had kept the Dark One's "mind control" from full possession of the host.—And 'twas me who, and again in their eyes, protected them even now from the Dark One's wrath.

As for me, Kyrie Fern, *Adjuster*, well all I wanted was to get it over with, once and for all. I wanted desperately to do that. I'd grown to love the planet: Murie, Rawl, Hoggle, the Boos; the whole damn crazy potpourri. But enough was *enough*! In the span of seven short months, I'd risked my life a thousand times, killed more in the name of peace, justice, and the humanoid right to a "quiet evolution," as taught by the Foundation, then I'd thought to ever *read* about in my lifetime, let alone commit myself to.

In essence, I was bone-weary, mind-weary. I wanted only to end it, to return to Glagmaron, marry up with Murie Nigaard, and then to sit back and watch the world go by for a decent length of time—*sans* goblins, monsters, magick, and the shadow of the Dark One's presence. . . .

I reveled in the all-consuming wash of self-pity. . . .

A young captain of Marack, together with a young captain of Om—fortunately all Marackians carry the three-cornered shield as opposed to the round one of the Omnians so we could tell them apart—rode up. They both dripped sweat and blood.

The Marackian cried to Fel-Holdt proudly, "We're at the city's gates, sir!" While the Omnian, he'd been fighting since seven that morning, said bluntly to Sernas, "But they're closed to us and the very air around them's frozen solid. We can't get through!"

Fifty pairs of questioning eyes shifted instantly to me.

I sighed, arose, took one last swig of cooling sviss and yelled, "All right! Let's ride!"

It was a force field. I'd known it would be. I tested it myself, at all four gates. On the walls above each gate the Kaleen's remnant hosts yelled down to us and shouted taunts. Fel-Holdt and Sernas marveled that they threw no stones, let loose no flights of arrows. I explained my theory that the Dark One was no tactician, let alone a strategist. He'd simply overlooked the above possibilities and had made the field too high. How high, we could only guess.

Whatever. One thing I knew. The field was his final effort. All remaining energies would now be directed toward the gateway!

We probed its every peripheral inch, and found nothing; no single crack or loophole—and the hours passed. Many of those whom we'd defeated during the day now came from forest and field where they'd been hiding, to join us; and others, too, who'd received the mustering message too late from their lords. And finally it was ourselves who numbered fifty thousand, so that we swarmed at each gate. Aside from the field, no Hishian could enter the city now and none came out.

Somewhat morose and filled with the dread apprehension of failure, I withdrew in the fast-falling twilight to sit apart from the others, excepting, of course, that Murie joined me. Indeed, she'd been ever at my side, a true shield-maiden. I leaned against a tree's bole. She rested her head on my shoulder. We passed a skin of sviss back and forth a couple of times. Once I started to speak, but she placed small hard fingers against my lips, and I was thankful. . . .

I closed my eyes to rest them—and Hooli came, or rather, the "collective." They were very grave. They had a right to be. "Collin," they said, "you've got but four hours. We dare to ask you once again to use your ship."

I relaxed my mind. I wanted to "see" them. There they were in the twinkling darkness, fat paws on fat bellies; little legs straight out before them. I dwelt upon their statement, then answered calmly, "As you have said, there's still four hours. If I must die—and I've yet to agree to your 'final solution'—I'll name the time, sirs, *and* the place. And how do we know the force field's not a 'bubble' so as to deny my ship an entry?"

"There is an entry—directly above the pyramid. How else, Kyrie, could he direct his creation's efforts?"

"Why, then," I said, "I could enter Hish itself, with the ship, land, and attack the temple!"

"If you fly your ship through the hole he's left for any purpose but to crash it, *instantly*—then he'll destroy *you* . . . And Fregis will be no more."

"All right," I said. "I'll *agree*! But I've still got four hours; therefore, I'll still name the time. Meanwhile, if an idea comes to us between now and *then*, I want instant contact with you. Do you understand?"

"Yeah, Buby. The code word'll be 'checkers.'" The voice was Hooli's, in a sad attempt at humor. Even he was depressed. No wonder. When I'd said the words 'I'll agree,' a soft, sick fear had touched on all my body. It was most difficult to control. I'd never fancied myself to be a martyr. . . .

During the next two hours we again probed every inch of the Hishian wall. To no avail. There was no entry. There was no exit. We retired then to one of the myriad small fires that now ringed the capital. The lords of Om were there; the lords of Marack—and my princess and all our stalwarts.

I told them softly then and in the simple terms of a magick they could understand, what the Dark One was up to; that the next two hours were critical; that if within that time no way was found for the introduction of twenty warriors, led by me, into Hish to attack the pyramid, that I, alone, must then crash the ship *and die with it*—lest all Camelot-Fregis perish.

How I explained the "ship" to them, I'll not go into. Suffice it to say that they understood me and were wide-eyed, white-faced, and stricken. Murie murmured simply at my side— "You know, of course, that I'll go with you."

Hoggle-Fitz was strangely silent. I envied him, for I doubted much that he'd understood me. But mayhap, too, he did.

Then young Lors Sernas rose unsteadily to his feet. Like all those around me, tears glistened, too, upon his sybarite cheeks. He spoke direct to me. "Well now, my lord," he said, "I'd hoped to avoid this since I am, as you know, sworn to the joys of our jolly Hoom-Tet God, and bound to keep his secrets. And, too," and a sickly smile touched on his lips, "I confess me, I had no wish to die—and in the Dark One's lair. . . ."

He paused and we waited, all eyes hard on him until his father spoke out loudly, ordering him to continue. . . .

"Well," he said again to me, after clearing his throat, "you are favored, sir, and that's a fact. For you gave of your gold and friendship to our gracious Hoom-Tet when none else honored him. Now hear me: Hoom-Tet, through me, returns the favor. For many years Hoom-Tet's been worshiped for the pleasure that he's given; this, in a land where such 'pleasure,' by law, was ever the Dark One's bounty. The peril of discovery of course was great. Therefore, and many years ago, a way was found to circumvent the Dark One's strict security. 'Twas but a small thing, and therefore quite likely overlooked by him. But for us it helped considerably." He drew a deep breath, exhaled and continued. "There's a way beneath the wall to reach our temple. The passage is sacred. What I risk in telling you, I know not—mayhap a life of deadly boredom, with thin wine and an absence of the textured flesh of women." He grinned. Color had returned to his cheeks. "Still, I'll pay my personal debt, sir—by going with you. Maybe I'll be forgiven. For Hoom-Tet, that satin-bellied rogue, is above all else a forgiving god; excepting for the Dark One, of course. For him our Hoom-Tet would never give a flimpl's turd. . . ."

I had arisen, said instantly when he'd finished, "Lors Sernas, we've little time to talk. But hear me: Should you go or not, if we destroy the Dark One, 'twill be carved in undying stone for all of time that you, sir, were central to the saving of this world. Hail now," I cried aloud: "Hail to this son of Sernas!"

All arose and pledged him solemnly.

"Who then," I asked, "will go with me besides my own? Twenty's needed. Eleven I have, for I'll ask Unghist and four of his swords to join me. For Yorns, too, are men and have a right to fight with men, against a common peril."

There were at least two hundred lords and captains around that campfire. The hafts of two hundred swords were offered. But I had no time for argument. I chose Lors Sernas and six young Omnians, a single Marackian student-warrior—and Breen Hoggle-Fitz, for he could not have stood it otherwise.

Time now, indeed, was running out!

We moved immediately toward the dottles, while I mentally said "checkers," and *Checkers*! you little son-of-a-bitch!" And even as my heart pounded and my pulse raced, I could still laugh at the act of shouting "checkers" to the wind while a planet's death lay so easily in the offing. It was something for the books.

"Hail, Collin!" Hooli's voice was sober at last.

"We've found a way, mud-ball. Twenty of us will enter the city within minutes. I want a diversion. And, since it will naturally fail, it's one that you should be able to do quite handily. Create a few fire-balls. Toss 'em at the gates. Something like that. He'll think it's me, the *best* I can do against

152

his shield. It should throw him off. *Keep it up for at least ten minutes!*"

"You will fight your way across the entire city, with but twenty swords?"

"Nope! There's a passage. It goes direct to the Hoom-Tet temple. We've but to charge the pyramid from there."

"The temple's full of warrior priests."

"So? That's not my worry, Hooli. My laser energy pack's weak. There should be two charges left, sufficient to blast an entry, if that's necessary—and to blast the Dark One, when I confront him. The last is my worry—*Will the laser beam destroy the Dark One in whatever form I find him?*"

"It will—*if* you can find him."

"He'll be in the one place he has to be. Indeed, he dare not be elsewhere."

"You speak true, Buby. But if you're killed—there goes the ballgame."

"Hooli," I said carefully—"and all the rest of you, too. By the time we reach the Hoom-Tet temple every man of mine will have learned how to handle the laser beam. In essence, the Dark One will have to kill us all before he's safe. He cannot do that, Hooli. Moreover, the chances now with the ship or with the laser should be exactly equal. What say you?"

He held a moment in thought, then said, "You're right, Launcelot." And then, "The best to you. And *whatever* he is when you find him, no matter if it's the Holy Grail itself—*blast it!* ya'all hear? Bye now, Buby. You'll get your diversion."

At my instructions certain young captains rode off instantly to alert their troops to the advent of Hooli's fire balls. "The force-field will remain," I told them, "and the fire-balls will be ineffective. But it will allow us proper entry without the Dark One scanning...."

Entry to the tunnel, built over a hundred years before by the hands of passionate, fearful, sybarites, was in a small grove some three hundred yards from the wall itself. Its guardian, the old man who owned the orchard—a Hoom-Tet worshiper you can bet—made the sign of his god when Lors Sernas and his six captains bade him open. He offered no resistance. More! When he was told by Sernas that we went to slay the Dark One, he wept for joy.

Two things then: I bade my Marackians to exchange their northern shields for those of Om—and Murie and Caroween dismounted, joined our group, and dared me with their eyes! Murie, for the record, had the grace to advise me firmly that,

"In this, the final onset, there was no question but that the royal house should have a part."

I nodded. There was no time for argument. Even as we filed into the down-sloping depths of the mile-long work, a fire-ball bounced harmlessly off the "field" before the western gate. In its bursting light the mass of our warriors leapt and howled and waved their weapons. . . .

I whispered mentally, "I thank you, Hooli." To which a tiny voice said sweetly, "You're more than welcome!"

We fell into a sort of trot. The tunnel's width allowed this. As we jogged, I explained to everyone how, in the event of my death, the laser stone at my belt could be directed toward the destruction of the Dark One. They understood, and told me so. And that was that. . . . Air vents had been built at points along the way, each lead to an erstwhile Hoom-Tet follower's domicile; though, according to Lors, this was most likely no longer true, since the tunnel had been built so long ago.

Fifteen minutes of jogging and the floor slanted suddenly upward, to end finally 'neath a grating in what we found to be the inner court of the Hoom-Tet temple. At a shrill whistle from Sernas the grate was lifted by a terrified young priest-neophyte. Obviously a visitation by twenty-two armed warriors, under the surrounding circumstances, was anything but appreciated.

We climbed out into a courtyard wherein the fountains and porno-statuary cast weird shadows 'neath the ghostly light of far-off Fomalhaut II which, I noticed, was also in a north-south line above the temple of the pyramid. . . .

The live-in priests and acolytes came running, summoned peremptorily by a now stern visaged Lors Sernas. They lined up against an inner wall which was one huge, ongoing mozaic of writhing, naked bodies, with copulation being the simplest scene projected.

"By the gods! Sir Collin," Hoggle-Fit said *sotto voce* in my ear. "What manner of place is this?"

Receiving no answer, he moved closer to examine a particular tableau, stared hard, muttered, and returned to my side.

There were forty priests, excited to the point of hysteria, thinking they'd been discovered. Ten of them were women, pretty, with pleasant, intelligent eyes. Murie and Caroween both glared at them. Lors Sernas introduced me and I told them briefly what was happening; that all the world was in revolt against the Dark One; that he held no spot of Om 'cepting the pyramid, which we intended to attack and seize, right now.

Some recognized me as the benefactor of the previous day who had given them gold. They passed the word and a single question was asked of me—"Would Hoom-Tet suffer, too?"

"Why so?" I asked in turn. "What harm has lusty Hoom-Tet done to anyone? I'd say, 'tis the opposite. Fear not, sir priests. I promise you, no harm will come to Hoom-Tet or his followers!"

"What then of Ormon?" Hoggle-Fitz breathed fiercely in my ear.

"No harm, old comrade," I said softly. "Hoom-Tet's no threat to him."

"He's a nasty, dirty, god, Father," Caroween intruded firmly. Rawl laughed aloud and got slapped, proving he'd shown some interest himself in Hoom Tet's pecadillos. Murie, her lips firm-pressed, glared at me furiously.

A final burst of Hooli's fire-balls lighted the western sky. "Lead on to the outer gate, sir," I told Lors Sernas. "And you," I grabbed two young acolytes with keys at their belts, "will open them." I raised my voice. "All other servitors of Hoom-Tet will stay precisely here, 'cepting for those whom your head priest will choose to send through the tunnel to act as guides to our army."

They bowed low.

I said solemnly to my small company, "Loose swords and follow me."

The outer gates opened, Rawl, Fitz, Unghist, Sernas, and myself, went out to view the pyramid. It seemed a pile of awful, stygian blackness. Moreover, its very height distorted the fact that its southern base was still two hundred yards away. I focused my contacts to ten mags. The entry doors were open. A faint light shone from the interior.

All around us was deadly quiet. Hish was a ghost city, its citizens huddling in stark terror in their homes; their doors double-locked against the death-throes of the Dark One— should he be beaten. The clear air gave a night-black, velvet texture to a sky wherein the stars were truly diamonds, blue-white and brilliant. Fomalhaut II, the size of a magnified Sirius, gave the starlight a ghostly intensity.

I threw an arm around Hoggle's shoulders for I felt a need to assuage his fears, his obvious confusion. Things had moved too fast: the Vuuns; the Omnians who were now "our friends"; the existence of new, unacceptable, gods whose statues must not be toppled. It was all too much for him. . . . "I count on you, old warrior," I told him softly, "to be the first with me to enter yon dread pile. I warrant you'll find sufficient devils there to last your remaining years. But whatever happens, friend, remember this: 'Tis our final battle. And we fight, not just for Marack, but for all of Fregis, too."

He came alive at that. His bulbous eyes actually gleamed in the starlight. "By the gods, Collin," he whispered loudly and with a tone of relief that I was not angry with him. "In this, I'm your man, and you know it. To test my sword 'gainst Ormon's mortal enemy is a thing I've lived my whole life for. . . ." He sniffed and wiped his nose; said gruffly, "And that we two shall be the first to enter is both an honor and a gift—for which I thank you deeply, Collin."

I called the others from where they stood next the shadowed, inside walls: first Sernas' six Omnian captains, then Griswall, Tober, Charney, and our new student-warrior, Onlis, with Murie and Caroween. Unghist's four Yorns brought up the rear. Rawl moved to join with Griswall and the princess.

My orders given, we jogged determinedly out upon the expanse of polished flagstones. We were twenty-two swords, two abreast in the starlight—*to bring down the greatest citadel in all of Fregis-Camelot!*

The sound of our passage was as the wind in heavy bracken; an occasional tinkle of well-oiled steel, the lightly cadenced pat of soft boots against the flagstones. At a hundred feet I bade them draw their swords. . . .

Six priest-warrior guards stood suddenly at the entrance, led by a cowled wizard. In my mind I had debated the question of parley in such a case—and then dismissed it! To reach the inner great hall, was to win us half the game. To be caught in the lengthy entry passage could be disastrous. And so I'd told them, "Attack instantly, when I attack! Leave not a sword alive behind us!"

And so it was.

At twenty paces, the wizard—and his cowl was by no means empty—called out to ask what we wished there—but we came on, rushing. . . . Their swords were out, but hardly raised. Five thousand years of nothing had in no way either sharpened their wits or their reflexes despite this, the Dark One's "crisis hour."

With one lightning blow I split the wizard's cowl and skull down to the breastbone. Stout Hoggle seized his man's sword-hand with his own huge paw to dash the fellow's brains out with his own sword's haft. The others were slain as swiftly. Two minutes at best, and we burst out of the ill-lighted, granite tunnel and into the magnificence of the hall. . . .

As we ran, two things had touched my mind: A moment's elation that I'd not been forced to use the laser and therefore now had a double-charge—and the hopeful thought that perhaps my tactically stupid Kaleen had emptied the pyramid of warriors, to serve his host.

The first was true—the second, a prayer for children.

As ants to the central command of the Dark One's control, the priest-warriors had instantly gathered in the great hall. A hundred awaited us on the polished flagstones. Others came streaming from all the corridors, the warehouses, barracks, and all the honeycomb of cells.

Seeing their line of blades, stout Hoggle-Fitz cried fiercely, "Well, now, Sir Collin, I'm bound to think we'll *earn* our victory!"

I'd called forth the pyramid's imprinted schematic to my mind's eye as we ran. The exit to the passageway which led to the second large room above lay across the great hall, in the northwest corner. Their strength, limned in the light of a myriad blazing tripods, plus a Kaleen glow from the high ceiling, was impressive.

Wasting not a second (we hardly broke our stride), we simply smashed into their line, broke through it, and headed for the exit.

There's a "high" one gets from bloody battle which is almost indescribable. For those who are prepared to die the "high" sometimes comes *before* the battle, and remains throughout. I've never felt it. Indeed, the only thing I've ever felt is a certain bone-deep fear, held down by the knowledge of my own superior skill (imposed neural conditioning and straining), and my strength which was twice that of the strongest Yorn. But Rawl has explained it. "To the man who has it," he told me, it adds to his prowess, gives him an unbeatable edge. It's a mind thing: you have to work at it. If the enemy, however, is equally skilled and is also possessed of a "high," a form of parity exists. The fighting then can become no-quarter, bloody, and terrible beyond belief.

Fortunately our enemy possessed no such "high"—and damned little skill. Their attributes were courage and desperation. But desperation is no substitute for confidence, nor does it replace discipline and control. Its drive is suicidal, actually, with those so smitten accepting the blade to prove their courage—by dying!

So we slashed through the first line—to find it replaced by a second, a third, and a fourth; becoming, finally, a mass of screaming priests who thought only to fling themselves upon our swords, to stop us. Whirling our blades in a lightning display of "murder," we "tacked" this way and that to avoid the crush of bodies, fallen or otherwise. The square of the hall was three hundred feet from wall to wall. I swear to the gods of all the galaxies that we had no choice but to carpet all that expanse with bloodied corpses. . . .

We were a "force" of driving, slashing, *winnowing* steel. *Nothing* could stand against us! A thing more terrible than the fighting; that which actually sickened *us*, was the shrieks of the wounded and dying. *For the hall was an echo chamber!* And, too, the heat of the place, the effect of it upon the burst entrails of a hundred slitted bellies, created a stench no man could stand for long.

We reached the exit, drove through it to the sharply inclined passageway beyond. Four swords abreast, we drove on and up, gained purchase, and paused for the first time to lean upon our weapons.

The greater number of warrior-priests had been cut off below; less than a hundred were above. But, as we quickly found, they were the pick of the Dark One's warriors. . . .

We breathed deeply, filled our lungs with the fresher air of the corridor. We'd lost just *three* of ours, a Yorn, our new student-warrior, Olis, and one of Sernas' captains—and that was all!

What was that ancient Terran story? One hundred Greeks had died at Marathon—*and ten thousand Persians!*

We'd slain at least a hundred; disabled as many more. All of us were wounded, but only lightly. To this day the carnage we wreaked in that *abbatoir* of the great hall of the pyramid, is a thing unreal, scarcely believed in our own minds.

The time factor now was slim indeed. We'd entered the tunnel at 20:45, Greenwich. Fifteen minutes there; fifteen more to the entrance to the pyramid, and a half-hour in the great hall. It was now 21:45. At 22:30 the stuff would hit the fan. The room above was at 200 feet. With an incline ratio of one-to-five, we had a thousand feet to go. . . . As a last resort, I'd use the laser!

Since we'd entered the pyramid, there'd been a thrumming in the air. What the Dark One sought to accomplish with it, I never knew. By that time I'm sure *he* knew that there could be no mind seizure in my presence. The thing he didn't do, however, which was the only thing he should have done; the only thing that would have made any sense against me, was to destroy the corridors and block all entrances and exits. There was no way I could *unblock* them. He *must* have known it!

I had little time to reason why he didn't. I was just damn glad such was the case. . . .

Four to the rear and four to the front. The advance up the incline continued. There were nineteen of us left. With only eight to fight at any given moment, we spelled each other off and saw to it that those our shield-men struck down *stayed* down, while we marched over them. Murie and Caroween shared the fighting. I never ceased to fear for them, despite the fact that excepting, Rawl, Griswall, and Hoggle-Fitz they were the equal of any of our company. The steel strength of Murie's wrist and sword arm was unbelievable; her speed and stamina, unmatched. At one point, when the Dark One's wizards led a charge of spearmen to come boiling up the corridor from below, it was Murie who tore the first spear from the hands of its owner, killed him with it, and drove the others back. On orders from me, the Yorns, under Unghist, charged the lower line and seized strong spears for all of us.

The pace and scope of the fighting, however, began to tell. A quarter of the way to the second chamber, we lost another Yorn. Then brave young Charney fell, cut to the breastbone by the wild swing of a huge, maniacal wizard. Rawl and two Omnian captains, who made up the shield front at that point, killed the man and led a charge to send his screaming cohorts back up the passage.

In another melee, wherein I led the foursome—Sernas, Tober, and a captain—we'd killed 'til our arms were tired and were then set upon by a solid phalanx of spears. I seized the first spear, emulating Murie, and the man who held it. I lifted him, hurled him flat, to be impaled upon the blades of his half-crazed companions.

We marched right over that "phalanx"; but in the process lost two of our captains who were pinned 'gainst the walls and slain by the thrusts of a dozen faldirks.

And so it went!

Stout Hoggle took a spear's thrust through the side, but still fought on. Another Yorn died, spitted by a dozen blades. His death screams were unsettling. I don't know why, except that they had an irdic, banshee keening to them. Caroween, blinded by a wash of blood, unloosed when a shield's edge cut her forehead, fell back to stanch the flow. Rawl, seeing, howled to the heavens—he'd thought her dead—and leaped into the very midst of an oncoming squad of red-robed wizards. Hoggle-Fitz, with a gerd-like roar to the *trinity*, and despite his wound, followed suit. The death cries of the wizards then joined with the Dark One's "thrumming," and the whole of it melded with the ghastly howls of the wounded and dying in that endless passage, blood-wet for all its length now, and filled with the gagging stench of opened bodies.

We lost young Sernas in the struggle for the entrance to the second room. We'd slain the last priest-wizard in the corridor, burst through the great doors so hastily barred to us— and were met by a double arc of spears to bar our way. A hurled shaft pierced his plate and hauberk; he'd not had time to get his shield up. He called to me as his life's blood poured around him—"Hey, now, my lord? What of your Ormon? Have I known him long enough for grace?"

Stout Hoggle answered for me, yelling, "He'll not reject you, young sir. Believe on it. He'll take you to his heart." And so saying, he sliced the spear arm from the man who'd done the deed.

"I do thank you, my Lord of Marack," the young man breathed faintly. And then softly to me, " 'Tis still a pity, sir, that our poor but happy Hoom-Tet has such little power...."

His eyes closed. We advanced—and the fighting raged beyond him. The exit leading to the final corridor and the room at the pyramid's top was, again, at the northwest corner of the room. This time, however, we had but a hundred feet to go.

Unlike the great hall the second room was more a privileged "club room" for upper priests and wizards. A soft glow from a hidden source outlined its every feature. It was thickly carpeted. Great leather chairs were strewn about amongst many tables for dining, games, and such. Along the length of the east wall was a bar of some sort, and with shelves of glasses, mugs and bottles to the rear. And, too, and this would have delighted our lecherous young Sernas, great tapestries hung on every wall; each one depicting scenes which outdid in every way the simple efforts of the priests of the Hoom-Tet. The Dark One most certainly catered to his wizard's tastes....

We were now thirteen, a baker's dozen. The thought intrigued me. I even laughed. 'Twas one of the rare, conceptual descriptions indigenous to all life forms—wherever bread is baked, that is.

The Dark One's protectors now numbered less than forty. We'd re-barred the doors against attack from below; though we hardly had to. Indeed, fewer and fewer of *those* had advanced to test us in the last two hundred feet. Their enthusiasm seemed to wane in direct proportion to a lessening of the Dark One's thrumming. I wondered about that, especially since I could scarce hear the thrumming at all now. . . .

The time was 22:15, Greenwich. We had but fifteen minutes to gain the exit, traverse the two hundred feet of corridor and seize the room with the Kaleen and his mechanism.

We threw ourselves into them, drove them before us. We were a small bristling hedgehog, using the spears we'd seized below. Then we lost our third Yorn and stopped to still our hearts and catch our breath. The pace, indeed, was becoming a thing no man could stand. . . .

Then the hoary Griswall—his surcoat and hauberk were now literally soaked in blood—announced in a rasping, whispered voice so only we could know, "Hear me now, Collin, and *you*, my princess. Each minute's precious. Man for man we are the better. And so 'twould be proven. But time's the thing, and *time* we do not have. But the room *is* large. There's space to maneuver. Therefore, I propose to challenge, and to plunge into them. When they're thus occupied—and of that you can be sure—then the rest of you must break up in twos and threes, dash 'round and through them and thus gain yonder exit. They'll be split in such a way as to be unable to stop you. And if they try," and he grinned wryly, "well, sirs, you're *still* the better!"

His logic was implicit. I quick-scanned the others. Their pleasure at his gambit shown bright in every eye. That he would go to his death was understood by all; especially Griswall.

I reached to touch his arm, and said softly, "Then go, old friend—and know that you have our hearts, and love."

Without a word he stepped easily out before our ranks; this, though I'm sure he had a dozen wounds. He stretched his arms and shook his shoulders to settle his hauberk, loosen his shield. He tossed his sword into the air just once, and caught it, and moved toward them. . . .

They had a shield front of fifteen, two deep, and some others still behind them. Griswall contemptuously dashed aside their spears with a twisting movement of his own shield, then whirled his sword high and plunged into them. Two he killed almost instantly, and then two more—And they fell back to form a half circle before him. Again he charged their spears. . . .

And precisely then we *split*, raced down their front, and around them, to either side. They watched, amazed, stunned, *fixed* for perhaps three fatal seconds by the fact that in their very midst our aging killing machine wreaked havoc.

We continued across the carpeted floor—but not without loses. Unghist and his remaining Yorn, slower than the rest of us, were caught first and pierced through with a dozen blades. Unghist took two red-cowled wizards with him. Hoggle-Fitz, also slow and awkward, bothered too by his wound, blundered against a table and fell to one knee.—He was instantly overrun by a half dozen pursuers. The young Omnian captain with him—he'd tried to lift Fitz up—was himself pinned to the floor by three heavy blades. But Hoggle, rising with the help of Tober, then stood his ground for two brief minutes and raging, slew the lot of them. Rawl, who was with Caroween and an Omnian captain, were pinned against the wall some thirty feet from the exit. A sad mistake on the part of his pursuers. He killed one with his shield's edge, split the head of another, then fell to one knee to literally "halve" a third. Caroween, lithe body twisting this way and that, dodged every weapon to spear three men in as many seconds. Their Omnian captain, an older, heavily muscled man, was likewise terrible in his wrath.

I saw it all since I'd reached the exit first. We, too, had had a running fight. In the last exchange, Murie, knocked flat in a clashing of shields, received a spear thrust through the thigh. She called from where she lay—"Collin, love! Go on! I command you!"

But I snatched her from where she'd fallen, saw with a red mist before my eyes the sweat of pain upon her forehead. I lifted her gently to my shoulder, protected the while by my hard-fighting young captain. I then killed two who sought his life while he, in turn, cut the throat of the wizard who'd wounded Murie.

At the exit—and a closed door barred our way to the corridor beyond—we were joined by a cursing Hoggle and Tober, then Caroween, Rawl, and their captain—and that was all.

Of our enemy, just ten remained alive. These huddled some distance from us, making no move to approach. I noted, curious, that the *thrumming* had stopped completely.

Scanning, I saw Griswall in the room's very center. He sat

quite dead against a table's leg where he'd dragged himself. Three spears still hung from his battered body. He faced us. His smile was peaceful. I'm sure he'd seen us make it to the door.

The door!

The seconds were ticking by. I turned to look at it, to test it. The thing was solid iron. "Well, now," I told the others, "I'd have been a fool to think it otherwise. . . . But stand aside. What little magic your Collin has will now be used."

"Collin?" Rawl questioned, his hand abruptly to my shoulder to stay me, "What beast is that depicted there?"

His voice, rasping-loud in the now deadly quiet, was instantly echoed by sneering laughter from the wizard-warriors. He'd referred to a drawing of some sort of creature etched strongly on the door.

"I know not," I answered; then jokingly, "Mayhap it awaits us on the other side. . . ."

They moved Murie to a safe distance down the wall. The doorway cleared, I expanded the laser beam to encompass it fully. The effect would be disintegration! As of that moment we had less than ten minutes.

I pressed the stone. Blue light coned out. The door disappeared in a whoosh of imploding sound. I waited. Dust motes glowed in the corridor beyond, but that was all. I sighed in relief, moved quick to Murie, brushing her cheek with my lips. "My love," I said. "I'll be leaving you now, but not for long. We've won so far. We'll win this last one, too."

Tears brimmed her eyes. She nodded and squeezed my hand.

And then, to the sound of clanking steel and a roaring, frog-like voice, the damned thing, *as etched upon the door-way*, came hurtling from the corridor!

Its momentum carried it a full thirty feet through the blasted door. It whirled, surveyed us, and with a gargoyle grin to show its teeth. It was a full nine feet in height. Its torso was massive, dressed in a rusted, steel-link shirt. Its arms and legs, the latter protected by greaves, were as the boles of small trees. Its iron shoes were weapons in themselves. The helmed head was humanoid, the eyes, blue-black, piercing, *intelligent*! Without a doubt it was the last, the ultimate guardian!

I knew instantly that there, indeed, was no matter-to-energy conversion, and back, of some Fregisian netherworld monster. The Dark One had created it—of bits and pieces!

163

The thing's liquid eyes passed over us, settled on *me*, and stopped; upon which it raised its mighty arms, one hand with a sword, the other a spear, and signalled a greeting. In moments of peril most humanoids exhibit a rare and personal telepathy. Each of ours knew instantly that the thing sought *me*. They therefore moved to bar the way to *me*, with their lives.

"Go!" Murie whispered. "They will not let him follow."

I squeezed her hand. And because I had to, I moved toward the door. But I didn't leave. I froze—to watch.

Tober and the two Omnian captains stepped forward, each with a spear and sword. And Rawl, too, and brave Hoggle-Fitz, though his wound had drained him, visibly, of blood.

Stout Tober, our dottle warden's son, thinking the thing would try to seize me instantly, attacked incautiously. He ran straight toward it, hurled his spear, and at the same time tried to chop a foot from the mighty legs. It dodged the spear and contemptuously crushed poor Tober's chest with a single kick of an iron-soled shoe.

The younger Omnian, he'd been with Murie and me, feinted his spear's point toward the monster's belly, then dodged the expected sweep of greatsword to run behind it. The second Omnian threw his spear, aimed for the eyes. It was dashed aside by the thing's own spear. But the captain's effort, too, was a feint, for he then leaped 'neath the creature's spear to plunge his sword to the very hilt up through its groin.

The roar from that cavernous mouth was hellish. Around came its sword to literally cut our courageous captain into two parts. Anther roar! The younger Omnian had thrust his sword deep into the flesh and tendons behind the knee. The monster whirled, hitting the captain with his spear's butt, sending his body sliding over the blood-stained carpeting.

Then Rawl attacked, doing what I would have done. He struck to disarm it. Hamstrung already, it faltered, stumbled, put out its sword-hand for balance. Whereupon my shield-man leaped and with one mighty blow severed hand from wrist and was instantly drenched in the creature's pumping blood. Around came the spear butt again to catch our blinded Rawl fair on the helm so that he dropped dead or unconscious to the floor.

And now it was left to Fitz, our brave but bumbling "theologian." And he need not have made that final effort; indeed, I yelled for him to hold. In no way could it prevent me now from reaching the upper room. Its left leg was useless; blood

164

poured in streams from the severed wrist and an artery in its groin. But Hoggle, drunk with his hatred of that epitome of all his nightmares, ignored me.

He roared in a voice to match its own: "Ho, now, Sir Fiend! You've killed my comrades! But by all the gods, I promise you'll take no joy of it. You've *me* to deal with now, sir!"

He stamped his feet. His eyes blazed with a templar's fervor. He advanced to within a few yards of it.

If he was killed, I reasoned, there'd then be only me in a race to the Dark One's room; the creature, sore wounded, would obviously lose. In no way, however, did I dare help him. If I did, and killed the creature, he'd never forgive me. He'd swear only that I'd robbed *him* of the glory which was his right!

Caroween, who'd come up behind me, put a hand on my arm. She understood her father well, for she said softly, "Stay, Collin. My father's made his choice." Tears brimmed her eyes.

And so I stayed. For if Fitz lost, the monster, though he could never race me to the Dark One, could still reach Caroween—and Murie.

Fitz had discarded his shield. He chose his sword over the creature's spear. I knew instinctively that he'd try to strike the spear from its hand. Instead, as he stepped in—and I'm sure now that our Hoggle's eyes were blurring from his blood loss—he *slipped* and hesitated so as to catch his balance. And the Dark One's creature, with an echoing roar to loose the stones around us, plunged his great shaft right through brave Hoggle's body.

I thought then, as I stepped forward, "Well, now I've no choice, have I? Here's Caroween, and Murie lives, and so, perhaps, does Rawl. What difference then does it really make to me if I kill the Dark One in his cloistered room while all I love in life are slaughtered here?"

Caroween had cried out behind me.

But Hoggle was not dead! With the momentum of its thrust the thing had fallen to its unwounded knee. The tip of the spear that had gone full length through Fitz' body now rested on the carpet. And Fitz, roaring a prayer to Ormon, was with a single hand, pulling himself up the shaft toward his hated enemy. The monster *saw* its death. Black fear and terror—perhaps for the first time—shone in its eyes.

Then our Lord of Durst (and no longer would he be a king in Great Ortmund), brave Breen Hoggle-Fitz, let go the shaft to seize his greatsword in both hands. He whirled it once with an effort that took all his remaining strength—and struck off the creature's head. . . .

I heard him say quite calmly then, "Well now, my *Lord*, to whom I've always prayed, I'm ready. And I truly thank you that 'twas given to me to send this Dark One's monster straight to hell. . . ."

And thus he died.

Tears washing my eyes, I went to Murie, saying to Caroween, "Stand now for these few brief moments of my absence and guard your queen to be; and your Sir Fergis, too, for I am sure he lives." Then, in a voice to equal Fitz's roar, I yelled to the remaining warrior-wizards: "You'll stay where you are, sirs—exactly there! I go to slay your master. If I fail, the world dies, and you with it. But if I live and return to find that you've moved one inch from where you stand, I promise you a death more terrible than this world has ever known."

Not a word did they answer. They simply stood, red cowls thrown back to disclose their terror-stricken faces.

"The charge is yours," I said to Caroween.

She put her head against my bloodied hauberk. I held her and kissed her cheek, then stepped through the ruined door into the corridor. . . .

I left shield and spear behind, holding only my bared blade as I went up the steep incline. The corridor for its full two hundred feet was empty. Moreover, when I think on it now, I hadn't really expected anything. The absence of the *thrumming* indicated that what ever awaited me was in the Dark One's chamber.

The time was 22:26, Greenwich!

The corridor's pervasive silence after the screaming and the interminable clash of shields was an almost tactile thing. It was as if the world had died around me, or soon would. Two hundred feet of tight spiraling corridor to end—where? And then a surprise. I spotted the chamber—and there was no door, just a general darkness tinged by what must have been starlight from outside the pyramid, plus a strange "blueness" from within.

Three minutes left. I crossed the threshold to the final mystery.

The carpeting was soft, luxurious; the room circular. A great arc bisected the pyramid's top, separating the east and

166

west sides. The width of the opening was perhaps twenty feet, its length, forty, which was the width of the room itself. Starlight flooded the interior, to mingle with "starlight" from another source. For the room's interior was as an inverted bowl, reflecting the night sky of an alien universe, as seen from an *alien* world. Strange constellations glowed in diamond colors. Stars. Clusters. Island galaxies; all were depicted. The effect of the alien universe upon the hemispheric dome was startling. Indeed, it was *the* single thing the Dark One had ever created that smacked of feeling—a bit of home, as it were.

At the room's center was a dais. Upon it was a bank of instruments, control panels and the like. Each stud and button glowed with a small light of its own. To the right and left of the controls were two great machines of a design I'd never seen before. The very lines of their contours wavered, became vague with a kaleidoscopic quality if one tried to trace them, to *see* them in their totality. They had one thing in common: each focused upon some given point in the true space that lay outside.

The instrument on the left controlled the power load, the right, its use. Both load and use—the instantaneous release of one at the exact point of accumulation by the other, was controlled by a single bar above a three-dimensional grid wherein I saw the tracery of Fregis-Camelot's magnetic lines, the faint connection to far Fomalhaut II, and the conjunctive, linear alignments of the small moons, Ripple and Capil. . . .

They were, or so it seemed, in conjunction now. But I knew they weren't. There were still two minutes!

"Well!" I said to the small, basketball-headed figure with fuzzy ears who stood quite casually before the control bank, "So this is it—the end of our bloody road." I'd switched my sword to my left hand.

"All things must end," Hooli replied in cliche. "Let's just be glad it did so in our favor. What do you think of this?" His accompanying gesture encompassed the control panel, the instruments, and the hemispheric projection. His voice, usually so intimate, was stilted now, reserved.

"Fantastic! But how's about the big blast? I figure less than two minutes to total alignment."

"Wrong, Collin. It's already over. Zero point was just before you entered."

"What happened?"

"Nothing. I stopped it, before."

"Then I'm off by three minutes."

"Apparently. . . ."

"Where is he—*it*?"

Hooli grinned. "You saw *it* die."

I frowned, uncomprehending. "That *thing*? That was the Dark One? It's hard to believe."

"Why not?" Hooli glanced down to the 3-D grid, moved even closer if possible, to the panel.

"That he would be *there*, below, in his supposed moment of victory."

"Supposed?"

Etched by the starlight, he stood statue-still against the instrument panel. I stared at him hard. Then I asked softly, "Hey, Hooli? How many whores did the Ripper actually kill?"

"The Ripper?"

Just before I pressed the laser stone a faint light shimmered, took form before him—a silvered shadow of the *Grail*!

Then both Hooli and the Grail were gone in a burst of light from a simple miniature laser power-pack disguised as an agate stone to embellish the beauty of a Terran *Adjuster's* medieval sword belt.

It took me exactly five seconds to mount the dais, slap the control bar, press buttons to right and left—and to then witness, gridwise, *the actual conjunction of Capil, Ripple, and Fomalhaut II.*

Nothing happened!

Seconds later my held breath exploded from my lungs. I shook my head, staring hypnotically at the puddled wetness on the stones before the grid. He'd played it cool. Indeed, he'd almost won! But with all his power, he'd not once been able to organize it properly; to concentrate it in the *right* place at the right time. He just wasn't smart. Moreover, like so many humanoids his very arrogance was a bar to thinking things out.

I sighed, breathed deeply of the fresh night air from the opened arc above. I could scarce take my eyes from the stars of our own universe. My feeling of euphoria was laced with the solid knowledge that now, at this very moment, in Hish, and outside, in all the towns and villages, and in Glagmaron, Gheese, Ferlach, Kelb, Great Ortmund, it was finished—*kaput*!

I sighed again and turned to rejoin my princess and the others. . . .

Hooli stood in the doorway, grinning.

I said, "You again?"

"Who else?"

I shrugged, nodded toward the wet spot on the dais. "He had no sense of humor."

"That was brilliant, Buby—the *Ripper* question."

"Your *Grail* would have done the trick."

"Possibly."

We walked down the spiral corridor toward the rec-room. I glanced obliquely down at him, *our* Hooli, with his one bootie and his pompon. "A question, meatball?"

He snickered. "The answer's 'five,' bubble-brain. So says the Ripper file in *your* fat head."

"Yeah." I said. "You get an 'A.'"

They were precisely where I'd left them, except they'd been joined by Rawl who held his head and seemed not to know me. Blood had congealed from his ears and nostrils. Hooli touched his shoulders, stared into his unfocused eyes; upon which Rawl looked up at me and smiled. He said, "It seems we've won."

I smiled back; this, while I kneeled to take Murie in my arms, and just before our weeping Caroween took Rawl in hers.

Hooli had but to crawl in and out of Murie's lap—and that was that! Indeed, the ensuing wave of Pug-Boo "goodness" turned on full blast, revived four of the Dark One's warrior-wizards, too, as well as a single Yorn named Olgit, who was ever after a leader of his people—and young Lois Sernas. Sernas, by falling in a certain way, had stanched his own blood's flow, thus saving his life 'til Hooli's "goodness" touched him.

The both of them had hardly rejoined us when Sernas' father and a half-hundred lords and captains of Marack and Um came softly, silently, swords bared, through the now opened dorway.

Joining us, they viewed the body of the monster with darkened brows, and waited. . . . Fel-Holdt saluted Hoggle with his sword!

We stood, hands clasped, the six of us, the sole survivors of the company. I said softly, "Sirs, m'lords. The creature you called the Dark One is dead. Your world is free!"

For the next hour or so those were the only coherent words to be spoken by anyone; such was the wave of euphoria that swept the corridors, the great plaza, and all the milling, joyous throng of populace and warriors:

"The Dark One's dead! The Lord of Terror has been slain!"

According to Fel-Holdt, the force-field had disappeared approximately ten minutes prior to my entry to the Dark One's chamber; apparently, to add to the needed concentration of energy. There's no way to describe the ensuing bedlam, the riotous feasting, the celebrating, wherein Marackians and Omnians, for one brief and shining moment, were joined in Fregis' history. The feasting, the drawing up of plans, pacts, and, etc., went on for days. . . .

On the same afternoon of the following day, however, I rode with Rawl to the scoutship to switch off its "null," while Murie and Caroween had silken tents pitched for the both of us on the green meadows outside the city. The air of late summer was sweet and soft, and we wanted nothing else but quiet and a chance to be alone together. Hooli was with Murie, but without the real Hooli, the host-occupant. So I kicked him out of the tent to be placed in the care of certain Marackian guards.

Lors Sernas showed up to dine with us, bringing with him, of all things, the lovely Buusti, Lord Haken's daughter. She seemed none the worse for having been ravaged by our lecherous comrade. Indeed, Hoom-Tet, I'm sure, had in no way lost a son, but, rather, had gained a daughter. Sernas had the good sense to say his "good nights" early, doing so with a most gay and wicked light in his liquid eyes. . . .

Later, when Rawl and Caroween, too, had gone, we revelled in the warmth of pillows, furs, and each other. I marvelled that not the slightest scar remained on Murie's gold-furred thigh where the spear had pierced it. I marvelled at many things! Later, too, small Ripple and Capil peered briefly in through the tent's flap, blown open by the night wind. A soft breeze raised her hair in gentle pats against her cheek where she slept against my shoulder.

I mentally sent out the code-word to the Deneb-3.

There was a delay of at least a minute, indicating that for them, too, the urgency was gone.

Kriloy's tone was mellow. "Well—well—well! *Kyrie!*" he said. "You know, we were thinking of coming down to get you."

"Wrongo!" I exclaimed. I was still a little high from both Murie and a surfeit of sviss.

"You did it again, Buby," Ragan chimed in. "When the

D.O.'s power weakened we took a chance, moved in to scan. You were beautiful. . . ."

"That wasn't very smart."

"Hey, Buby! Nothing about this whole charade's been 'very smart!'"

"We'll talk about it."

"When are you coming up?"

"Got a few things to do yet. Gotta go north to Marack; return Hoggle's body to Durst, then get the five fleets in motion to retrieve Marack's army. I doubt me much that the Vuuns will so much as lift a claw to fly 'em back, now that the battle's won."

"So the Dark One's really had it."

"Yup."

Kriloy intruded. "I had mixed feelings about you and that dinosaur. I was worried. But once you were in his mouth, I figured he had an even chance."

I groaned.

"You really are a bloody bastard."

I didn't like that, not even in joke. "You could have taken my place any time, baby."

"With the princess, too?"

"Watch your mouth. I still owe you one for burning my brain."

"Stop the crap, Kyrie," Ragan said. "We love you and you know it."

"You gotta be debriefed," Kriloy said.

"Yeah. After my marriage—early Spring. After that, well maybe I'll bring the first delegation of Fregisian Alphians along."

Ragan asked, "Did you ever find the source of Camelot's 'magick?'"

"Nope," I lied. "But I'm working on it. You'll have an instant tape on everything in the next few days."

Then we chatted for a bit more, but they could sense that my heart wasn't in it, so they let me go.

"Just one thing," Ragan said. "There seems to be some kind of action in re the original gateway on Alpha. We're going to do a forty-eight hour, in-and-out, and check it off. We'll buzz you when we return."

"Good. I'll save the tape."

"Bless you, Kyrie."

"Bless you both," I intoned.

"You'll be promoted," Kriloy said. "Diamond Star!"

"Hey, man," I said, in Hooli's vernacular, which he'd

sponged from *my* head; which was ancient earth, "I am *the* 'Collin,' man! I don't *need* your damn diamonds!"

"Out, Kyrie!"

I closed my eyes for sleep, but then *he* came as I had sort of expected he would. He wore his mortar-cap and gown, and large sunglasses. This time he marched into my consciousness to a far-off choral background of the "Eroica." The scenario was a graduation ceremony. I, apparently, was the "graduate." Seating himself in front of what he assumed was my mental line of vision, he adjusted his robe, one bootie protruding, polished his lenses, and said, "Hi, there!"

"Hooli," I asked, with a new intimacy, "Why do you do all this?"

"Why not? It's the thing I've enjoyed the most. All life evolves somewhat the same, Buby; excepting that *humanoids* are a wee bit different, more complex. Where, might I ask you, in all the myriad of intelligent, saurian worlds, is there a single *face* 'to sink a thousand ships'?"

"Hmmmnn. So you're *not* humanoid?"

"Nope. I told ya."

"So what's up now?"

"Loose ends. We owe it to you."

"Great. Let's begin with the bubble."

"A ploy, to attract your starship, so they would tell you, so you would decide to go to Hish."

"You were that sure?"

"*Buby!* You're predictable!"

"But why not the Deneb-3, Hooli? It could just as easily have blasted the temple. Why all this nonsense? Our Fitz died, you know, and Griswall, and one helluva lot of others. I'd like an answer."

He smoothed his pleats, said solemnly: "The Dark One's gadgets, as your Foundation will shortly find out, are for the moment indestructible to your science. A totally different physics is involved in their creation, a different math. Any attempt against them by an alien force (you), before they were deactivated could easily have produced anti-matter, with the end product, unimaginable. That they were also flawed, is true. They would have done precisely what I said they would—fall short of containing the released power of an alien sun. To stop it, there was but one way: They had to be *manually*, if you will, redirected; in effect, turned off by their own switch!"

"And only I could do that?"

172

Hooli smiled.

"Why then did you ask me to crash the scoutship into the temple?"

"To *spook* you, Buby! Martyrdom, for a hero type, is unacceptable. You may have thought for one brief sparkling moment that you were committed to it. But no way! What you'd really committed yourself to was the alternative choice that the temple and the gadgets could be won in a way that would also save *your* ass. And 'to save your ass,' Buby, *you'd fight ten times as hard*!"

"Which is what you wanted?"

"Yup."

"You're one miserable son-of-a-bitch!"

He winked behind his shades. "Would it help to say that I know of no one else who could have done it?"

"Sheeeeeh!"

"It's true."

"Look, Hooli." I took another tack. "Our goal was a one-on-one confrontation wherein, hopefully, I'd blow the bastard away. Still, am I right in concluding that he was tactically stupid, incapable of using his power properly?"

"His basic problem was that he'd never been taught *not* to play another man's game."

"Your game?"

"No, Buby, yours! The game of *war* in all its phases, is the game wherein you humanoids excel. Example: jacks, tennis, soccar, all have simple rules; but all are won primarily by physical skill. Chess, on the other hand, and *war*, have an almost four-dimensional quality—time, politics; what you ate last night, etc. The logic of both must be *learned*. No thinking entity, unfamiliar with the concepts, could ever expect to win the first time out."

"As for the improper use of his power—no doubt about it. But it would have made no difference, except in the last instance. He figured you for power. How else, in his mind, could you have deflected lightning bolts, shifted the clouds around, blown his wizards to hell, etc. He had decided to retain a sufficient amount of his own to take you out, with the remainder being channeled, for his life's sake, into the gadgets. In effect, you'd of cancelled each other out. There was always the chance that you would have blown him first. But we couldn't risk it. So we let him *see* me—and told *you* about it!"

"You *let* him see you?"

"We sure did, Buby—right after we'd planted the *Grail*

173

idea in your head. I even let him *see* a piece of my mind, a bit of the potentially available 'goodies,' so to speak. I linked you to them, too, along with the thought that it would be to his interest to keep us both alive.

"He then did what we'd thought he'd do. He was even more predictable than you. He used his remaining power to change his form to resemble me, so's to hold you in check for the last few critical moments."

I grunted.

"Actually," Hooli grinned. "His best weapon was himself. If he'd given you one buggering peep at him in the *original*, you'd have been flat on your back with instantaneous metabolic imbalance. In essence, if he'd only known it, he could have won—and lost, and taken all Fregis-Camelot with him, in that order. . . ."

I thought about that. Then I asked curiously, "What *did* he look like?"

"*Me*, Buby! The real *me*! It's not too late. You can still have a peek!"

I sighed. "I'll take a rain check."

"Well, what else?" Hooli asked.

"Dahkti, Chuuk, Jindil?"

"Gone. Oh, there'll still be Pug Boos in the five northern kingdoms. After all," he grinned, "everybody loves a Pug Boo."

"I've wondered about that."

"I'll bet you have," he exclaimed softly. "Here's an old paradigm, Kyrie. Stick it up your personal memory bank: Where humanoids evolve there are eventually puppies in the yard, and teddy bears in the play room."

"What the hell is that supposed to mean?"

He was up and pirouetting. "Well *you* said it," he grinned over a black-gowned shoulder. "You told your princess that except for Pug Boos, *all* animals on Fregis have six legs."

"Jesus-Og!" I said.

"That's going to change, though. From now on, Pug Boos, like Alphians, will actually reproduce themselves."

"Bloody Buddah!" The enormity of what he was suggesting suddenly hit me.

"Sort of shakes ya, doesn't it?"

"But the Vuuns told me—"

"The Vuuns are dreamers Buby."

"Show me, goddamn it. *Prove* it!"

He did. He managed a sort of "cake walk" with sundry

174

bumps and grinds. Then he suddenly reached to whip his gown aside and shout: "See! *No belly button!*"

And sure enough his hairless tummy disclosed an area equally barren of anything resembling the mark of a one-time umbilical attachment.

He returned with a heel-and-toe, buck-and-wing, slanted his mortar-board forward against his shades and said softly in my ear, "It's about that time, Kyrie. I've got to go."

"Will I see you again?"

"That's hard to say. We'll try. . . ."

"Sheeeeeh!" I shook my head.

He said, still softly, "I'll miss you, Kyrie."

"I'll miss you, too, Hooli."

He then made a couple of skating motions so that his small, round figure began to fade. His voice came faintly—"Good-bye, *Collin.*"

I said, "Goodbye, Mr. Chips."